Hyperdimensional Beings!

Butch was never sure exactly what happened. He was in the middle of his sentence, he knew what he intended to say, and part of him remembered saying it. Part of him remembered a flurry of activity, of the strange hyperspatial aliens rushing in all directions, of trying to take aim with his sidearm as they moved too quickly for him to take a bead—but he also had no memory of saying the rest of his sentence, and in an eyeblink he was alone. Ophelia and the rest of the aliens were gone.

BOOKS BY COLLIN R. SKOCIK

Voyage Into the Unknown
Station Post One
LOVED AND LOST

Collin R. Skocik

Cover art: Jonathan R. Skocik

Visit the author's website at
http://www.lulu.com/spotlight/voyageintotheunknown

VOYAGE INTO THE UNKNOWN:
STATION POST ONE

LOVED AND LOST

CHAPTER 1

"Is this what you wanted, Ophelia?"

"Yes, Mr. McCrae. Is. I you thank."

"You're welcome."

Butch McCrae felt himself flushing as Ophelia took the Casimir torque from his hand, and the brief contact with her skin sent ripples of excitement through him. He had never been a shy man, but something about this ethereal alien held off his usual bluster and bold advances. He hesitated to put a name to his blossoming feelings for her; after all, she was not human. Her blue skin, blue hair, wan body, and enormous blue-black eyes were a constant reminder of that. Yet none of that detracted from her extraordinary beauty.

He also wasn't sure how she thought of him. She was here to work with Dr. DuBois; how did she feel about this pilot who occasionally ran errands for her? And how pathetic did he look by continually offering to run those errands?

"Uh, listen, I was...uh, I was wondering how much longer you'll be working on this. I mean, today. How long till you knock it off for the day."

She eyed him quizzically with her large, luminous eyes—eyes that seemed too large for her skull, but somehow seemed proportionally *right*. "Me forgive. Your word 'long'—strange is me too. Time an alien concept is."

"Sorry."

"Apologize do not. Come we different worlds from. Come understand each other to challenging is it. But pleasurable is it, you not do agree?"

Butch smiled—a wide, boyish smile that embarrassed him, but he couldn't help it. "Yeah, I agree."

"Needs does DuBois Doctor a kevlon-tau converter work to finish."

Butch took a moment to mentally rearrange her words... *Dr. DuBois needs work to finish a kevlon-tau converter.* "Sure, I understand that, but around here—I mean we human beings can only work so long before we need a break. I guess that's a reference to time again, isn't it?"

Ophelia smiled; that wide smile, revealing perfect white teeth, was the most human thing about her. "Is it. Thinking am I...rest...rest... resting in future put rest now."

"Sorry, I didn't quite get that. What are you saying?"

"Rest I will *future* in—future is time ahead of now, right?—and feel effects now."

"Wait a minute...are you saying you can take a *retroactive nap*? I mean, you feel rested *now* because you *will* rest later?"

"Yes." Ophelia's voice was musical, always accompanied by a sort of bell-like ringing sound. Butch thought of a fairy tale character from classic literature...*Tinkerbell*.

Butch searched for words. He tended to freeze up around Ophelia—quite atypical for him. He wished he could be as smooth around her as he was around everyone else. What the hell was the *matter* with him?

"Uh, listen," he stammered, "uh, I'm hungry right now, and I can't feel, uh, a meal I will eat in the future. I've gotta obey the ol' cause-effect rule. Arrow of time and all. I was wondering if you'd like to, uh, take a break and, uh, join me for lunch."

Again that smile. "Yes! This will I do."

Butch wondered if she had known ahead of time that he was going to ask her that. There was so much about these strange beings that eluded human understanding.

Ophelia turned to Dr. DuBois with a remarkably graceful and fluid motion. Even her hair moved gracefully, as if she were under water. "DuBois Doctor—"

"Go ahead," DuBois said with a save of the hand, "take a break. You've given me enough material to keep me busy studying for the rest of my life. An hour won't hurt."

"An...ower? Okay." Ophelia turned to Butch, smiling. "Human things me show."

Butch smiled and extended his arm. "I'd be more than happy to." Then he realized she had no idea what the gesture meant.

But she slipped her hand into the crook of his arm just as a human woman would have done in centuries past. Butch smiled at her and led her from the Wheel.

As they walked, he admired the way her feet seemed barely to touch the floor, as if she were walking on some sort of force field—or hovering, or flying on angel wings, or...or maybe it was his imagination.

Her grace was indeed remarkable, though, and others had noticed it. Not only she, but all the aliens who had come aboard the station, moved with a fluidity that made them look like animated characters a little kid might create using Real As Life software.

Their proportions were so humanlike as to be caricatures—again, as if they were animated characters. Ophelia had, at least by appearance, the same equipment as a human female, though ridiculously well-endowed. Yet it did not look ridiculous, it looked natural on her. Her eyes were so huge they seemed to leave not enough room for a brain, yet they looked somehow normal. And a brain she certainly had! Her understanding of quantum physics and relativity outstripped any human being—but that was quite natural, considering the world from which she had come.

Her most apparent aspect, of course, was her blue skin and hair. She looked, in fact, like a human woman seen under water—right down to the way her hair flowed.

It was as if she and the other aliens were obeying different laws of physics than humans—as indeed they may be. Although they had been removed from their own environment and come aboard Station Post One, surely their bodies carried some portion of their bizarre and inexplicable homeworld with them.

Ophelia's name, of course, was not Ophelia. Butch could not pronounce her name; no human could. An assortment of clicks and whistles that sounded like a whale's song, any attempt by a human to pronounce it would sound comical. So Butch named her Ophelia because "Juliet" was too on-the-nose.

At the same time, he hoped his own—would the right word be "relationship"?—with Ophelia would end a little better than Shakespeare's star-crossed lovers or Hamlet's ministering angel. What possible future he envisioned for himself and this unearthly creature he could not have explained, only that he was smitten with her in a way that he had never been with any woman before.

When she had first come on board, he, like all the humans, had been struck by her beauty. But there were lots of beautiful women on the station—*human* women. (Few admitted it, at least not openly, but there had been speculation that physical attractiveness had been one of the Selection Committee's qualifications for the survivors of Earth....)

There was something else about her. Her musical voice, with that bell-like jingling that accompanied her every word. Her huge, expressive eyes. The way she turned her head. The way her hair flowed as if under water. The way she gestured with her slender fingers as she spoke. Her compassion. Her grace. Her curiosity about his world and his curiosity about hers. The juxtaposition of her total alienness with her uncanny humanness. He didn't know. He couldn't place it. Only that something about her resonated with him.

Sometimes things she said, or the way she said them, or the gestures she made as she said them, provoked a sense in him almost of irritation, or as though he were embarrassed on her behalf because she had made a fool of herself and he was embarrassed to have seen it, and this was followed by a wash of excitement, or perhaps compassion...or something, some feeling he couldn't define.

It was far too early for him to say that he loved her, or was even infatuated with her. He only knew that he kept thinking about her, and that her presence, or any thought of her, filled him with a sense of excitement and self-consciousness. When in her presence—or anyone else's, as long as she was on his mind—he was acutely aware of his own behavior and appearance, and found himself going out of his way to be more impressive, more efficient, more debonair than usual. He paid more attention when combing his hair in the morning, when brushing his teeth, when donning his uniform—making sure it was cleaned and pressed—and taking special care to make no mistakes on the job and to conduct himself with the crisp and flawless efficiency of a proper Dock Deck Chief.

He took special pride in himself, and was glad he owned a respectable position on the station. Oh, he would come into more contact with Ophelia were he a scientist, but he did what he was good at, and he went the extra mile to demonstrate his skills.

Yet he also went out of his way not to mention Ophelia, or to force his way into her presence. He thought of her constantly, yet made an effort to give no outward sign that this was so. But he would find himself daydreaming, making absent-minded mistakes, ignoring people's reports, neglecting some of his daily tasks—and when he caught himself, he would quickly attend to correcting any errors, but with a strange and warm sensation that paradoxically made him shiver.

Could he be attracted to an alien? Ophelia was a biped, her limbs of roughly human proportions. Her head was larger than a human head, but not ridiculously so. Her eyes were enormous, but her facial features corresponded to human features. In other words, though she could never be mistaken for a human being, she was certainly not the most alien being he had ever seen. Her chest expanded into what sure looked like breasts—*big* ones—and on her midriff was a depression that looked like a belly button.

The aliens wore slim garments about their waists, the females a kind of metallic bra-like thing. Aside from that—nothing. Butch watched the way Ophelia's muscles moved, analyzing their similarity to human structure, and although her limbs were thinner and more delicate than human limbs, the way they worked seemed to be engineered much the same. Her hands each had four fingers and thumb, though longer and slimmer than human appendages; her feet each had five toes, though she had no fingernails or toenails. What went on beneath the clothing was a total mystery to him...

...yet he found himself wondering.

And on the third night of the aliens' presence on the station, as he lay in the darkness of his privacy pod, he allowed himself, with the thrill of the forbidden, to be attracted to her, to fantasize about the exploration of her unearthly body, and to spill his seed on his mattress.

And so, as unobtrusively as he could, he began to offer his services—first to DuBois, and then, very much in passing, to Ophelia. And the first time she accepted his service, the first time she turned those large eyes on him and smiled at him, his legs almost buckled beneath him. He was conscious that his voice had risen two octaves, and he left feeling flushed, faint, and certain he had acted like an idiot.

But Ophelia was never anything but kind to him. Whether that kindness transcended into a deeper awareness of him he didn't know, and didn't know how to ask. But he kept thinking of her, and hoping to grow closer to her.

He guarded his behavior around Elmer Tepper. His partner and rival would leap at any chance to make fun of him, and his attraction to a bizarre and inexplicable alien would provide Tepper's unsophisticated sense of humor with hours of entertainment. Oddly, although Butch and Tepper spent hours together, whether on duty on the Dock Deck or on a long mission aboard the *Frontier*, they had rarely talked about women. Butch was sure his tastes and Tepper's did not mesh; he imagined Tepper was into grungy women with low-class tastes and nonexistent IQ. Butch preferred class and intelligence.

He did not anticipate any real relationship with Ophelia, but if such a thing did occur, he would be neither embarrassed nor ashamed. But at the present time, he had no reason to think such a thing could happen, and so he did not intend to make his feelings known to anyone—not even Ophelia.

It wasn't that he was shy; he never had been. Ordinarily he would stride up to a woman and say, "Hi, I'm Butch and I'd like to take you out to dinner." Well, not quite, but he had never been timid about his feelings. In this case, however, he found himself, not embarrassed, but *private*. And

Tepper was the last person in the galaxy whom he wanted invading his privacy.

What Butch didn't know was that others noticed his behavior, and Commander Damon Kramer was becoming concerned about it.

CHAPTER 2

Ophelia and the other aliens were known as Etuknips, and their homeworld was not a planet. In fact, it was not a physical object in space, but a mathematical abstraction, a one-dimensional line—a cosmic string.

Dr. Ebor DuBois had been driven to hysterical jitters at the thought of studying life forms who lived on such an exotic world, even as he expressed disbelief that life could exist there. Life, after all, was a complex process resulting from chemical processes. A cosmic string went beyond simplicity into a realm where matter, and even energy, were too complex to exist.

Cosmic strings, when they had first emerged, spanned the length of the universe. In 1976, Thomas Kibble looked for supersymmetry in the young universe, a way of explaining the irregular clumping of matter and energy. His solution: spacetime defects, like tiny cracks in the universe that formed as it expanded and cooled.

Tiny though they may be, cosmic strings were *dense*. Dense on the order of neutron stars or black holes. But they also vibrated, shedding energy and ultimately fragmenting and disappearing. Few still existed. The first cosmic string fragment had been spotted by the Barry Barish Space Interferometer in 2078, a fragment only ten kilometers long. It was right here in the Milky Way Galaxy, and so there was a distinct possibility that the homeworld of the Etuknips was that very fragment.

The Valdor, typically, were silent about the location of the cosmic string fragment. The Etuknips, for their part, had difficulty communicating; it was a laborious process to get them to think in terms of linear time. It seemed that their world was timeless; they lived in past, present, and future, and even saw alternate timelines. Their mode of existence was so fundamentally different that, although they had quickly learned English, they had considerable difficulty with tense. Even placing words in the correct order in a sentence was a real problem for them. But the Etuknip ambassador, whom Butch McCrae insisted on calling Ophelia, was friendly and forthcoming and promised to cooperate.

So far, however, she had been unable to provide much information on her homeworld. She had been very helpful in developing the kevlon-tau converter, but her inability to comprehend linear time had restricted discussion of almost any other subject.

One thing was clear, though—her transtemporal nature, her ability to see alternate timelines, and the Valdor's own testimony about her origin, indicated that there was no mistake: the Etuknips had indeed originated on a cosmic string—or cosmic string fragment.

DuBois was familiar with theories as to how life could evolve in two-dimensional environments, and indeed had encountered just such life on a neutron star (the so-called "Antimatter Lords"). But life in *one* dimension?

Obviously the question was academic, since the Etuknips did exist—but as a scientist he had to ask the question, *why* did the Etuknips exist?

That gravity existed on a cosmic string was obvious. And gravitational lensing and severe spacetime distortion would certainly take place as one grew close to the string. The illusion could well exist of entering another universe—and in fact the gravastar theory suggested certain scenarios in which entering a black hole would place one in a holographic simulation of the real universe. Could such a thing be true with a cosmic string? Perhaps...

But a whole civilization? Beings who, when removed from the string, became three-dimensional, humanoid beings complete with blood and DNA? How in the *hell* did that happen?

DuBois could only formulate one hypothesis, and he had no way of testing it at this time. Since the string was vibrating, there must be oscillations along its surface. It was possible, just possible, that those oscillations could be assigned arbitrary values of ones and zeros, and so a basic binary language could exist there—and therefore information could exist.

Life was, at its most basic level, information.

What if the Etuknips had not originated on the cosmic string? What if they had once been biological life forms who evolved on a planet, like everyone else in the universe? Perhaps—no doubt long, long ago—they had gone into space and encountered the cosmic string. What would happen to them if they wandered too close to it? Most likely they would have been torn to bits; but was it *possible* that their knowledge, memories, and genetic information might be integrated into the oscillations of the string's vibration?

Doubtful.

More likely they had somehow deliberately projected that information into the string, loading their complete information into the one-dimensional storage medium. If so, though, they had given no such indication.

And why would they encode themselves into a storage medium that was self-destructive? Cosmic strings inevitably broke up, faded away.

Yet with their timeless nature, their ability to see alternate timelines, and their inability to understand past, present, and future, perhaps the inevitable destruction of their world meant no more than the existence of the outer hull of Station Post One meant to DuBois; harmless as long as you don't go through it. Perhaps the Etuknips could wander at will across the "past" and "future" of their world just as humans could wander at will across Station Post One's interior.

Despite the difficulty in communicating with the Etuknips, DuBois had gleaned a few insights, enough to know there were two factions of Etuknips: the Sweg and the Leira. Both existed in a portion of the cosmic string which could only be described as "now." As some of DuBois's equations had hinted, there was a focal point of quantum gravity around "now"—after all, despite the time twistings of relativity, one thing everyone in the universe agreed on was that Now is Now. Entangled communication, which allowed signals to be sent and received instantaneously, no matter how far apart, had collapsed the notion that simultanaeity did not exist.

With the Etuknips' ability to wander freely through time, the Sweg were fearful of invasion, not from other factions or from other countries or other worlds, but from other *times*. Superstitious and mystical, the Sweg even had a cultural archetype, a bogeyman, a pirate from the future whom they feared would invade "Now." Therefore they huddled together in "Now" and discouraged any wandering into other times.

The Leira, by contrast, had no superstition and devoted themselves to science and mathematics. They encouraged exploration and research, and they explored other times and had mapped the cosmic string. Except that "mapped" was the wrong word. Ophelia had tried to explain what they did, but DuBois did not follow. Whether it was a linguistic barrier or a barrier to the limits of human comprehension he did not yet know. But the Leira peeked into parallel timelines, wandered through the realities, mapping as many outcomes as possible and studying the fabric of spacetime in a way that DuBois could only imagine.

All of the Etuknips now aboard Station Post One were Leira; Sweg would never dare leave their cosmic string. But the Leira, under Ophelia's leadership, had struck out to see the universe beyond their one-dimensional infinity, and to explore a three-dimensional world which they could barely fathom.

Their intuitive understanding of higher dimensions and quantum gravity and parallel universes was, in fact, the reason they were aboard Station Post One. The Valdor had quickly realized that the Etuknips' knowledge might enable them to understand the humans' enemy far better than any human could.

Until two years ago, the destruction of the Earth had remained a mystery. For twenty-one years, scientists had wondered why the Sun, good old G-type Sol, a happy little main sequence star with five billion years of life left to it, had exploded in a supernova. It was impossible, but it had happened.

Well, twenty-one years after that destruction, what was left of the human race had encountered the Valdor and their interstellar Community, and learned of the Thermians—extradimensional beings who had a habit of infesting main sequence stars, injecting superplasmic energy from their own high-energy universe, and driving those stars to supernova. No one had ever seen a Thermian. No one had ever spoken to a Thermian. No could even guarantee that Thermians existed except as mathematical concepts. But their effect on the universe was very real.

The Etuknips were the most Thermian-like beings ever encountered. To describe them as "higher-dimensional" may not be precisely true— the opposite, in fact: they were *lower-*dimensional. But they seemed to have the freedom to wander higher dimensions.

Their ability to see alternate timelines (parallel universes) did not, by itself, indicate they had access to the Thermian universe; those were two different types of universes. Alternate timelines existed on the same brane as this universe. The Thermian universe (according to all the math) existed on another brane. DuBois entered a new timeline every day, every time he did anything. Every decision fragmented reality into multiple timelines, multiple *universes*, in an infinite multiverse, but all in the same higher-dimensional brane.

The Thermians were somewhere else, in a universe totally dissimilar to this one, where energy had a different value, where gravity operated differently—where spacetime itself likely had a different meaning. Nothing was known about the Thermian universe except that the energy level there was much higher—or perhaps, more accurately, the energy:gravity ratio was different than in this universe. Either way, the Thermians commanded great energy, and through them, the creatures that had been emerging throughout the galaxy, called the Dreb.

That was what had brought the Etuknips here; DuBois' lost love Natasha Fairbanks had discovered a way to harness the energy of the Thermian universe in the same way as those strange wizards known as the Dreb. Organic beings who had somehow been blessed with "powers"—including teleportation, mind control, shooting of energy from the eyes, and transubstantiation of food—it now seemed that the Dreb had no intrinsic powers, but had only the ability to tap into the high energy of the Thermian universe and direct it through their bodies.

Natasha had done the same...briefly, before she was killed. Based on her research, DuBois had developed the NCT—the Natasha Continuum Tapper—which duplicated the device that had been destroyed with her.

Now the Etuknips were here to help to develop a device that might combat the Thermians, or even to destroy them. This was something the Community had sought for centuries.

DuBois was itching with curiosity to learn something of their invisible enemies; for all the rest of the human race, or whatever was left of it, the drive was more basic: they wanted revenge for the destruction of the Earth.

CHAPTER 3

It had been a rough time for Station Post One, and Commander Damon Kramer hoped that the coming of the Etuknips would mean a change for the better. But the situation was complex—politically complex.

Ever since the Doomsday War, the station—and the entire Community—had been in a state of constant chaos. Although the Alternative Alliance had fallen, a group of renegade Throrb called the Fantasmata, who refused to accept defeat, continued to wage a foolish, doomed, and irritating war against the remnants of the Community.

The Dreb of Derringer-9, who had become Station Post One's allies, had failed to defend the Community during the war because the Alternative Alliance had obtained Modified Partial Superplasmic Activity Reducers (MP-SARs), which deadened a Dreb's "powers." And then Argo, the Dreb Priest King who had pledged his support to the Community, had disappeared. His brother, Cercone, an avid follower of the Thermians, had taken over.

Cercone was now dealt with, and was a prisoner on Station Post One—though he had to be subjected regularly to the MP-SAR lest he regain his "powers" and escape.

But Cercone's takeover of Derringer-9 had one benefit: he had ordered the Book of the Dreb to be translated for humans to read. (Actually it turned out that Argo had originally ordered the translation, even though Cercone, for his own reasons, had delivered it.)

The Book's description of the Thermians had left Ebor DuBois stunned; it seemed that the Dreb religion was consistent with the equations discovered by Natasha Fairbanks.

The Dreb belief was, in brief, that when a star became a supernova (induced by Thermians) and destroyed an inhabited planet, the inhabitants who had been granted the Dreb powers would "transcend," eventually becoming stars themselves. And in time they, in their turn, would become infected by Thermians and would supernova, at which point they would transcend to the ultimate form, becoming Thermians themselves.

DuBois' studies indicated that this was indeed possible, or at least within the realm of the wild world of physics Dr. Fairbanks had discovered.

It was clear now that the Dreb had no "powers." They were ordinary organic beings. Argo and his Dreb, who had not possessed the Book of the Dreb, had believed their powers came from nature (and in fact it was his learning of the Thermians that prompted Argo to give his support to Station Post One). Other Dreb believed that the Thermians granted them their powers.

The truth was somewhere in the middle.

All life forms emitted some degree of black body radiation; although perfectly black, nonreflecting objects were the most efficient emitters of black body radiation; most life forms were reflective to some degree, and the majority were also opaque. Most of the radiation emitted by the human body was infrared, but some black body radiation was emitted. As long as some electromagnetic radiation was absorbed, some black body radiation would be emitted, since the body's temperature varied. (Even cold-blooded animals emitted black body radiation, since they too could absorb electromagnetic radiation and then be heated by external sources.)

As had been known since the thirty-fifth century, the black body emissions interacted (via a quantum Lorentz Force) with the vacuum energy surrounding the body. In the case of inanimate objects, this meant nothing. But in the case of living beings, the implications were immense; it meant that all knowledge, all memory, all genetic information, everything that made a person a person, was stored in static form in the very vacuum of space. In fact, what twentieth century mystics had called the "quantum hologram" was literally real.

What Dr. Fairbanks had discovered was, in simplistic terms, that the quantum hologram interacted via quantum entanglement with the high energy of the Thermian universe. This was true for all living things—but the Dreb had been given the power to tap that energy. In their case, this had been done by the Thermians themselves, by sifting energy from their universe into the Dreb brains, altering their genetic structure, arranging their brain cells to, through a complex process, receive and conduct energy from the Thermian universe. Since the Thermian universe had a much higher energy level, this amounted to an almost limitless well of energy for the Dreb to use as they wished.

According to Dr. DuBois, when a Dreb was killed, his information was preserved in his quantum hologram—and that information was duplicated in the Thermian universe thanks to quantum entanglement. It was possible that, like in this universe, it remained static and useless. But given the high energy of the Thermian universe, it was quite possible that the Dreb would live on in that universe. With the vast well of available energy, and with the entanglement with our own universe, a deceased Dreb (or ghost Dreb) could inflict great changes upon our universe by sifting power through microscopic wormholes, exciting vacuum energy. This was, in fact, the principle behind superplasmic energy, the "supernatural" energy which had destroyed the Sun.

DuBois theorized that the Dreb could influence gravitational attraction in dust clouds and nebulae to jumpstart the births of new stars. In a way, they might indeed "become" stars, just as their religion suggested.

It was a stretch, but the coincidence was certainly compelling, especially given the undeniable powers of the Dreb.

All those aboard Station Post One had seen those powers. The Dreb could vanish and reappear elsewhere in the universe. They could shoot destructive beams from their eyes. They could alter people's will, turn them into mindless slaves. And Kramer had no doubt they had other abilities; Argo was silent about the full extent of their power.

Dr. Natasha Fairbanks had discovered the well of energy between this universe and the Thermian universe, a field that Dr. DuBois insisted on naming the "Natasha Continuum." But Natasha had taken her discoveries to the ultimate expression; she had invented a device that did the same thing as the Dreb brain, and she had given herself Dreb power.

She, and the device, had been lost in battle with the Dreb. But DuBois had reconstructed her thinking and developed his own device, which he called the Natasha Continuum Tapper (NCT.)

The NCT's potential was demonstrated in most dramatic form aboard the Valdor Artificial World, when it had been stolen by a crazy Hyron on a Vengeance Quest against his own commander. He had given himself power beyond even the Dreb—so much that he had vaporized himself.

Dugrow, the Valdor Administrator, in typical fashion, blamed the humans for inventing so destructive a device—but even he recognized the benefits of the NCT, and by a happy coincidence had recently negotiated the Etuknips' entry into the Community.

He believed that the Etuknips could develop a device to convert kevlons to taus. That was important; kevlons were a type of lepton suggested by Natasha's research—and verified by many confrontations with the Thermians—which played an important role in the Thermian universe. Taus were leptons common to this universe, with a one-half spin and negative electric charge. DuBois had joked that they were electrons on steroids. Taus had been used in the past to construct exotic atoms, such as tauonium. Fiercely penetrating, and associated with the tau neutrino, taus were, according to Natasha's equations, incompatible with the physical processes of the Thermian universe, and therefore perhaps lethal to Thermians.

In other words, the kevlon-tau converter *might* be the long-sought Thermian Destroyer.

Before the arrival of the Etuknips, Kramer had contacted the Seers. Bloblike inhabitants of the planet Menchie, the Seers had been thought at first to be mindless animals. But they had proved not only to be intelligent, compassionate creatures, but among the strangest life forms ever encountered: their bodies extended into higher dimensions. They claimed to be able to *see* Thermians.

Kramer did not understand how this was possible, and DuBois had been unable to explain it, but their ability to see in higher dimensions had come in handy more than once. And so Kramer reached out to their Seer contact, Watcher, to ask if he could verify that the Dreb lived on the Thermian universe, and if there was any validity to their belief that they could become stars, and eventually Thermians.

But Watcher could not answer that question. "Our ability to see the Thermians does not extend to discerning such subtleties," he said.

Well, perhaps the Etuknips could. The Seers, whatever their abilities, were evidently tied to linear time, like everyone else in the rational universe. The Etuknips, incredibly, manipulated spacetime at will as part of their metabolism. Kramer wondered if that ability would still exist once they were transposed into the three-dimensional universe.

Like everyone else, he had been struck by the beauty of the Etuknips. Their glistening blue skin, flowing bluish hair, and large, luminescent eyes struck him as angelic. Not for the first time, he wondered how many Earth myths could be attributed to the life forms of the cosmos. How many magicians in Earth's past had been Dreb? And could the Etuknips have visited Earth, perhaps to tell of the coming of a savior?

CHAPTER 4

The Valdor were the most unhelpful and hostile of all possible allies. It was easy for Kramer to forget that the Valdor were indeed allies and not enemies. Dugrow was gruff, rude, uncommunicative, and constantly accused the humans of violations of the treaty with the Community.

Kramer understood that the Valdor had made a concession in allowing Station Post One to be established in their space, but it was the most convenient way for the human race to become Community members. But the Valdor had been specific about the terms of the arrangement: the humans must recognize Valdor primacy.

It was a commonsense enough condition, but what bothered Kramer—and everyone else on Station Post One—was the *way* the Valdor insisted on it, the way they dwelled on it, and the way it seemed that anything less than a constant state of worship of the Valdor was a failure to recognize their primacy.

Ever since the war, Kramer had abandoned any pretence at honoring that condition. The Valdor had allowed the war to escalate into a catastrophe unlike anything the galaxy had ever experienced. Many entire worlds had been destroyed when both sides had unleased naked starships—faster-than-light ships that did not keep their lethal gamma ray surges in check with electromagnetic dissipators—and the Valdor Artificial World had itself been half-destroyed.

And now, like hyenas pouncing on a dead carcass, the Hyron Empire had moved in, annexing the Community—and, ironically, naming Station Post One as its capital!

Well, the Valdor were not taking the new situation well. Kramer didn't like it either, but he did enjoy seeing the Valdor put in their place. Anyway, it was hard to respect them as the leaders of the Community when it was their bad judgment that had led to the destruction of the Community. They had lost their legitimacy and everyone saw it. The Hyrons had, so far, successfully enforced their annexation as well as Station Post One's new position as capital of the Community.

The Valdor hated it, but they were too consumed with the reconstruction of their Artificial World, and the massive evaluation of the damage to other Community worlds, to fight the Hyrons. They were weary of war, and for the time being they accepted that they were no longer in charge.

But there was no question that Dugrow held the upper hand in the relations with the Etuknips. It was he who had negotiated the Etuknips' admission to the Community, it was he who arranged the Etuknips' visit to Station Post One, and it was he who gave the Etuknips the means to contact the humans. And therefore it was he who had the power to place any conditions he wished on the relations between humans and Etuknips.

"I think the days of Valdor primacy are over," Kramer had laughingly told the Valdor Administrator.

Dugrow leveled his glowing eyes on Kramer. "How dare you—"

"You said you came to discuss Dr. DuBois' NCT."

Dugrow's eyes noticeably dimmed. He turned away from Kramer and said, "Yes—Yes, I did come to discuss that. The Centralized Committee has reviewed the mathematics which Dr. DuBois printed for us. We have concluded that Dr. DuBois..." Dugrow's voice dropped to little more than a mumble. "...might be on to something."

"Oh, you have?" DuBois asked. "Well, tell me, can this information be of general use to the Community and any other Community worlds that could possibly help us?"

"The answer is yes to both questions. There is a world which recently became a member of the Community, but it is neither a planet nor a space station. It is, in fact, a cosmic string."

DuBois was astounded. "A *cosmic string?!*"

"You know what a cosmic string is—a one-dimensional hyperspatial filament."

"Yes, I know what a cosmic string is."

Butch said, "Uh, my cosmology's a little rusty. What is a cosmic string?"

DuBois thought for a moment, then said, "Picture taking a singularity—the center of a black hole—and stretching it out to almost infinite length across the universe. It's basically a remnant of the Big Bang."

"Elementary particles are the key, as I understand it," Dugrow said. "The creatures who live on this cosmic string have a mastery of them."

"*Creatures* who live on a cosmic string?" DuBois asked, dumbfounded.

"They're called Etuknips, and they perceive an infinity on the surface of their cosmic string, even though from the outside we could perceive a one-dimensional length with no thickness, no depth. Remove them from the cosmic string and they, astonishingly, resemble organic beings, much like us, with metabolism similar to ours. They even have DNA."

"That's extraordinary!"

"Not really. It was once theorized that all matter in our universe was two-dimensional, was merely a projection in a giant cosmic computer program."

"That was disproven centuries ago," DuBois said.

"But it fit the mathematics. In the case of this cosmic string, it is true. The Etuknips have proposed utilizing your discoveries to develop a device which converts kevlons to taus. This is incredibly significant because it would seem to match the Thermian influence on our universe."

"In other words, if we could develop an energy source which is identical to the Thermians, we might find a way of fighting them on their level."

"Them and the Dreb."

"The NCT is only capable of giving us Dreb powers briefly, but the device you're talking about—"

"This device could be the long-sought Thermian Destroyer!"

And so the arrangements were made, the Etuknips contacted, and Kramer had waited for their transmission.

Once it came, though, Dugrow had more conditions to level.

It came after Kramer had tried unsuccessfully to file a complaint with the Hyron government against Zoran, the crazed Hyron commander who, Kramer had suspected, sent an assassin to kill him.

"Well," Dugrow said, "it seems you don't have the control over the Hyron Empire that you thought you did."

"I never claimed to have control over the Hyron Empire," Kramer protested.

"But you *did* claim to wield control over the Community. Perhaps it's time for the Valdor to reassert themselves. So let me make myself clear: when the Etuknips come aboard your station, you may find that they have internal difficulties—difficulties that, knowing you, you will have a hard time resisting interfering with! So let me just say this: our relations with this newly discovered and exotic species cannot be jeopardized by your whimsical, self-righteous interference. You will stay *out* of their affairs. There is to be *no interference!* You will obtain from them the technology necessary to develop the Thermian Destroyer. Beyond that, *stay out!"*

"I had no intention of interfering in their affairs."

"I've noticed that your *intentions* rarely translate into reality!"

"You realize the Hyrons won't take kindly to your asserting this kind of control over Station Post One."

"From what I've seen here today, you can no longer rely on the Hyrons to be your muscle—and even if you can, the Valdor are prepared to take that chance! I will take my leave of you now."

Dugrow clattered out of the room, leaving Kramer exasperated, confused, and exhausted.

He went to his privacy pod to squeeze in a quick power nap before finishing his shift. But he found his realscreen flashing with a recorded message. The mysterious Etuknips had contacted him.

CHAPTER 5

The face of politics had changed little in the past four thousand years, and probably longer. Politicians were short-sighted fools, and bureaucracy won the day with often mind-numbingly stupid decisions. Kramer had seen many of these decisions, if not firsthand, then at least secondhand.

He had been very young when the Space Star *Silver Streak* had fled the Earth twenty-two years ago. In the middle of his primary school years, he had been roughly displaced at age 15 when his family had won their ticket to survival, and for a year had been forced to suspend his education—before the *Silver Streak*'s own education system had been firmly put in place and into operation.

In those early days, he had paid close attention to the goings-on in the Congressional Council, and one of the first things that had happened after the destruction of the Earth was the civil unrest, threats of violence, and even a number of assassination attempts on Council members. And so, to safeguard their own lives, the Council had passed a new measure establishing a secret ballot—an emergency measure, but one that had never gone away. To

this day there was no record of which way
senators voted. It was unjust and contrary to the
ancient rules of democracy—but crisis always
stripped away the norms of freedom.

Another dumb decision had been a weird
compromise between public relations and the
requirements of security: the bridge of the *Silver
Streak* was open to all who wished to visit at any
time—but that fact was not disclosed to the
general public. The convoluted reasoning behind
that was, since the *Silver Streak* was a civilian
ship that would have to function as a world, the
civilians ought to have access to its nerve center.
But recognizing the reality that it would be
dangerous for anyone at any time to wander onto
the bridge, the fact that people had that freedom
was kept secret; and so, in practice, that freedom
did not exist at all.

That bizarre rule now extended to Station
Post One, whose status was ambiguous at best.
Was this a civilian station temporarily leased to
the Command Section? Or was it a military
station that kept a civilian contractor on board?
Before assuming command, Kramer had assumed
that had all been tidied up and there would be no
conflict—but was he ever wrong! He had clashed
with Intercore's CEO, Zach Mortimer, since the
day the station had been deployed.

But now, in opening relations with the
Etuknips, he had been forced to accept another
perplexing condition: the Etuknips would take
over the station's security.

When Dugrow had told him of that condition,
he had openly laughed in the Valdor
Administrator's face—or whatever passed for a
face. He would have to be insane to place alien

beings about which nothing was known in charge of his station's security. But Dugrow was adamant; it was a part of Etuknip culture that they were to oversee their own safety and the safety of their hosts. To refuse this would be the height of discourtesy—and these relations were far too important to risk offending the aliens.

And so Kramer agreed, though not without a great deal of trepidation. The Valdor had agreed to take responsibility for any security breaches—a remarkable concession for the arrogant, crablike aliens—so he felt constrained to accept this unwelcome situation.

The Etuknips were among the most alien life forms ever encountered, and they thought very differently than humans. The overall mission of learning about the Thermians and the Dreb—and defeating them—took precedence over short-term security concerns. It wasn't a good deal, but it was one Kramer felt he had to accept.

The Valdor had sent the Etuknips to Station Post One on this condition among others; the way Kramer saw it, the alternative was the Valdor would deal with the Etuknips directly, and that was unthinkable.

So he chose to learn from the Etuknips rather than digging in his heels and clinging to his own notions of security. It was a risk, he knew, but he hoped the benefits would outweigh the risk.

Anyway, by trusting the Etuknips to develop their ultimate weapon, he was already entrusting the security of the universe to them; it didn't seem so unreasonable in the scheme of things to entrust to them the safety of his own little space station.

Kramer's Deputy Commander, Tobey Dingell, saw things differently, of course—but he had the luxury to see things differently. He didn't have the responsibility of the station on his shoulders, and of the delicate interstellar relations with the Valdor, the Community, and now the Etuknips.

Fortunately he and Tobey worked well together, handled their disagreements civilly, and rarely clashed.

Station Post One's duty schedule was divided into three shifts: green, yellow, and blue. Green shift ran from 0700 to 1500, yellow from 1500 to 2200. Kramer and Tobey were on duty through green and yellow shifts—an unreasonably long shift which for that reason gave them great latitude to leave the Prime Hab Center any time they wished as long as the station was on level three alert status (the minimum alert level). They were both rather casual about when they reported for duty in the morning, and often left PHC early in the evening in order to finish the daily reports in time to take *some* leisure time before going to bed and then getting up to do it all over again. But even given these privileges, the fifteen-hour day was grueling, and it would be all too easy to lapse into bickering.

Fortunately Kramer had chosen his second-in-command well. He and Tobey were good friends, anticipated each other's needs, were sensitive to each other's moods, and were too emotionally mature to let disagreements devolve into shouting matches.

But the long hours and constant emergencies were a strain on their psyches, and they both wondered how much they could take before they both suffered nervous breakdowns.

CHAPTER 6

Long ago, the human race had been divided into four races. As an avid reader of ancient literature, Butch McCrae was well aware of the divisions along ethnic lines that had caused much needless hatred and suffering in antiquity.

The ancient scientific classifications of australoid, caucasoid, mongoloid, and negroid had defined, respectively, the black-skinned Aborigines of Australia, the fair-skinned Europeans, the tan Asians with their characteristic pinched eyelids, and the brown-skinned Africans. And these divisions had fluctuated over time, with other ethnic groups claiming their own racial identity, others merging, and of course all of them disappearing over the past two thousand years.

Today, of course, there were still gradations in skin color, but few people identified these with ethnicity, though ethnic origin was a source of pride for many people. Philippe Stargazer, the *Silver Streak*'s famous chief scientist, was so proudly French that he had become a joke to others. Jerome Flynn, chief of Station Post One's Battlehab and chief engineer of Intercore, wore his Irish heritage as a badge of honor and spoke with a thick Irish accent that, Butch had been amused to note, none of his family shared.

Tobey Dingell and Zach Mortimer undeniably had caucasian ancestry; Commander Kramer appeared to have some perhaps caucasian and black in him; Dr. Ebor DuBois maybe some caucasian and Asian. It was so hard to tell. Elmer Tepper's brown skin and curly hair would have likely identified him to the ancients as black.

Butch had looked himself in the mirror and tried to decide which race he most identified with—but the many generations had blurred the color lines in his family to such an extent that he could claim none as his own heritage. He knew that the name *McCrae* had Scottish ancestry, but that had been diluted by generations upon generations of Maxwells and Robinsons and Blakesleys and Breens and Gilmans and Loomises to the point that it meant nothing. That saddened him; as a student of Classical literature, he would have liked to lay claim to one of the ancient ethnicities.

But those old divisions were not only meaningless today, but had always been meaningless. The human race was *Homo sapiens*—there was no genetic difference between the races. Perhaps that wasn't true; Butch had read somewhere that before the races had merged, the caucasian race had been identified has having a trace of Neanderthal DNA that the other races lacked, and certain races were more susceptible to certain diseases; for example, sickle-cell anemia had been peculiar to the blacks.

Either way, though, skin color and facial characteristics had been a ridiculous reason for human beings to hate, enslave, and kill one another, but it had been done throughout history.

It was a testament to how meaningless racial divisions had become in the forty-first century that Butch could tease Tepper about his blackness without offending him; though Tepper was so ignorant of history that he might not even know that he would once have been classified as black. But Butch was also aware that there would have been a time when his teasing would have been not only socially unacceptable, but cause for his dismissal from duty, for he would have been considered "racist"—a person who judged people based on their race.

It was all very distant and incomprehensible, even to a student of history like Butch McCrae. He read about it, but didn't fully understand it.

He did know that the ancient United States of America—not the New United States, but the Original United States, the United States founded in 1776 and broken away from England—had been built on slave labor based on race. Blacks had been hired—no, that was the wrong word—*bought*, literally as property, owned by the masters of plantations, to work long hours for no pay, in miserable conditions, and treated worse than animals.

The increasing controversy over slavery had been a direct cause of America's First Civil War. Abraham Lincoln (whom many people today were surprised to learn was a real person) had freed the slaves and reuinited the country after the war, but the blacks were a far thing from truly free for a long time to come—centuries, in fact, according to some social historians. First there was the dishonest practice of sharecropping, then came the Ku Klux Klan who took it upon themselves to murder "uppity" blacks in terrifying night raids called "lynchings," and then came the Jim Crow laws (though Butch had never figured out who this Jim Crow had been) which imposed legal restrictions on the rights and freedoms of blacks.

The whole subject of race had come to Butch's attention, though, through his interest in ancient literature, and it had taken him a long time to figure out the early twentieth century entertainment known as the "minstrel show."

He had laughed because he sensed he was supposed to laugh, because it was absurd to see people with their faces painted jet-black with big clown lips, walking funny and talking funny. But if he was honest with himself, he didn't understand the humor, and he laughed because he always tried to respect ancient works of art and entertainment. And so when he had begun to research the origin of the minstrel show, he had been disconcerted.

But the ancient divisions and hatreds had few traces in today's world, and so although he had been dismayed to learn that a piece of comedy he sometimes enjoyed had its roots in hatred, he nevertheless felt none of the strong emotion that someone of an earlier time might, and no one on Station Post One had any cause to object to his enjoying those ancient shows that would once have held the dreaded title "racist."

Today, where there was no race, there was no such thing as racism. And so no one, even the identifiably black Tepper, had the slightest objection when Butch gave one of the Etuknips the name "Sambo." Butch could not help smiling when he watched the alien walking with a rather comical waddle, and talking in a manner that evoked the ancient minstrel shows.

It was up for debate whether it was a good thing or a bad thing that the human race had so forgotten race and racism that Butch's attitude offended no one—or it *would* have been up for debate, were race a thing to which any human being gave the slightest thought anymore.

Sambo took no offense at the name bestowed upon him, but then he had little contact with the humans. He had little contact with Ophelia either; he was merely one of the security officers who had come to take charge of Station Post One's security.

There were several positions to fill—security chief was a buff Etuknip whom Butch had named Hulk, Dock Deck security chief was a slight female much tougher than she appeared, for whom none of the humans had a name. Through some casual conversation—and some very subtle manipulation of timelines—Sambo had arranged to be placed in charge of the Control Booth during blue shift. Alone on duty during Station Post One's nocturnal shift, when most people were asleep, Sambo was in charge of coordinating arrivals and departures. There were few overnight, as most Community members respected the humans' day-night cycle.

But Sambo was expecting one—one that the humans were not.

CHAPTER 7

The Rec Pod was not the most private place for a romantic date, but Butch would take any place he could be in private with Ophelia. The Rec Pod was certainly not *private*, but so long as he sat at a table alone with her, most everyone left him alone; he only prayed Tepper didn't come in here.

"I hope you don't mind my calling you Ophelia," he told her in a tone much softer and more tender than he could recall using with anyone else. "It's just that I can't pronounce your real name."

"I mind not do."

Butch smiled; he was aware that he would have quickly grown annoyed with any other alien who mangled the language the way Ophelia did— and in fact he *did* grow annoyed with all the other Etuknips. But he never failed to be charmed by this beautiful female, and by everything about her.

"Where this Ophelia name did from come?"

Butch wondered how to explain an ancient play to a timeless alien. How could she understand his fascination for the ancient when she had no concept of ancient? Would she even understand the concept of a play, which was a story told in linear time in which the audience was unaware of the ending? "It's from a piece of human entertainment," was all he could think of.

"This entertainment phenomenon—interesting find it do I."

"Well, good! I'd be glad to treat you to a performance of *Hamlet*."

But if he did, wouldn't that mean she was already aware of it? Was there any part of her life that she did not already know? Could she be taken by surprise?

But then there was the fuzziness of reality, the quantum cloud, the other timelines.

At the moment Butch was more puzzled by Ophelia's biology—the fact that she had a biology at all! She was unable to eat most human foods, though she did drink water. The Etuknips had brought packets of some sort of high-energy substance which they drank. But now Ophelia ingested neither food nor drink, but light. She shone a small flashlight into her eyes, and Butch could see her retinas glowing.

"Oy, that freaks me out," he muttered.

"Problem is?"

"No, I just don't understand—well, how your body works."

"It different is yours from."

"You can say that again!"

"Again? Repeat twice in same timeline—yes. It different is yours from."

"No, that's not what I mean—oh, never mind."

"Communication difficult is between two species our, but easier somehow it you with is."

Butch smiled. "Well, I'm glad to hear that. I guess I was just wondering how you can derive nutrition from light, but then I guess that's no big thing. Plants do it, there's no reason in the world why you can't. But is there a lot of light in your world? I wouldn't think light would be possible on a cosmic string."

"Is it. From outside perspective, light only one direction travels along membrane, but once membrane laid out is in...*this* way..." She made a fist and then spread her long, slender, blue fingers out to spread her palm flat. "...then light is...what word is?...omnidirectional."

It was useless to inquire further. Even Dr. DuBois had trouble understanding Ophelia. Even normal conversation was challenging; her explanations of the physics of her native world was entirely baffling.

Still, in spite of the linguistic barrier, Butch found an easy camaraderie with this beautiful alien, a camaraderie that he didn't think existed between any of the other Etuknips and humans. Ophelia was friendly, warm, and kind, but his admitedly biased perception was that no one else enjoyed the same warm and comfortable companionship with her that he did. Was the attaction, he wondered, mutual? It was almost too much to hope—and even if so, what could they do about it?

"Different our species are," Ophelia told him regretfully. "Communication challenging is. Cannot even tense agree on."

"Yeah, well...no reason we can't be friends, is it?"

Her expression brightened; despite the problem with language, her expressive face always conveyed her meaning—more eloquently, in Butch's opinion, than a human face. "Oh, yes! So this is! Friends is!"

Butch smiled at that and lifted his glass in a toast. "To friendship." And he immediately realized she would have no idea what the gesture meant.

"Friendship our in a cup is?"

Butch laughed. "No, no, just a human custom." And now that he thought about it, Butch had no idea of the origin of the custom of the toast; he would have to research it. Certainly there was no way to explain it to an alien who had yet to grasp the concept of time.

And yet none of these gaps in their knowledge of each other, none of the awkward lapses in communication, none of the disconnect between their entirely dissimilar backgrounds cast a pall on the enjoyment they took in each other's company—or at least the enjoyment Butch took in Ophelia's company. At this stage of their budding friendship, he didn't dare ask if she returned his feelings.

Often during their conversations they fell into silence, neither able to think of anything to say. But these were not awkward silences; they were comfortable silences in which they—or at least *he*—reveled in the companionship. Usually when this happened, they smiled at each other and said, "Long silence."

Butch was beginning to feel like a teenager enmeshed in a torrid high school romance. He liked the feeling.

He fell into the habit of meeting Ophelia for lunch each day. Dr. DuBois didn't seem to mind; in fact he enjoyed the break. As brilliant a scientist as he was, his human mind was still too small to try to absorb the concepts Ophelia was imparting to him.

Butch was flattered that Ophelia not only made him part of her daily routine, but had made the effort to understand what a daily routine was in order to spend time—time! What a laugh!—with him.

"Differences lots," Ophelia said, "but many things same emotion."

Butch was puzzled. "What are you saying?"

"Saying you me friends."

Butch smiled. "You bet we're friends."

"DuBois Doctor scientist is, I scientist is. But closer and friendlier you and I is. Peculiar say you?"

Butch still wasn't entirely sure what Ophelia was getting at, but he thought she was confused as to why she had made friends with Butch rather than a fellow scientist. He hoped she wasn't saying that he had inflicted an unwanted friendship on her.

"No, no, not peculiar at all," he said. "People meet, they click or they don't. Job's got nothing to do with it." At least...*usually* it didn't. Or sometimes. Most of his friends were fellow pilots. Back on the *Silver Streak* he'd had some friends who were fellow students of Classical literature and music. But certainly when pursuing a romance, job never entered into it. Right?

"Anyway, anybody can meet and be friends no matter what their job is."

"Klay," Ophelia said.

Butch had heard her say that before and had not asked its meaning; he assumed it would take longer for her to explain than for him to deduce the meaning from context. It seemed to be generally a term of acceptance or consent.

"But interest to do with it does. I not do care about fighting or spaceships flying."

Butch had to admit, he would have taken offense had anyone else said that. He would have indignantly protested the joy of flying, the beauty of a fine ship, the intellectual and physical superiority of that species of human called *pilot*. But when Ophelia said it, he only felt warmth and compassion.

"Well, that's okay. You've got, I don't know...class and inner beauty that..." He trailed off. He hadn't meant to be so open with his feelings. But then again, how long should he hold back? If he never told her how he felt about her, then how would they...

That thought led down dark corridors. How would they *what?* He still didn't know what he expected, or even wanted, from this strange, otherworldly figure. Surely they couldn't have any kind of relationship. Even if they were of compatible species, which was clearly impossible, and even if bestiality were socially acceptable, the fact was she wouldn't be aboard the station for long. Eventually she and the other Etuknips would fly off to their cosmic string, and Butch would never see her again.

"And you a self inner have," Ophelia said. "More there is to you than fighting and spaceships flying."

"Yeah, yeah, there is." Butch felt himself flushing. He was glad she had noticed; he wasn't sure how he had put his "self inner" on display for her, but she had proven as insightful as he had suspected. "I guess not a lot of people see that."

He stared at his lunch, realizing he hadn't taken a bite in many minutes. It was hard to take his eyes from the ethereal beauty before him, and to stop studying and gauging her reactions to him. He took a bite of now-cold dijon chicken—not real chicken, of course; only the colonists on virgin planets were reduced to eating animal meat, but the old names lingered.

When he looked up, he saw that Ophelia was still staring at him with those dark yet somehow luminous eyes. Such unplumbed mystery behind those eyes, such an exotic world; and yet she seemed perfectly willing to open herself to him. He wondered why.

His mind inevitably wandered back to the beautiful words of the Bard. And he then found a way to speak his feelings without taking too great a risk, for he could always quite truthfully claim he was just quoting.

"Oh, she doth teach the torches to burn bright!
It seems she hangs upon the cheek of night
Like a rich jewel in an Ethiope's ear."

Again blissfully unaware of the racial context of the quote, he spoke the words of pure and simple love as innocently—and perhaps as naively—as had Romeo.

"This is?" Ophelia asked.

"Uh...just a quote.

Did my heart love till now? Forwear it, sight!
For I ne'er saw true beauty till this night."

"These words related are to what talking we about were?"

Butch was embarrassed. "I guess....ah...what I'm just saying is, uh, I think you, uh, mean a lot to me."

There. He had said it. Okay, he hadn't confessed his love—except in the words of Shakespeare—but he had told her in plain and simple language that she was more to him than a lunch companion.

But then that wasn't such a bold step, since they had been talking about friendship anyway.

"Klay," she said again—and again he interpreted it as an affirmative. "And...you a lot me to mean."

When Butch went back on duty, Tepper gave him a lot of funny looks, but never asked why he kept smiling through the rest of shift.

CHAPTER 8

The most persistent argument aboard Station Post One was also the oldest: who's in charge? As far as Zach Mortimer was concerned, the answer was obvious: *I am.*

Commander Kramer didn't see it that way, and so they had locked horns ever since the station had been dropped into space by the Space Star *Silver Streak*. But of course the antipathy between the two men went back to before the station's deployment—a year before, actually.

Zach Mortimer was the CEO of Intercore Corporation, a leading technological company based aboard the *Silver Streak*, the Omega Colonies, and several other colonies. For years, Mortimer had tried to secure a bigger portion of the *Silver Streak*'s defense department—and with that end in view had developed a replacement Carrier. To his great dismay, and his company's calamitous financial loss, he had lost the contract; though the investment had finally been recouped when that Carrier became Station Post One's Dock Deck.

Intercore had also designed a new type of space fighter, the D-4000. The *Silver Streak*'s captain, Richard Cameron, had assigned Kramer, then the chief of the Operations Center, to investigate Mortimer's company with the specific objective of finding a reason to reject the D-4000. Kramer had wormed his way into Mortimer's graces on the pretense of working with him to solve integration issues between the D-4000 and the Carrier's computer systems.

Kramer had accomplished his mission, finding numerous flaws in the D-4000 (all of which were now solved, and *would* have been solved without Kramer's interference), and thus he had lost that contract too.

It all turned out well in the end; Mortimer still marketed the perfected D-4000 to the Command Section the following fiscal year, and now the new fighters were in use aboard Station Post One along with the QV Fighters. But he had never forgiven Kramer for his duplicity—even though he acknowledged that it was just business, and he would have done the same in Kramer's position.

But he would never let Kramer have an easy job running the station that Intercore had designed.

It was Mortimer who had first approached the Valdor about establishing a human space station in their space. It was Mortimer who had pushed the Congressional Council and Captain Cameron to approve it. It was Mortimer who had given up his comfortable office on the *Silver Streak* and left behind the bulk of his assets to live in this little station. And it was Mortimer who ultimately made the decisions—at least in his own mind.

More recently, he had reached a separate peace with Kramer. The Doomsday War had taught everyone an important lesson—and its aftermath left little room for petty arguments.

And there was another, more subtle reason for the softening of Mortimer's relationship with Kramer, and it was a strange thing indeed.

One of Intercore's innovations, driven by Mortimer's own fiery passion, was a transduct, a device that could instantly transport a person across many light years of space. It was originally a Valdor device, but Mortimer had copied the technology, and with the help of Jerome Flynn had developed a working model.

The transduct was supposed to transport people to other transducts. But Mortimer had tested it himself—and found himself in four different places simultaneously, some *without* transduct units. With the Valdor's help, the multiple Zach Mortimers had been reintegrated into one man, but the effects of that experience had never entirely gone away.

Ever since then, he had felt different. It was a disconcerting feeling, but not an unpleasant one. In fact it was a very pleasurable feeling, though the source of that pleasure was something he could neither identify nor explain—and he did not dare discuss it with anyone.

He felt a sense of companionship. Even when he was alone, he felt there was someone with him, someone watching after him, loving him. He worried over this feeling, wondering if he was going mad. Sometimes he said things and did things he had never done before—things he didn't even *want* to do. Striking up friendly conversations with people he didn't like. Helping people with personal problems when he really didn't give a shit about them.

And in dark moments, like his time as a prisoner on the Valdor Artificial World, or on Strikton, he had felt that presence stronger than ever—like the way Christians felt the presence of Jesus Christ—as though there really were some sort of invisible deity caring for him. It didn't change his luck, and he didn't pray to it...but it had a name.

Fweery.

He didn't know what it meant, and it scared him. Or at least it *started* to scare him until that presence washed the fear away and consoled him.

Still, business went on. And the last few days aboard Station Post One had been very interesting with the Etuknips on board.

He made sure to keep in close contact with Dr. DuBois, following closely the development of the kevlon-tau converter. He wished he could develop the device himself, but right now there was nothing more he could do than try to keep up with all the developments, and hope one of his own engineers or scientists could make the final breakthrough before DuBois did. To patent a real, honest-to-God Thermian Destroyer would make Intercore a fortune to rival the Clanton Plasmium Company!

Even if his people failed to beat DuBois to the final development, it would still be possible to manipulate DuBois into selling him the patent. DuBois was not a business-savvy man; he was a scientist who worked day and night for the sake of science. He cared nothing for money or business; sometimes Mortimer wondered if he even really cared about defeating the Thermians. DuBois cared only about knowledge.

Mortimer felt no disdain for DuBois; he cared about knowledge himself. That was, after all, what drove his company's innovations, and his own considerable wealth. He just felt that DuBois was blinkered. But that was fine, since it meant DuBois could be manipulated, and manipulating people was a large part of Mortimer's job.

Don't think that way, Zach. It's wrong.

Mortimer often had to shove those thoughts aside these days, the voice of a conscience he thought he had long ago suppressed. In business, the only ethic was *making money*. And making money was all about manipulating people in one way or other—manipulating them into handing over their money, or manipulating people to place other people in the position to be manipulated into handing over their money.

So far he had failed to manipulate Commander Kramer. He had some hopes for Tobey Dingell; Kramer wouldn't be the commander forever, someday Dingell would take over—and Mortimer sensed a trace of instability in Dingell, a shade of potential corruption, a weakness that could be exploited.

But that day was not yet. For now he must deal with Kramer.

Ever since the war, he had deferred to Kramer's authority. Both men were tired of the repetitive "I'm in command" arguments, and so for that and other, more complex, reasons, Mortimer had granted Kramer the victory in this case. But he was not finished. He still wanted his slice of Station Post One.

Intercore, like all forty-first century corporations, was a collective—meaning it was employee-owned. There were no such thing as shareholders in the modern world; that was as barbaric a concept today as lords and serfs. Mortimer was accountable only to his customers and his employees, and his employees could fire him as surely as he could fire them.

Of course, like all systems from the feudal to the capitalist to the communist to the fascist to the modern collective, power eventually conglomerated at the top, and those on the bottom found themselves powerless. The situation usually changed only with sudden, and often violent, revolution—and then the cycle would begin again.

Yes, his employees could *theoretically* vote him out at the next quarterly meeting, but they never had, and he doubted they ever would. He still stood as CEO in spite of standing trial for war crimes, for heaven's sake. He had served as CEO for a solid thirty-two quarters, and he expected to continue in this role until he retired. He was the most experienced—and he knew how to bribe. Even if he was voted out, it was likely the company would instantly feel the pain of the loss of his experience, and he would be voted in again the next quarter. Although he was technically just a cog in the wheel, an employee like any other, for all practical purposes Intercore was *his*, and he thought of it as *his*.

If any part of Station Post One was *his*, it was the Dock Deck. The two Habs had been designed to operate as weather stations over colonies, and had been adapted as components of a larger, self-sufficient, deep space station.

The Dock Deck, dammit, was *his* Carrier. It was only the Dock Deck because the

Congressional Council, on some stupid whim, had decided they didn't want a saucer-shaped warship—which was just stupid. It fit just fine in the *Silver Streak*'s Carrier Bay, it was lighter and more maneuverable than the old Carrier, its technology was more up to date, and the circular shape and larger launch tubes optimized it as both a command center and a launch center, and allowed for the launch of many different types of ship.

Well, so now it was serving a vital role on Station Post One, so Mortimer had the last laugh. Soon that old Carrier on the *Silver Streak* would wear out, and the Council could drool with envy as they watched Station Post One.

He felt a strong emotional connection to the Dock Deck, and he didn't like that it was operating under Kramer's command and under the supervision of that crass idiot Butch McCrae. But right now the Dock Deck was under full control by the Prime Hab Center, the Battlehab Center, and Butch McCrae's office.

Mortimer could gain access to any of those locations, but he lacked the startup codes and access keys, and so could only command Dock Deck operations while logged in to someone else's account. He could hack those accounts, but someone would always catch on.

He wanted those startup codes and access keys, and at the moment had no strategy to get them. But his eyes were always open, his mind always calculating, always searching for an opportunity...

...even as that insistent voice in his head said *Enough, Zach...you've been greedy all your life... the time has come to be generous....*

CHAPTER 9

Although Butch was unaware of it, everyone around him had noticed his infatuation with Ophelia, including Commander Kramer. Leaving Tobey Dingell in charge of the Prime Hab Center, Kramer went down to the Rec Pod to lunch by himself, and found himself sitting near Butch and Ophelia. He did not mean to eavesdrop, but there was no mistaking the giddy tone in Butch's voice, or the lovesick expression on his face.

Well, Ophelia didn't seem to mind his attention, but Kramer would be damned if he allowed a silly romance to mess up Station Post One's relations with the Etuknips. The prospect of developing a Thermian Destroyer was too important—and equally critical, the Valdor had made their own opinions on the matter *quite* clear.

At the same time, Kramer recognized the emotions which Butch was so prominently displaying, and he sympathized with the lovestruck Dock Deck Chief.

His mind went back to the *Silver Streak*...all those planetary missions he had monitored from the science lab, working in close proximity with Kiani Fulquist.

To the best of his memory, he had never spoken to Kiani, but he had watched her out of the corner of his eye; she had worked at the next table over, and he had always tried to catch glimpses of various parts of her anatomy as she moved. He had known nothing about her in those days—and even now what he knew was restricted to what was on her gab on the SPACEWEB.

Of course, even then he had known she was in the biological sciences (he knew now she was a biophysicist), and for some reason something about that turned him on. *Everything* about her turned him on; she was, without exception, the most desirable human being he had ever seen.

But as near as he could tell, she was never aware of his existence. And he had never dared approach her. No one had ever accused him of being timid, but for some reason Kiani Fulquist was more terrifying to him than a hull breach or a radiation leak. And so although he watched her every day and dreamed of her at night, he did nothing about it.

But then, when he had joined the colony on Fresno-B IV, he had met Jill Freeport. It was a funny thing about Jill—she wasn't that pretty; her skin was mottled with freckles and large pores, her nose was an unattractive hook shape, and her jaw was too prominent and too square. But somehow she was attractive anyway, with her bright eyes, infectious smile, musical laugh, and black, shiny hair. And her *body*—her body was *perfect*, one of the most perfect models of the ideal human female he had ever seen.

She was his supervisor in the Space Tracking Center, which kept the colony in touch with the other colonies and monitored the skies for asteroids or, God forbid, hostile aliens. Consequently, unlike Kiani Fulquist, he had frequent contact with Jill, and she was always kind, friendly, and easy to talk to. It didn't take long for him to consider her a friend.

He learned quickly that she was engaged to Bobby Fredericks, so he entertained no thoughts of a relationship with her—well, all right, he *thought* about it, but he was quite aware that those thoughts were mere fantasies.

But then one day she came to work visibly depressed. She nitpicked his work, snapped at people, and was generally unpleasant to be around. He was irritated and decided he had overestimated her; but then, by chance, he ended up having lunch with her. They sat in silence until he noticed that she was crying.

It wasn't in his nature to ignore a crying woman, so he asked, "Hey, you all right?"

She nodded. "Sorry." She gave a nervous laugh and said, "I broke it off with my fiancée."

"Oh, I'm sorry!"

She shrugged. "It wasn't working. He's a great guy, but I'd been thinking for a long time that we just weren't right together."

Kramer was ashamed of himself for taking sheer delight in the news. He shouldn't revel in her pain—especially since he still had no real plans to date her himself (after all, she was his supervisor). But he took great pleasure in comforting her that afternoon, and counseling her to the best of his ability. He felt he was rather clumsy about it, searching for the right words and often stumbling over himself, but eventually he found himself giving her a heartfelt speech about how she had made the right decision, that it might hurt right now but she had to make the right choices in her life—and, what the hell, he told her someone as attractive and as kind as she was would have no trouble finding someone else.

People came and went through the break room, but seeing the rather intense conversation, they tended to grab their lunch and move on to the patio to eat, so Kramer and Jill had a modicum of privacy to talk. It was the most sincere and intimate conversation they had ever had, and it left Kramer feeling both embarrassed and proud of himself—and pleased that he might, just might have opened a new chapter in his relationship with this endearing woman.

Wiping her eyes, she said, "Well, thanks for letting me bend your ear. Sorry I've been such a bitch today."

"Oh, you haven't been!" Actually she had been, but well, what else was he going to say? "I just hope you're feeling better."

"Oh, I will."

They went back to work and spoke nothing more of the encounter.

But a few months later, Kramer worked up the nerve to ask her if she would like to join him for Christmas dinner. She agreed.

He never referred to their dinner as a "date"; he never intimated that it was anything more than a dinner between friends. But when he picked her up, she was wearing a dazzling blue sleeveless dress with sparkling crystals, and a softly glowing tiara that was all the rage that year.

He took her to Griselde's Restaurant, the finest restaurant in the colony—which still was no match for even a fast food joint back on Earth, but afforded them a chance for an intimate, one-on-one meal unaffected by their work relationship.

It was funny how well they got along; they really had little in common. Aside from their mutual fields of study, their interests diverged wildly. She wanted a large family; he wasn't sure he wanted one at all. She was fanatic about aerobics (which no doubt explained her perfect figure), where he found the subject more dull than a slowly drying bucket of paint. She was politically conservative, he was politically progressive. She was a devout Indo-Christian, he was an atheist. In fact, they agreed on practically nothing; yet they never argued. In fact, they took pleasure in their disagreements and the lively conversations they stirred.

After that, he could no longer deny his romantic feelings for her—though he didn't allow this to affect his work relationship with her—and a week later, he told her how much he had enjoyed their dinner and asked if she would be interested in another date...and this time he used the word "date." His legs nearly collapsed under him as he waited what seemed an eternity for her answer—while she sat, staring at the ceiling and chewing her cheek. It was probably no more than a second, though it felt like an hour, before she smiled and said, "I'd love to!"

The second date was very different from the first, as there were no pretentions that this was anything less than a romance. Rather than filling the night with chatty small talk and jokes, she effusively complimented his appearance, talked about how much she enjoyed his company, and while they were waiting for their dinner, slipped off her shoe and ran her foot up his leg—stopping short of the critical erogenous zone.

By the time the meal was over, both were breathless with passion, and they adjourned to her apartment outside the colony, where they made love all night.

The one thing they seemed to agree on was what pleasured them, and their lovemaking was in near perfect synchronicity. If a relationship could be only physical, theirs was—except that despite their myriad differences, they enjoyed a close friendship that grew closer by the day. He wasn't sure how to account for that, and he often wondered how long it would be before their first big fight.

Yet four months of steady dating went by and this never happened. They reveled in each other's company, laughed at each other's jokes, and loved engaging each other in debates that left both of them thinking.

Not that he didn't have moments of impatience with her, and he was sure the same was true for her. But this generally happened at work; sometimes she nitpicked his work, or told him to do something when he was in the middle of something else, and he would just wish she would shut up and leave him alone. And sometimes he would go into the supervisors' area to ask her a question and she would give off the unmistakeable vibe that he was interrupting her. And there was that awkward time when she had presented his efficiency report in the boss's office, and had to lay out his areas for improvement. The criticisms would have stung under any circumstances, but coming from her they felt almost like betrayal.

But they were both mature enough to leave such concerns in the office, and to understand that such things were bound to happen and they meant nothing.

By May (which was actually the colony's deep winter), he had begun to consider a life with Jill.

It seemed premature, as they had not even decided that they were in a steady relationship; technically there was no formal understanding that they couldn't date anyone else. He wasn't sure she didn't consider him just a good friend who was good in the sack. And if he were really honest with himself, he wasn't entirely sure he was *in love* with her; she was a very, very good friend and he had a great time having sex with her, but he didn't really feel that rush of endorphins that accompanied love.

But the more he thought about it, the more he thought that didn't matter. There were all kinds of love. He loved her as a friend and as a lover, and he was sure she would be a good wife and—if she got her way—a good mother. Was anything more really necessary?

Even under the strange circumstances of their sort-of relationship, they began to mention the possibility of marriage. He didn't remember which of them brought it up first, but they discussed it casually, sometimes as a possibility for the future, sometimes as an inevitability they both took for granted. In a number of ways, they already acted like a married couple.

So one weekend, after a partcularly blissful day together followed by a night of breathless thrashing in bed, Kramer went out to the shopping district to find a wedding ring. There was nothing fancy in the colony; he settled for a bronze ring with a heart shape carved on it. But he knew she would understand the circumstances; he only wondered if she would accept. Even if they both assumed that marriage lay somewhere in their future, was this the time?

Well, he was never to find out.

As he watched Butch McCrae with his big puppy dog eyes and goofy smile, he felt a certain contempt for him, and a feeling of jealousy as he thought of his ill-fated romance with Jill...and of his unrequited passion for Kiani.

But he also felt a welling of compassion, for both of them. Compassion, sadness, and pity— because there was no way their love story could end well.

CHAPTER 10

People of the twentieth and twenty-first centuries would have thought that future historians would consider the greatest scientific discovery of their time to be general relativity. But historians of the forty-first century, though they acknowledged the revolutionary contributions of Einstein, Hawking, Dirac, and Heisenberg, considered the twentieth century's most important contribution to humankind's knowledge to be something that few laymen of that time had ever heard of: Planck's Constant.

It was true that light speed, artificial gravity, and antigravity were applications of quantum relativity, the direct descendant of Einstein's theory, but none of them would be possible without Planck's Constant. Nor would lasers, interstellar communication, quantum computing, plasmium, or most of the other technologies that enabled civilization to survive post-Earth.

It had long been theorized that energy, like matter, was made of tiny particles. If matter was made of atoms, it stood to reason that energy itself, and even light, were made of packets. It was Max Planck who, in 1900, experimented to find the solution for two competing theories about black body radiation, and measured the precise energy of those packets: 6.626×10^{-34} Joule seconds.

Though not as well-known as $E=mc^2$, that number described the precise energy value of a single packet, or quantum, of energy. No more, no less. And that constant governed the behavior of the universe.

Since the orbit of an electron around the nucleus of an atom was synonymous with its energy level, it was physically impossible for it to exist between energy levels. To do so would violate Planck's Constant. And so, in order to move from one shell to another, an electron must jump instantaneously—*without traversing the intervening space*.

Every time a laser was turned on, electrons were "teleporting" from higher energy levels to lower. Every time a superconductor was used (for instance to collide atoms and create a singularity for the Gravity Propulsion System), the energy dissipation speed limit came into play—which was linked to Planck's Constant.

It was why the elements existed and why they bonded to form molecules. It was why the brain worked and why it was susceptible to manipulation by the Thermians, and so it was how the Dreb obtained their powers.

The "spooky action at a distance" that popped up in Einstein's equations was found by quantum relativity to be the same phenomenon as the electron tunneling demanded by Planck's Constant—and that made interstellar communication possible, as there was no other way to transmit signals instantaneously, without running up against that pesky speed of light.

Every aspect of forty-first century technology was based on that number discovered at the dawn of the twentieth century. And it was Planck's Constant—along with quantum relativity, which was itself intertwined with Planck's Constant—that made the world of the cosmic string possible. Quantum relativity had also revealed that Planck's Constant applied not just to spacetime and matter-energy, but time; for time itself had a smallest possible particle. It was called a chronon, named for a hypothetical shortest possible unit of time first proposed by Robert Lévi in 1927. In quantum relativity, it was a unit of time that was indivisibly small, and was identical to the Planck Time, the amount of time it took for light to travel the Planck length: 5.39×10^{-44} seconds. And like an elementary particle, the chronon was measurable as both a point of time and as a wave, with its greatest probability lying in the moment of Now.

Sambo knew these things intuitively. On his world, spacetime was a material thing, as mutable and changeable as a blanket or a cloth in the three-dimensional universe. He had the same difficulty as the other Etuknips in adjusting to human time references, but in addition to adjusting, he had also to overcome his fear. He had been specially trained for this mission, but one doesn't simply turn off an eternity—past and future—of fear.

For Sambo, unlike the other Etuknips on Station Post One, was a Sweg.

The Sweg feared all times but Now—Now being that one moment, that chronon of time, in which all the Sweg lived their lives. The Sweg feared invasion from other times and from other timelines.

And these three-dimensional creatures, these *humans* who lived outside the Infinity of the cosmic string, they represented an invasion as frightening as the mythical pirate from the future.

It had not been easy to fool the Leira, but determination and persistence had won the day. It would be difficult for a human to understand exactly how Sambo had wormed his way into the Leira's confidence, but suffice it to say he had shifted the timelines in subtle ways so that he had been friends with one of the Leira leaders for a long "time"—though that in itself was an inaccurate measure of life on the cosmic string.

Upon leaving the cosmic string, he and the other Etuknips had discovered a world, a whole way of being, unimaginable to them. Here they were locked into a single reality, a single timeline. They moved inexorably and without control from past to future. Cause led to single effect. Only one decision could be made, and once made, was irrevocable. It was a hellish existence, one with no freedom.

But it was also exhilarating. Most of the Leira reveled in it, even as they feared it; such was the curious mind of a Leiras. But Sambo was not exhilarated; he was terrified.

Cautiously, he reached out and made a tiny tweak to the timelines—just to assure himself that he could. It was comforting to know that his physical structure still contained enough of the cosmic string's properties that he could still shift realities if he must, could still fold time and space even if only to a small extent.

That also increased his chances of accomplishing his mission—though he had to use his abilities sparingly; the Leira could trace any spacetime tinkering. So as much as possible, and preferably all the time, Sambo must follow the laws of this universe.

That was why he had arranged to be placed in the nocturnal shift in the Dock Deck. From here, he could arrange the arrival of the Sweg ship—for yes, both the Sweg and the Leira had developed spaceships, specifically for this mission.

He wished he could communicate with other Sweg—find out how things were going, or just to hear a friendly voice. He could disappear into the future if he so chose, but the risk was too great—his spacetime resonance would cause a disturbance in the gravitational fabric of Now. In fact the effect would be multiplied, for Now appeared to be an even stronger focal point here than it was back home. All consciousness was drawn to it, with very little variability.

There was *some*; past, present, and future became fused with distance because of the speed of light. But for all practical purposes, Now was Now, as fixed as a singularity, with little freedom to escape.

Sambo could escape if he wished, but if he moved more than a few seconds from Now, the other Etuknips would know.

So he played by the rules. He acted as a three-dimensional being. He pushed buttons, he communicated by intercom and by transmitter, and he spoke this incomprehensible language with its constant tenses and continuous references to the passage of time.

And he waited. Soon the Sweg would come, and he could escape this frightening, disorienting assignment...and go home.

CHAPTER 11

"Having trouble gettin' a date, Butch?"

"I'm ignoring any comments about my personal life, *Tepper*."

"Cuz I'm just sayin', I mean, you know, there are *human* women on the station, you know."

"I am above this kind of thing, *Tepper*."

"I'm just wondering what a strange creature that evolved on a cosmic string, who doesn't even have our anatomy, has to offer that, say, Tammy Streit or Calista Redgrave don't."

"I happen to be interested in her culture, *Tepper*."

"Oh! Her culture. Of course."

Butch had known it was only a matter of time before Tepper caught on to what was going on between him and Ophelia—and the fact that it had taken this long reinforced his opinion of Tepper's intellect, if not his nose for gossip.

But he was prepared for the needling; he had been ever since he had first developed an interest in Ophelia. Even if he'd had a crush on one of the human crew members, Tepper and the others would be teasing him. He could take it. But the fact that Ophelia was not human only made it worse, because really he had no business having a romantic interest in a nonhuman.

He had heard stories in the past about men having sex with dogs or horses, and he had come across bizarre corners of the SPACEWEB promoting animal porn—or animal/human porn. He had always found such things not only bizarre, but sickening.

And yet now he not only engaged in nightly sexual fantasies about Ophelia, but was rapidly developing a definite intention to make those fantasies come true. How was that different from lusting after a pig or a donkey?

Yes, she was intelligent—but so were whales and elephants, and he would never harbor a sexual thought about one of them, even were he to develop a deep friendship with one.

She *looked* generally human, despite her blue skin and the fact that her "hair" was not hair at all, but a complex sensory web. But the great apes looked human too, and he found them repulsive.

So what was the difference? Why had he okayed his own sexual and romatic feelings for this creature—who had far less in common with humans than apes or elephants or donkeys or dogs or horses?

He didn't know. Even though she was not human, he somehow thought of her as human—or as an uber-human, an embodiment of human potential.

There was likely a certain level of human arrogance in his discrimination. Apes were very human-like, but they were behind humans on the evolutionary scale. No matter that they had arms and legs and expressive faces with eyes, noses, and mouths in the right places, and thinking brains only a little behind *Homo sapiens*—they were, nevertheless, identifiably and unambiguously *animals*.

Ophelia, though considerably less human than an ape on the genetic scale, *looked* more human than an ape did, and had a far more sophisticated mind than an ape—*or* a human. And she could talk. Butch had to admit that made a difference; he asked himself if he could be attracted to an ape who could talk, and he wasn't sure he could answer honestly. (The fur would probably ruin it for him.)

The answer was probably much simpler than all his philosophical and genetic musings; Ophelia may not be human, or related to life on Earth in any way, but she *looked* like a blue-skinned human. It would be easy for a woman to paint herself blue and pass for an Etuknip. The other clues to Ophelia's nonhuman nature were unmistakable, but subtle.

In fact, those very features seemed to enhance her humanness, not detract from it. Her enormous eyes, for instance. No human being had such eyes, but eyes of that kind had existed in human artwork for millennia, going all the way back to the Egyptian heiroglyphs. Her large breasts—which were not breasts at all, but some sort of sensory gland peculiar to Etuknip females. Her perfect hourglass figure—which all Etuknips had, even the males—as if the Etunkips were an idealized version of human.

Butch thought about the old stories about aliens visiting Earth in ancient times, and couldn't help wondering if there was some truth to them. If the Etuknips had visited Earth, then they could only have been taken for angels. He wondered what Tepper, with his religious upbringing, would think of that.

Yet Ophelia had denied that the Etuknips had ever visited Earth, and she seemed certain. So the phyical resemblance between Etuknips and humans must be coincidence—or deception. Butch did not think Ophelia was deceptive, but it was possible they had somehow assumed the most practical form to come aboard Station Post One.

More likely their present form reflected their original organic state before they had gone to the cosmic string. Dr. DuBois felt sure that the Etuknips had originated as three-dimensional beings, had evolved on a planet like most normal life forms, and had, by accident or design, gone to the cosmic string and somehow been transferred there and survived. Human-like life was not unknown in the galaxy; scientists generally agreed this was a result of different planets, and different solar systems, constantly exchanging meteoric material. Many worlds of different star systems must have been delivered a serving of the same genetic soup that had jumpstarted life on other worlds. From that origin, similar climatic conditions had led to similar life forms.

And then there were many planets that may or may not be lost Earth colonies. Could the Etuknips be a lost race of humans who had set off from Earth and stumbled into a cosmic string?

"Given the timelessness of the Etuknip world, seems to me it's a possibility we can't discount," Butch said to DuBois one day when Ophelia was in a meeting with the other Etuknips.

"I don't think so," DuBois said. "Yes, it could be that the Etuknips only entered the cosmic string last week, and all their history took place in a single moment, but I don't think the nature of their world would allow for the kind of biological evolution we see in them. That kind of thing takes time. Real time. So even if they've existed in the cosmic string for a very brief period by our measurement of time, I think they would have needed millions of years, at the least, if they had evolved from humans. And our species is only about three hundred thousand years old—and the very first known interstellar missions from Earth were only two thousand or so years ago."

So Ophelia evidently had no relation to life on Earth, unless there was remote panspermic commonality.

But Butch could not deny his attraction to her. He didn't care about Tepper's taunting. He didn't care how he looked to the other pilots—well, yes he did. When he wasn't with Ophelia, he was even more gruff and blustery than usual. He even, much to his shame, joined Tepper, Peters, and Summers in making fun of Ophelia one morning. Summers put on a fair imitation of the way Ophelia walked, and Butch joined in the laughter and did his own impersonation of the way she talked.

"Not having sense walk this of me to," he said to the guffaws of the others.

He wasn't proud of it, but in that moment he preferred to make fun than be made fun of.

That was the only time, though. When he was with the guys, he tended to focus his attention on the job, and not talk about anything but spaceships, flight patterns, fuel chemistry, and sports. And of course he always reserved time to show off his knowledge of Shakespeare and Beethoven.

The truth was he was sensitive about his feelings for Ophelia. It would not be true to say he was embarrassed, but he was sensitive and didn't care to draw attention to his blossoming love story. He knew that in time he would have to own up to his fellow pilots—*if* he and Ophelia were to become a couple.

But that in itself seemed unlikely. He didn't even know if that was what he wanted; somehow it seemed hubris for him even to consider being the Significant Other of this fantastic being from the stars. She didn't belong to him. How dare he even ponder pretending to make her his?

Yet he did ponder it. He pondered it every night. He pondered it every time he spoke to her, every time he had lunch with her. Every moment with her he was a breath away from telling her his feelings...but he always stopped short, terrified of rejection, terrified of acceptance. His life with her existed only in his own head, and he wasn't sure it should go any further than that.

But Tepper had obviously picked up on it. "Sure looks like a romance to me."

"If it is, it's my business, *Tepper*."

"I don't know, I've been involved with lots of women," Tepper said. "I remember puberty like it was yesterday."

"In your case, it *was* yesterday."

"Ha-ha. Look, I've been involved with women before. They're hot, you have fun, but the whole love thing—it's a symptom of insanity."

"*Love?!* Aren't we getting a little ahead of ourselves?"

Tepper laughed. "You wouldn't have jumped out of your seat like that if I wasn't onto something!"

Now Butch *was* embarrassed. Evidently he had said or done something to betray his feelings. He hated that he felt his face burning, and he was sure he must be beet red. "Well, what the hell ever. Whatever the case is, it's my business!"

"I'm not saying it's not! Just mark my words: love is a symptom of insanity. It's gonna land you nothing but trouble."

CHAPTER 12

Butch wanted to take things to the next level with Ophelia—but he didn't know what the next level was. He was reinventing the whole notion of romance. He was dating a timeless alien with a completely nonhuman biology. He knew nothing of her dating customs—let alone her reproductive system!

But he knew that having lunch in the Rec Pod no longer satisfied him. He was looking for more, but he didn't know what that would be. So he settled for a more private, and moderately more romantic, setting.

The problem was, Station Post One had to be one of the most unromantic places he had ever been. Cramped, utilitarian, and functional, every room spherical, every available surface covered with equipment, all the lighting harsh and white, and every place filled with buzzing or hissing or rushing sounds as pumps and ducts and fans did their work, the station had been built to sustain life and do a job. Romance had been the farthest thing from Zach Mortimer's mind when he had conceived of orbiting weather stations and a replacement Carrier, or when he had stumbled on the idea of putting them together into an outpost in deep space.

So Butch had to employ his own imagination, which he felt was fairly active, to create a romantic place.

The problem was, the only place on the station large enough to serve as a reasonable facsimile of a romantic restaurant was...the Wheel. Ophelia's workplace.

Butch arrived in the Wheel before shift (after posting a notice on the station's gabsite that he might be late for work), and began to inspect the area for possibilities. As he walked around the Wheel, he realized it was a smaller space than he had thought. He didn't come in here very often, and he thought of it as a vast and cavernous place; but on examining the details, he was chagrined to realize it was not much less cramped than any of the pods; it just ran in a circle around the Prime Hab. And that wasn't even a very big circle; it took him less than a minute to walk a complete circuit.

The door opened and Dr. DuBois entered. There was surprise in his voice as he said, "Good morning, Butch."

"Ah. Morning."

"What are you doing here so early?"

"Oh...nothin'..." Well, since Ophelia wasn't here, and everyone had caught on to his preoccupation with her anyway, and he was looking for ideas... "Actually...I was hoping to, ah, turn a part of the Wheel into something like a, I was looking for a...I was hoping to..."

"You want to take a girl on a date?"

Though DuBois must surely know exactly who they were talking about, Butch was grateful that he didn't mention Ophelia by name. "Ah, well, yes, yeah."

"Well, you're in luck. Come with me."

Fortunately Dr. DuBois had already laid the groundwork. His doomed romance with Natasha Fairbanks had led him along similar trains of thought as Butch, and he had subdivided a section of the Wheel and turned it into something resembling a quiet, softly lit restaurant. It was no bigger than one of the science cubicles, but it let in jut enough light to emulate the shade of the *Silver Streak*'s V.I.P. Restaurant, which was just what Butch had been aiming for. DuBois threw a makeshift tablecloth over the work desk, and set up two emergency lanterns to serve as candles— and from there it was just a matter of ordering up palatable food from the selector. And that depended on what Etuknips could ingest.

So when Ophelia arrived, he was ready to take the plunge.

"Um, Ophelia."

"Morning good, Butch. The right expression that is?"

"Yeah, sure is."

"Time hard me for to get used to, but think I early this is you to for appear here. Different this is?"

Butch was momentarily lost in the word salad of Ophelia's scrambled sentence, but he quickly got the gist of it. "Yeah—see, I wanted to talk to you if you've got a minute."

"A minute? Yes, extra minute can I you give."

"Somehow I've got a feeling you meant that literally. No, I mean I just want to talk to you for a minute."

"Oh. Klay."

"Uh, rather than having lunch—or, I mean, I'd be glad to still have lunch with you, but, what I mean is, I was thinking, if you'd like to, I was wondering if after shift or when you're done for the day or whatever, if maybe if you like you can join me for dinner."

"Oh. Klay."

As simple as that. He grinned. "Yeah? I mean, what I mean is, I mean I'm inviting you to a romantic dinner. What we humans call a date."

"Oh. Klay."

This was easy. Too easy. He was afraid she wasn't getting the concept. Well, maybe it was just as well. "Great! Uh, how 'bout nineteen hundred hours? I'll drop by your privacy pod and take you to a nice spot I know and we can just, ah, have a nice, softly lit dinner and spend the evening just the two of us."

"Nice that would be. Looking to it forward will I."

She seemed to understand; she just wasn't making a big deal out of it. He wondered what that meant. If anything. "Great! I'll see you then."

It was the longest day of Butch's life. He tried to fill the day with as many activities as he could, but there were only so many landing gears to check on, so many fuel pumps to inspect, so many flight computers on which to run diagnostics. He kept looking at the wall clock as the minutes crept by.

Rumors about his coming date had not spread, and he was grateful to DuBois for keeping his mouth shut, for he knew Tepper would not have let up on him for a moment—or worse, might have shown up at the dinner to spoil it.

He was grateful when a problem came up with a pressurization check on one of the external ammonia tanks. With DuBois occupied in the Wheel, it was up to Butch to take a Nautabot out and fix the problem. That killed a few hours.

Then another hour on post-EVA analysis... and soon the chimes signaled end of shift.

Just a few hours to go.

Butch went to his privacy pod, changed to his casual uniform, and read for a while. Then he went to the Rec Pod and joined a couple of the pilots in a mindless game of darts.

At last it was eighteen forty-five...time enough to stop by his privacy pod, freshen up a bit, and then on to pick up Ophelia. He took an extra five minutes brushing his teeth, then noticed with irritation that damned stray lock at the back of his part standing on end like it tended to do when his hair got too long. He combed it down and spritzed some HairConquest on it—that should hold it!

And then he headed off for Ophelia's privacy pod. His felt as though he were in his cockpit pulling out of a dive as he anticipated what the evening would bring. Nothing, probably; a few hours of stimulating conversation. But you never knew....

He rang the doorchime. He bounced on his heels as he waited for the door to open. Nothing. Was she in there? Had she forgotten? Had she been detained in the Wheel?

But then at last the door opened.

He gaped.

Rather than wearing the usual Etuknip garments, Ophelia was clad in a sparkling white dress adorned with blue sequins. Her hair was bound in a ponytail bound by a white bow. She stepped toward him, her dark eyes wide and glistening, her smile as irrepressible as his own.

"Hello, Butch."

"Hi! ...Wow! Uh, where'd you get the getup?"

"Get up? Got up did I when doorchime heard I."

"No, the clothes, the clothes, we've got nothing like that on the station."

"Do. Borrowed did this I from Stephanie Osborne."

"Oh." Of course. Stephanie Osborne was notorious—accurately or not—for sleeping around. Butch had never had her himself. But if even part of her reputation was true, it stood to reason she had some nonregulation clothes on board.

"Well, anyway, you look great—sorry I showed up in my uniform; it's all I have."

"All right it is. Good look you."

"Glad to hear it. Well, uh, shall we?" He extended his arm, remembering that once before she had placed her arm through his exactly as though she knew the custom. Perhaps she did; the easy way she wore the dress and hair indicated she had done some research on human dating rituals. He wondered if she had given any thought to the mating aspect of the human custom.

Well, it was only a first date. Probably too early to worry about that.

He escorted her to the Wheel, ignoring the looks of people they passed in the hall; what the hell were they looking at anyway? At the same time he felt some pride; Ophelia may be alien, but she was still quite a looker, and of all the men on the station, she had chosen to go out with *him*.

He found their booth in the Wheel already prepared with a tablecloth, placemats, and bottle of Champaign. The emergency lanterns were lit and stood on end like candles. There was a note:

BUTCH AND OPHELIA—

HAVE A TERRIFIC EVENING!

—EBOR

Butch smiled, showed the note to Ophelia, then folded it and put it in his pocket. He pulled out a chair for Ophelia, and on his look, deduced that it was for her. She sat.

He sat across from her, picked up the bottle, and eyed it critically. "4093. Well, I guess if that's the best we can do. Uh, can you drink this?"

Ophelia handed him her glass. "Willing I am anything to try."

"Great." He poured first her glass, then his own. "To a terrific evening."

Again, she showed that she had done her research. She held up her glass and said, "To a terrific evening."

As they clinked their glasses, he noticed that the bell-like clink was exactly the same sound that formed the undertone of all of Ophelia's words.

Suddenly he was self-conscious about having brought Ophelia to her own workplace for dinner. "Great panda bears...I know the place you've been working in isn't the most romantic place, but well, this is a space station, and the Wheel's the most open and spacious place—and you can't beat the view." He gestured to the wide observation window with its expansive view of the stars of the Valdor Sector. With the light in this cubicle muted, there was little reflection or glare, and the stars shone brilliantly. It was a reminder to Butch of the infinity of the universe, the mysteries that still lay out there to be discovered.

And how wonderful it was to be here, having dinner with one of those mysteries.

"I love it, Butch." Ophelia's voice was soft, her tone sincere. Either she had done a lot of practice faking human vocal qualities or she really meant it.

"It's the best I could do. I just, ah...really want to show you a good time."

"A place does not a good time decide. A companion a good time decides."

Looking across the table at Ophelia, at her large and expressive eyes, flickering in the light of the lanterns, at the play of light around her blue face, at her sweet smile, suddenly all of Butch's apprehension seeped away. He felt comfortable, as cozy as if he were curled in a warm chair in front of a fire on a winter night on Earth. And so it was without self-consciousness that he said, "I've never known anyone like you, Ophelia."

"That is because no one like me visited your station before has."

Butch smiled, shook his head. "Oh, what you're doin' to me."

He had finally spilled to her how he felt, how he *really* felt, and in the moment suddenly realized he had taken a chance in doing so. And she hadn't understood him. But the evening was young and the mood had not been broken.

"I never felt like this. –Well, of course I've felt like this—well, I don't know." He cleared his throat, saw that she was waiting expectantly, patiently, for him to say something that made sense, and he started over. "Ophelia, do your people have...love?"

"We have all the emotions you have...and a few you don't."

"Do you have marriage?"

"Not known to me is term that."

It had never occurred to Butch that marriage was a difficult concept, but now he found he could not explain it. "Togetherness..." No, that was wrong. Togetherness was what they were doing right now. But somehow describing it as a legal contract in which they were entitled to each other's property didn't seem appropriately romantic. "I mean...I've thought about it since you've been here...hell, I haven't thought about anything else."

Whoa, boy, this is going way too fast! He had only just now accepted the real possibility of a relationship with her, and now he was talking about marriage! But now that he had started, he found he couldn't stop.

"I don't care what planet or dimensional plane you're from; I want to be with you. Live with you. Raise a family with you."

"That may be difficult, since I lay eggs."

Butch didn't know if that was meant to be a joke, but he laughed. At himself more than anything. By human standards, he had moved too quickly—talking about marriage on a first date was a quick way to drive the woman out the nearest window. But Ophelia was not human, and somehow, at the moment, that made honesty easier.

"Whatever it takes. I don't know, maybe I've gone crazy. *Tepper* says love is a symptom of insanity. I can't help it, Ophelia, I'm in love with you."

Wow! I've never said that to anyone before, and here I blurted it out before hors d'oevres!

He wondered why he was being so open and frank with this alien. Why was he so comfortable expressing his inmost thoughts and feelings? Was she doing something to him? Was it her earnest curiosity about him? Or was he just so smitten that he didn't care about the risks?

After all, he thought, *Romeo and Juliet were planning their marriage the night they met!...*

"And I love you in ways you cannot even understand," Ophelia said.

Butch's heart sang at that. This was too good to be true; was he going to wake up at any moment?

"In past, in present, and in future, love you do I like part of my own dreams."

What a heartbreakingly beautiful way of putting it. Butch looked into Ophelia's eyes, then realized he was starting to tear. He blinked, wiped at the corner of his eye, pretending he had an itch.

"I don't know much about your anatomy, but I want to show you something that we do to express affection."

"Show me."

Butch leaned across the table, placed a finger under Ophelia's chin to move her face to meet his, and kissed her. He kept his eyes open, watching her reaction. First there was a slight frown, then she began to participate, angling her head and pressing her lips against his with more urgency. He allowed the kiss to linger for just a moment; he was astonished, embarrassed, and giddy at what he had done. He returned to his seat, trying to gauge her reaction.

At first she had none. She watched him with those large, unfathomable eyes, and said, "Strange custom, but not unpleasant. May I show you what we do?"

Butch smiled. "Sure!"

What happened next was an experience Butch could not describe. Although nothing happened, and his watch insisted that only a microsecond had passed, he felt as though he had experienced a lifetime of bliss—sexual, emotional, spiritual, philosophical, in every way he could think of and a few he could never comprehend. It was as though every moment of pleasure he had ever experienced—and ever would experience—had become concentrated in that one moment.

He also realized he had ejaculated—in fact his groin hurt, as though he had ejaculated multiple times. But that was impossible; there had barely been time to get an erection, let alone ejaculated several times...but the puddle in his crotch didn't lie. Unless he had peed—but he knew the difference.

He was left breathless, drained, dizzy, faint, and happier than he had been in his life. "Whoa," he gasped. "Whoa! What was that?"

"That was—" Ophlia made a sound in the Etuknip language, a sound like the tinkling of a bell combined with the braying of a whale. "A compressed point of time in which we pleasure each other into one concentrated moment of experience."

If Butch was understanding her correctly, he had just experienced a lifetime of sex in one moment. No wonder he felt as if he had ejaculated several times. There was probably nothing left in there now! "Whoa, that was...that was...wow! I wouldn't want to say anything was better than sex, but if anything is, that is."

"Sex?" The expression of puzzlement on Ophelia's face was all too human.

Now *that* was strange; she had obviously researched human dating rituals. How could she not know about sex? "Uh, mating."

"Cannot mate. Parts...do not match."

"No...Well, I've got nothing against trying." *Whoa, why did I say that?* But he had already brought up marriage, kissed her, and experienced his entire life's supply of orgasms, so why not? It was obvious that whatever image he had of her as a superior being with whom he had no business was clearly in his own head. He meant something to her—he wasn't sure what, but she had made clear he was important to her. Maybe as important as she was to him. Was there any reason they should not explore each other's bodies? What harm could it do? The taboos and restrictions and psychological hangups about sex were a purely human phenomenon; all other known life forms just did it when they felt like it.

Of course, it might take him a while to reset now....

CHAPTER 13

If Sambo understood human time references, and he wasn't sure he did, then "tonight" was the night. He had reached the point in linear time in which the Sweg ship was to arrive. This was the moment for which he had been trained.

Back home he could simply have taken a look over there and seen the consequences of the coming actions, as well as all alternatives, or at least those in sight. But here he was virtually blind, restricted to a single timeline, a single point in time, moving from the past to the future at almost a fixed rate only slightly alterable by velocity.

It was a risk; the humans had made clear their displeasure at turning their security over to him; moreover, the human Control Booth Chief obviously didn't like or trust him, despite his attempts to emulate human courtesy.

The feeling was mutual. The humans were like the Leira—always tinkering, always exploring, always curious, heedless of the dangers of the universe, ignorant of what they might stir up in their ceaseless adventuring. And look what it had gotten them; they had contacted aliens about which they knew nothing, formed an alliance with them, and allowed themselves to be drawn into a doomsday war which had destroyed both sides. It was a miracle that Station Post One survived.

The Sweg were not so careless. If the exploration of other timelines, and of past and future, had proven anything, it was that if one probed far enough, one found doom. It was inevitable; even humans understood that entropy increased in a closed system. The same was true with timelines and the same was true with the three dimensions of space. As long as one stayed put, one knew one was safe. A stationary ship would never collide with anything.

The Sweg were content to remain in one time, one place, to live lives of quiet contemplation of the Glory of Creation. Their existence was the eternal paradise that some humans craved in their religions. The Sweg lived in an Eternal Moment, a moment of joy that never ended, for they need never move past that instant of happiness.

In human terms, if a person could choose one moment of happiness in his life—such as Butch had experienced in his first date with Ophelia—and make that his heaven, then the Sweg had chosen their own. The specifics of the moment were different for each Sweg; for Sambo, it was the Theridimian. It would be impossible to explain the Theridimian to a human, but it was possible to express an equivalent concept with which a human could identify.

The Theridimian could be expressed as a festival where many people gathered to watch a spectacle of the universe, a lensing of the starlight that occurred when a red giant passed near to the gravitational field of the cosmic string, creating an astonishing light show in the skies of the timelines.

This had only happened once, but Etuknips could revisit any time, any experience, as often as they wished. As for Sambo, he simply stayed there, living forever that night of the rainbows and auroras and flashes and infinite sheets of colored light. Playing word games with his—the word "brother" might be the closest human approximation. Getting seribi (an Etuknip delicacy that might be compared to an ice cream cone) and eating it during the long walk back to the matapis (hotel? House? Something like that...)

A single night that represented for Sambo the epitome of happiness. He lived in it, reveled in it—and, like all Sweg, developed a fear ever of leaving it. What lay outside his moment, his temporal home, was the Unknown, and was a source of terror. Somewhere out there, somewhere in the timelines, in the future, was the Pirate, the Thing that would rampage in and terrorize the Sweg, destroy their idealistic world, smash their comforting and comfortable view of the universe.

And so Sambo had demonstrated extraordinary courage in taking this assignment, in leaving the Theridimian, leaving the Cosmic String, entering an unknown and incomprehensible universe.

But the fear of the consequences of the Leira's action outweighed the fear of leaving home. The Leira had reached out beyond the World—beyond the very Universe—into an irrational place, a place so infinite, and yet so constraining, that every moment in it took constant willpower for Sambo not to go mad.

The Leira had contacted beings, creatures utterly alien, creatures who roamed at will through the physical dimensions and had no freedom whatsoever in the temporal ones. Creatures whose very language was impossible to master, where the contraints of time layered every facet of their lives. Clocks, shifts, actions, decisions, relationships, all done with no awareness of the future, no awareness of alternate timelines, and always the pedantic measurement of the passage of time; for here time simply flowed by like a river, uncontrolled, invisible.

A human might understand Sambo's fear by picturing being in the driver's seat of a vehicle, blindfolded, hands and legs bound tight. You know you are moving and moving fast, but have no idea where and no control over the vehicle. It would simply end up where it ended up.

Sambo had his assignment and he performed to the best of his ability, but it was maddening not to know how events would unfold. It would be possible for him to cheat and take a look, but the others would know; he dare not risk it. It was ironic; one who took solace in huddling in one particular time now wished more than anything else to break free of this moment and see where he was going and what were all the possible outcomes.

But he was stuck, speeding forward through time—through one timeline—and hoping that things panned out as planned.

The scanner registered an incoming ship. He knew that the Battlehab Center and the Prime Hab Center would also be picking it up—and again he wished he had some foreknowledge of how the humans would react.

Fortunately the nocturnal chiefs in both Hab Centers were Etuknips, and they trusted him when he told them he would handle it.

He recognized the ship; it was transmitting the beacon he had been told to expect...*squeak... squawk...groooaaaaann...squeaksqueak...clatter.* Yes, it was the Sweg ship.

He spoke to the Sweg captain in his own language; it was more convenient, and should the humans investigate, they would not understand what was said.

The Sweg captain replied. Sambo gave landing instructions.

With no announcement, nothing on the arrival schedule, and half the nocturnal crew dozing in offices and cubicles, the Sweg ship was able to land without being noticed. Still, he reached out and exerted the slightest nudge, just the slightest, imperceptible jolt, a minute bump against a few electrons, enough, *just* enough to knock this timeline into one in which no humans entered the bay at this critical time. The Leira would never notice.

He left the Control Booth and descended the stair to meet the Sweg as they disembarked.

They exchanged greetings. Sambo asked how they were going to conceal the ship; the captain explained that the pilot would take it back out again and, when the time was right, superposition it so that it would momentarily be in two places at once.

Sambo verified that the deal still held—he had done his job, and so now he could leave this hellish place with the other Sweg. The captain confirmed that this was so. Sambo was satisfied.

———

Butch was not satisfied.

Still feeling euphoric from his date with Ophelia, he reported to the Dock Deck in the morning to be immediately confronted with a mystery—and that mystery was the log dump.

Every shift had a duty officer who entered relevant information in the scrap log; Butch would later go over the scrap log and prepare the final log which was then submitted daily to Kramer. A lot of trivial information was whittled down that way.

The computer automatically created its own log—a ponderous, tedious log that recorded everything. Every event, every circuit status update, every button pushed, every setting changed, every change in atmospheric content, every variation in pressure, and so on and so on and so on. And some poor schlep on every shift was required to go through this mess of minutiae in case something interesting had happened that the moronic computer had failed to alert the human crew.

On this particular morning, something interesting had indeed come up. Ben Crowley, the nocturnal recordkeeper, had the unenviable duty of going through the log dump. Butch, knowing what a tedious job it was, rotated the wretched duty among all his people; though the overnight crew was smaller, and therefore all the nocturnal guys got a double dosage of it. Crowley had just gotten the duty on Friday; now it was Tuesday and he was stuck with it again. Butch felt bad for him, but that was one of the pitfalls of the nocturnal shift.

The log dump indicated that there had been a cleared arrival at the station—but the written log indicated nothing. It was inconceivable that an arrival had not been noted in the log. Crowley had no access to the master security scan; only Butch had the code. So Crowley delivered his report to Tepper before going off shift, and Tepper brought it to Butch as soon as he arrived.

So Butch went into his office, Tepper trailing behind him, and plugged in the code for the security scan. It verified that there had been a cleared arrival—but the security camera had not caught it. That was even stranger than the arrival not being noted in the log; the security cameras were configured automatically to swivel toward the entry tubes as soon as the clearance code was transmitted. If the arrival had been cleared, the camera should have caught it.

Moreover, although the security scan verified that there had been a cleared arrival, it did not specify *who* the arrival was. There was no scheduled arrival, and any unscheduled arrival's identity obviously had to be verified before it was allowed to dock with or enter the station. That was not only standard procedure, it was common sense.

"Whoever cleared this shouldn't have," Butch said. "Who was on duty last night?"

"Sambo," Tepper said. "The Etuknip."

Butch clenched his jaw, punched the side of the console, and said, "That does it."

"Oh, you're not gonna go shoot your mouth off at Commander Kramer, are you?"

"I sure as hell am."

"Well, okay. I guess that'll just bring me one step closer to taking over your job."

But Butch was already out the door.

CHAPTER 14

"I'm not sure I understand your objection, Captain McCrae. From my observation, you have absolutely no problem with the Etuknips."

"I didn't say I had a problem with them, Commander. What I have a problem with is them handling our security."

"I have a problem with it too. It just happens to be one of the provisions of our agreement with the Valdor to have the Etuknips here."

"Yeah, yeah, we've been through that, I didn't like it then and I don't like it now."

Butch knew better than to angrily confront the commander in the Prime Hab Center, so he had instead brought copies of the scrap log and the log dump and asked to speak to Kramer in private. So now they sat in Kramer's privacy pod, the log dump on Kramer's desk, the suspicious portion circled.

"I'm not diminishing your concerns," Kramer said, "I'm pointing out that you have a close relationship with the Etuknip ambassador. Why not just ask her?"

"I intend to, but she might not know anything about it. There's a fracture in their civilization—"

"All right, stop right there. That's another condition the Valdor imposed on us. Dugrow told me there are political complications in their civilization, and we are to stay out of it."

"Well, Commander, I think our agreement to stay out of it is nullified if it results in unregistered guests on our station!"

"All right, fine—*are* there unaccounted visitors on the station?"

"Well, I don't know! With the Etuknips in charge of our security, how am I supposed to know what the hell is going on?"

"Don't get smart, Butch. You still have the security codes."

"And I'm telling you the truth: I don't know. I'd have to run a complete security rescreening of the entire station, and that'll take time. I sure as hell haven't had time to do that this morning."

"Well, get on that then. Is there anything I can do to help you?"

"Well—"

"Short of abrogating my agreement with the Valdor?"

Butch sighed. "No, I guess not. But with all due respect, I think it's high time you put the security of our station above your stupid agreement with the Valdor. What the hell are they gonna do? They're diminished in the Community, and as you just pointed out, I've got it in with the Etuknip leader."

"Well, then ask her."

"I will—but as I said, there is a schism in their society, and that's what I'm worried about. Ophelia's group represents one faction, the Leira, and there's another group called the Sweg—"

"Look, Butch, the less I know about that the better. Let's just deal with our own station. If there are unauthorized Etuknips on board, find them and I'll deal with it."

"Well..." Butch stood. "I hope you do. Sir."

Butch knew that Ophelia was busy in the Wheel working with DuBois, so he went back to the Dock Deck; he would be meeting Ophelia for lunch and would ask her then.

The first thing he did on reaching the Dock Deck was to locate Tepper, who was in the common area writing flight schedules.

"Hey, *Tepper*, how would you like to get off the paper-pushing for a while?"

"Paper-pushing?"

Butch sighed; another term from classic literature of which the sergeant was painfully ignorant. "I want to do a security rescreening of the entire station. Want to join me? It'll be fun."

Tepper clicked "save" and shut down his linkpad. "I'd rather be flying, but what the hell. It'll break up the monotony."

"Monotony? Good, *Tepper*, you've moved on to four-syllable words."

"Oh, ha-ha."

"But I guess you haven't gotten as far as clever comebacks yet."

The first step in the security rescreening was simple: print out a list of everyone, human and Etuknip, who was supposed to be on board—and then require that everyone present him- or herself in the Dock Deck in order to verify facial recognition, fingerprints, retinal prints, and DNA. Fortunately, Etuknips had all of these.

"Why check the humans?" Tepper asked. "There are a hundred people on this station.

We're looking for Etuknips; why not just check the Etuknips?"

"Two reasons," Butch said. "One, we don't want to offend the Etuknips, so officially this is just a standard precaution and we're checking *everyone*. Two, if these creatures who live on a one-dimensional world can become three-dimensional beings, then I wouldn't put it past them to impersonate humans. I know, I don't have any reason to think they can do that, but I'm not taking chances."

"Yeah, but checking *everyone*'ll take forever."

"Nah. Couple hours, tops. A hundred people plus ten Etuknips isn't much."

In practice, Butch turned out to be very wrong. When he called PHC and asked for everyone to gather in the Dock Deck, Kramer said, "Butch, you're seriously overestimating the volume of the Dock Deck. Yes, it's a big section, but with all the subdivisions and ships and equipment, there's no way you'll squeeze a hundred people in there. And besides, every person on the station is a trained specialist, each involved in a particular project. Some of those projects are very sensitive. We can't just knock off all that work at a moment's notice. We'll have to rotate schedules to check their identification."

Butch remembered then that the initial security screening, back before Station Post One had been deployed, had been done in the *Silver Streak*'s cavernous landing bay, which was larger than all of Station Post One. "I guess nobody thought ahead and anticipated a mass rescreening," he grumbled. "Okay, wait here, *Tepper*, I'll draw up a new plan of action."

Butch's new plan of action started with a test check of himself, Tepper, and the top security personnel.

"Why am *I* not conducting this rescreening?" was the very legitimate question from Security Chief Moulson.

"Because this is a Dock Deck problem," Butch answered gruffly, "and I'm the Dock Deck Chief."

And so Butch ran the identification checks on the small group, then had each of them verify the results, so that he knew he had a core group of people he could trust. Then he drew up a schedule rotating members of this group to stand as guards in the area subdivided for the screening—section three, specifically. The first to be posted were Tepper and Moulson.

Butch went himself to lock the surrounding emergency bulkheads in order to seal off the section and prevent anyone from sneaking in—or out. When he came back, Tepper and Moulson predictably gave him a hard time, grilling him for password, DNA test, urine sample, ordering him to pull down his pants for a rectal exam...to which Butch replied, "A reminder, *Tepper*: I write your schedule."

Tepper immediately stood aside for Butch—though his grin didn't vanish.

By the time all this was done, it was time for Butch's lunch with Ophelia.

The rush of pleasure at being with her contrasted with his sudden distrust of Etuknips; his instinct to treat her gently and with courtesy and chivalry warred with his instinct to give her a rigorous grilling.

"I've gotta ask you something, Ophelia, and I hope you and I have gotten close enough that you can give me an honest answer."

"This will I do, Butch. Honesty us between important to me is."

"Good, good...and I hate to mix business with pleasure. But I have to ask, did any Etuknips come aboard outside of the ten of you? Was there an arrival last night that you knew about?"

"No!"

Butch's affection for Ophelia compelled him to believe her; but his pathological distrust of all suspects had him searching her face for signs of lying. And being Butch McCrae, he found those signs. Her overdone surprise, her unwarranted exclamation.

"Know nothing this of do I. Etuknips on board are there other than my group?"

"Well, that's what I'm trying to figure out. Why did you guys insist on taking over our security?"

"Decision that was outside my purview of. Responsible I am scientific work for. Arrangements for the details our visit of belonged to—" A series of whistles and tones formed the name of one of the other Etuknips.

"Well, anyway, one of your guys was in charge of the Control Booth last night, and that's when an unidentified ship landed. But there's no ship there and there's nothing in the log, so it's obvious to me there's a shenanigan going on and I don't see who could be behind it but you guys. So that's why I'm asking you to be honest with me."

"Honest with you being am I, Butch. Promise you, would not I to you lie. If dishonesty going on is, being it conducted is one of my people by without my knowledge. Or a Sweg trick is it."

Butch nodded. "Yeah. I thought of the Sweg. That was my first thought, except I'm guessing there are no Sweg in your party."

"Unless one planted was."

"Could be, could be. Okay...I believe you, Ophelia. I don't think you'd lie to me."

It was not like Butch McCrae to take anyone's word for anything, particularly a security issue, but something about Ophelia disarmed him every time. He had no good reason to trust her, but he did, implicitly.

After lunch, he returned to section three, now designated the Headcount Station, where a line had already formed for phase one of the rescreening. He pulled Tepper aside and laid out his plans for the next phase.

"Phase two will involve isolating everyone in their privacy pod and doing a sonic search for heartbeats. I'll make arrangements with Kramer to work in a time tonight to terminate all routine work and have everyone, on all three shifts, go to their privacy pods."

"Hope that won't cause too much havoc aboard a space station involved in many different projects."

"Nah, as long as everyone knows it's coming, they can make sure nothing sensitive is going on."

The rescreening took the remainder of green shift and most of yellow shift. The personnel being tested walked through the Headcount Station and filed to the end of the corridor where the two guards were posted, then waited until the entire station was in line, could be accounted for, and were cleared.

Because of the scientific experiments being done in the Wheel, and some of the engineering projects being conducted by Intercore right here on the Dock Deck, there were inevitably some people who could not be away from their stations for any period of time. Butch and Moulson personally went to them, counted them, and checked them out—but only after everyone else had been accounted for.

Kramer checked with each of the section chiefs and determined that 2200 hours was a suitable time for everyone to be in his or her privacy pod; after all, the heartbeat check would only take a few seconds, and then anyone involved in a special project could get right back to work.

In the event, it took fifteen minutes to get everyone to their privacy pods, which was a concern for Kramer, as he realized they had never run a full station evacuation drill since the Station had been expanded; if it took this long for everyone to get to escape pods, the station could be in real trouble.

"Heartbeats check out," Tepper told Butch after the scan was complete. "One hundred ten heartbeats on the station."

"Hmmm." Then what the hell was going on? Could Etuknip intruders conceal their heartbeats? Or should be accept the results of the scan and assume the anomaly in the log was some sort of glitch? "Well, we'd better be doubly certain tomorrow. We'll take a small group of the checked-out people and conduct a complete station sweep, section by section. No announcement."

"Good enough. It'll be a more exciting way to start the morning than reviewing the overnight logs."

Butch met Tepper in the morning and they conducted the screening—first each section of the Dock Deck, then the Battlehab, and finally the Prime Hab. It took five hours and it turned up nothing.

Butch finally had to admit reluctantly that there were no unauthorized personnel on Station Post One. He wrote up a detailed report to Kramer admitting this finding, but closing with,

"Considering the abilities of the Etuknips, I still cannot rule out the possibility of hidden intruders, and I recommend the station maintain level two security alert."

Kramer did not respond, and the alert light in the Dock Deck remained on "3" for the rest of the day.

CHAPTER 15

To: Damon Ezekiel Kramer, Commander, Station Post One

From: Ebor Xavier DuBois, Chief Science Officer, Station Post One

Subject: Kelvon-Tau Converter

The Kevlon-Tau Converter is now assembled and attached to minireactor 2 in Wheel section ten. Primary power test was completed at 1120 hours this morning (060294). Test was successful, and I have enclosed details: *ktcpt1*

If our analysis of the Dreb "powers" is correct, and if we have correctly identified them with the behavior of the kevlon particle, then any use of that energy source in the vicinity of the Kelvon-Tau Converter should cause a pertubation in the flow of particles that can be identified. I should point out that such a perturbation could have many causes, but there are a number of specific configurations that should allow us to identify the specific use of Dreb powers.

Not only will this enable us to locate the use of those powers in our own universe, but also in the Thermian universe.

There was never any question that the Dreb powers originated in the Thermian universe, but the thing that I have learned, which is particularly interesting, is that if a Dreb is killed, his electromagnetic resonance does not, as we previously thought, remain encoded in surrounding vacuum energy (quantum hologram). (*See Schoderhov 4/266l.*) Death is death for a dreb as for a human. The only way his memories, knowledge, and ability to effect change (kinetic energy) can remain post-death is if he is infused with a tremendous amount of energy directed into his quantum hologram at the moment of death.

To clarify, it is not enough merely to be vaporized by a supernova. There has to be a direct infusion of kevlons, tau neutrinos, and imaginary virtons (the energy particles that are the primary components of Dreb powers) into the quantum hologram. That is not something a dreb can do by himself. He can conduct energy through his body and direct it in a number of useful ways, and he can teleport via quantum entanglement, but direct interface with his quantum hologram is impossible. He would need a "push" from the Thermian universe. Most likely a Thermian would need to consciously provide that push at the moment of death.

I would like to point out that almost this exact thing was done when the entity known as James Wilcox Lowell—who was no more than the knowledge and memories of a colony of humans encoded into vacuum energy—became a godlike being with the assistance of the Space Star *Silver Streak*, which supplied antimatter to enable the transformation.[*]

This is the first solid indication of a discrepancy in the Dreb religion. A supernova does *not* provide a Dreb with "transcendence." If that transcendence occurs (and I am not entirely sold on that concept) it is the Thermians that do it, not the supernova.

This data was achieved by an analysis of the behavior of kevlons though the subdirectional scoop of the Kevlon-Tau Converter and the shower of particles resulting from the kevlon-tau conversion. The Etuknip ambassador verified the results and agrees with this interpretation.

Zach Mortimer had not been cleared to look at DuBois' report, but he didn't care. He had ways of obtaining information from the Command Section; this was, after all, his station, and he wanted to know the results of all those experiments going on in the Wheel.

DuBois, in his scientific naïveté, had already shared more with Mortimer than he was strictly supposed to, so Mortimer knew exactly where to look for the report. He knew where to look each morning to find out if such a report had been filed.

Do not allow your desire for profit to overwhelm your sense of right and wrong, his mind whispered to him.

He frowned, shook his head. He didn't know where all those thoughts were coming from these

---

[*] *See the novel* Voyage Into the Unknown (*Lulu, 2013*) *chapters* 24-27

days, but he refused to go mad. Sanity was, he believed, a choice. Insanity was a sign of weakness, and he was not weak.

Why elevate the concepts of weakness and strength above concepts of morality, Zach?

Shut up! He went back to the report, referred to the details of the test. He clicked on the link DuBois had provided, which took him to a CLASSIFIED warning. He bypassed that with his own six-digit code, which he had programmed to override *most* of the security barriers on the station, and the detailed report appeared.

As he had expected, it was a barely comprehensible gibberish of numbers and impenetrable scientific jargon. He prided himself on his scientific knowledge, but he knew he had no hope of understanding. Nevertheless, he saved the report to his hidden files; if necessary, he would show it to his scientific aides on condition of absolute secrecy.

The main report told him what he really wanted to know. The Kevlon-Tau Converter was operational, at least the prototype stage, and had already yielded results. He was interested in the findings regarding the Dreb and their relationship with the Thermians, but that merely satisfied intellectual curiosity; he didn't see any way that it would benefit Intercore. But then again, you never knew.

But if—*if*—the Kevlon-Tau Converter was the first step in developing a Thermian Destroyer, then Mortimer intended to be the one to market it.

What is your personal profit against the preservation of all intelligent life in the universe, Zach?

Where is that voice coming from?! Mortimer growled, balling his fist. If he was becoming schizophrenic, at least he was aware of it, and therefore he could control it. There was no need to mention it to Dr. Lazarev or anyone else.

And if he was really honest with himself, he would be sorry if the voice was exorcised. The feelings of love and companionship, irrational and imaginary though they may be, were genuinely comforting. He supposed it was okay to be just a little bit crazy—as long as it was harmless—if it brought him some measure of happiness.

Just as it was okay to reap a profit as long as one was already saving the universe.

He thought of Butch McCrae; everyone on the station was aware of McCrae's bizarre romance with the Etuknip ambassador. If McCrae could pursue a relationship with a one-dimensional blue line, then Mortimer could take solace in a voice of comfort even if it was wholly in his mind.

Yet the *feeling* that came over him when the voice was present—it felt so much like love.

Zach Mortimer was not a sentimental man, and he had long ago decided that his business took precedence over any romantic pursuits. He was fully aware that he might one day regret poring his life into his job, but then his job filled him with a sense of fulfillment more than any of his disastrous dates and one-night stands ever had. There had been Cynthia Green—that had been going well—but she had gone and gotten herself killed on Cerberus, so even when it went well it ended badly. Women cheated, left, or died. His business would always be there.

So if Mortimer were going to fall in love—which he indiginantly denied even to himself—it might as well be with a figment of his imagination.

Enough of this sentimental stuff, he chastised himself. *Back to work.*

He was intrigued by the fact that the Dreb religion was wrong after all. It had been disconcerting to hear Ebor DuBois, a scientist, quoting a religious text and using it as a guide to understanding physical principles. Mortimer was relieved, though not surprised, that DuBois had been chasing a false lead.

So far, all the evidence had pointed to the fact that the Dreb had no "powers"—all their abilities filtered through from the Thermian universe, perhaps even from the Thermians themselves. It occurred to Mortimer that this was a significant discovery for several reasons; it could shatter the faith of the Dreb's followers, it could certainly make the Dreb easier to fight—and it occurred to Mortimer that if the Thermians were directly responsible when the Dreb used their powers, then that power could be turned back on the Thermians. In other words, just as the Dreb used Thermian energy to strike at their enemies, so their enemies could thus use the Dreb to strike at the Thermians. It was a titillating thought that made Mortimer cackle with glee in the privacy of his office.

But dammit...his use of his personal security code to access the report reminded him that he still didn't have access to the whole station. *His* station. He wanted the startup codes and access keys to the Dock Deck, and he wanted them *now*.

Patience, one thing at a time. He didn't need that mysterious voice in his head to remind him of that. He was a pragmatist, and he would take the gift that had just been delivered to him—or that he had stolen. This report might just be the key to Intercore becoming the galaxy's supplier of the Thermian Destroyer.

He smiled as he imagined the headlines. *Zach Mortimer, Savior of the Universe!*

CHAPTER 16

Butch had decided tonight was the night. He didn't know how he was going to broach the subject with Ophelia, but he was comfortable enough with her, and felt that their relationship had progressed far enough, to take things to the next level. She had, after all, shown him the Etuknip way of expressing affection—in spectacular fashion! He didn't see that he would be violating propriety by showing her the human way.

He wasn't sure anything could really happen; as Ophelia had so eloquently pointed out, "Parts don't match." But he still looked forward to lying down with her, undressing her, layering kisses all over her body. He had to admit to some curiosity to examine her anatomy and learn exactly how it differed from a human woman. He wanted to see if his touch could pleasure her; he already knew hers could pleasure him! Most of all, as much as he had enjoyed the lifetime of orgasms she had showered on him, he wanted the simple pleasure of hugging and kissing, touching the way human males were instinctively programmed to do it.

Naturally, he said nothing to Tepper or anyone else. He had already endured quite a bit of ribbing, as the gossip about him and Ophelia spread all over the station. It was what he had feared as soon as he had become aware of his infatuation with her; but now that they were officially dating, there was certainly nothing to be embarrassed about. In fact he felt a certain pride; he alone had managed to attract one of these ethereal beauties.

But he was not one to brag about sexual conquests; Butch McCrae's romantic sentiments were steeped in the flowery trappings of ancient literature, and he carried with him a sense of courtesy and chivalry that had made him something of an oddball in his dates with human women, and certainly outside the mainstream of the other pilots. He didn't know whether he was going to go to bed with Ophelia tonight or not. He didn't know if she would agree to experiment with the concept. He didn't know if he could make the "parts" match. He didn't know if he would walk away fulfilled or disappointed. As of now, there was nothing to brag about. And later, if they had a night of sheer bliss, it would be nobody else's damn business. It would be a personal and private encounter between him and Ophelia.

That was how he would have been with *any* woman—but especially Ophelia.

It took a little work to program the autotailor to produce a fortieth century sartori suit; the cravat, long coat, and waist coat were so out of style that there was no program for them. He had to purchase the styles from a historical brochure on the SPACEWEB, the same brochure he had used to design costumes for plays back on the *Silver Streak*. The outfit the autotailor produced for him was not quite what he had in mind, but it was the best he could do with the sparse resources of Station Post One.

Perhaps he was being too hasty with the elaborate formal wear; she might even laugh at him—no, that was doubtful. There was no reason for her to laugh. She knew nothing of human fashion styles. At worst she would observe that he was dressed differently and ask for an explanation. Come to think of it, he had never heard her laugh; he wondered if Etuknips could. Or if they had a concept of humor. Strange that it had never come up.

DuBois was already gone when Butch arrived in the Wheel, and Ophelia was talking with two of the other Etuknips. He held back respectfully, listening in pleasure to the hauntingly musical sound of their language.

But she glanced his way several times, smiling each time, and finally said something that broke up their meeting. The other two Etuknips left, and Ophelia approached him with her arms spread. "Seen this have I your visual records in. A hug believe I called this is?"

Butch embraced her, then held her close, enjoying the odd scent from her neck—a sort of fresh car smell was the only thing he could compare it to.

As they parted, he said, "Well, I'm off watch. Care to come with me back to—"

"Someone is here."

Was it his imagination, or was there a note of alarm in her voice? She turned silently, her head moving back and forth like a radar machine scanning the air.

Even now, in his evening clothes and in anticipation of a night of sexual ecstacy, Butch refused to go anywhere without his sidearm. He reached into his suit pocket and wrapped his fingers around the grip. "You sure? Where?"

"This way." Ophelia took small, vaguely dance-like steps around the curvature of the Wheel. Butch stayed close to her side, allowing her to lead the way but prepared to jump in front of her if necessary.

Although the Wheel was large and spacious, the many cubicles, cubbyholes, and masses of intrumentation provided a lot of hiding places—and, he now noticed, a lot of shadows.

"Could be *Tepper* playing some stupid practical joke." He hadn't mentioned his intentions to Tepper, but it wouldn't take a genius—and Tepper certainly was not one—to notice that he had big plans for tonight. He could imagine Tepper crouching in one of the cubbyholes, a camera ready to record Butch's efforts, and to broadcast them the next day to the whole station. Yeah, Tepper would find that hilarious.

"No," Ophelia said. "Know I feeling this. Felt I this before."

"Feeling what? What do you mean?"

"How should say it I? Vibrations? Small ripples in gravitational distribution your station of. And—know I not describe it how to. A sense suppose I humans that have do not."

"I'm not sure I follow you."

"Going I *this* way. Fine you are doing."

"No, no, I mean I'm not sure I understand what you're saying."

"Explain it cannot I. Language your words has no to explain it. But sure I am that—"

Her words were cut off by a—a *something*—from one of the cubicles. Butch thought at first it was sort of beam weapon that caused a refractive effect in the air, but then he realized that space itself was distorted. It was as if he were watching a black hole cross the room—or, no, not a black hole...a *cosmic string!*

"Sweg!" Ophelia cried. "You supposed to be here are not!"

Butch saw them now. They were Etuknips, they looked just like Ophelia and her group, but they wore different outfits—long robes that looked like sack cloth. They were crouched behind the cubicle; Butch had the sense that they were having a meeting. He aimed his sidearm at the cubicle. "Hold it!"

"Out of this stay, Butch," Ophelia warned.

"Like hell! I've put up with your own guys taking over my security, I'm sure as hell not gonna—"

Butch was never sure exactly what happened next. He was in the middle of his sentence, he knew what he intended to say, and part of him remembered saying it. Part of him remembered a flurry of activity, of Etuknips rushing in all directions, of trying to take aim with his sidearm as they moved too quickly for him to take a bead—but he also had no memory of saying anything past "gonna," and in an eyeblink he was alone. Ophelia and the Sweg were gone. And *nothing* had happened.

What had happened? He shook his head, blinked heavily, tried to concentrate. But only one thing really mattered: Ophelia was gone.

Gone where?

He ran to the nearest wall intercom, opened a small hatch underneath, and thumbed a red key. The alert klaxon sounded. He hit the key for stationwide announcement and shouted, "Intruder alert! Wheel section two-nine!"

How could Ophelia be gone? Where had she gone? Where had the Sweg gone? They had to be here—if not in the Wheel, then at least somewhere on the station. They couldn't have left; it was impossible. Even if they had the ability to see other timelines...

Could they have slipped out of our reality into another timeline?

No! Fantasy!

He would once again have to take an accounting of all the heartbeats on the station. Surely with an attack by enemy intruders, Kramer would give him no trouble this time.

CHAPTER 17

To: Commander Damon Ezekiel Kramer, cc.
Executive Officer Tobias Christopher Dingell
From: Captain Randal McCrae
Subject: Security Rescreening, intruder alert

As per Commander Kramer's approval, the second rescreening of the entire station was conducted from 0700 to 0030 on 060394.

Section Three of the Dock Deck was subdivided, the bulkheads closed, and top personnel cleared and posted as guards. With Commander Kramer's approval, all work was terminated and everyone on the station ordered to their privacy pods. The heartbeat scan was conducted while Sergeant Elmer Tepper and I personally inspected every pod on the station.

Heartbeat scan shows the presence of one hundred eight (108) heartbeats. Analysis confirms this to be one hundred humans and eight Etuknips. All Etuknips' identity confirmed. So all humans are accounted for and all Etuknips are Leira. No Sweg were detected. Two Etuknips are missing. These are the Etuknip ambassador we refer to as Ophelia, and the Etuknip security officer we refer to as Sambo.

I personally saw the Sweg in Wheel Section Two, but cannot produce evidence of this encounter except for the disappearance of Ophelia and Sambo. Obviously those Sweg must have come aboard with the cleared arrival that was not noted in the log. Sambo was the Etuknip in charge of arrivals on the night in question.

Reaction to a second security rescreening was mixed. Some groaned; they had just been through this—why were they going through it again? Others agreed with Butch's concerns; the station had been attacked, and clearly security had been lax and it was time to crack down. Generally the scientists were irritated at having their work interrupted again, where the engineers, security, and pilots, though annoyed at the hassle, agreed with Butch.

Butch and Tepper delivered their report during a command staff meeting to Kramer, Tobey, DuBois, Dr. Lazarev, Flynn, and (to Butch's annoyance) Zach Mortimer.

"So Sambo's gone too," Tobey said. "I can't say I'm exactly shocked."

Butch, staring at the tabletop, grumbled just loud enough to be heard, "I'd sure like an apology from someone who had a problem with my objections to putting Etuknips in charge of our security."

Kramer sighed. "I know how you feel, Butch, and I agree with you. But those were the conditions of the Etuknips' visit. Was it a mistake? Obviously. But I have to deal with certain political realities that you don't."

"Well, the disappearance of Ophelia is not a *political* reality, it's a *real* reality!"

"That's enough," Tobey warned.

"It's okay, Tobey," Kramer said. "Butch, was Sambo by any chance among the Sweg that you saw?"

"I don't know, Commander! I just didn't have time to register it all! It happened so fast I'm not even sure what happened."

"All we know for sure then is Ophelia is gone," DuBois said.

"Yeah, she's gone." Butch couldn't keep the bitterness out of his voice.

"Hey, I'm sorry, man," Tepper said.

Butch just nodded at that.

"Well, fortunately the Kevlon-Tau Converter is essentially complete," DuBois said, "and the other Etuknips have the necessary knowledge for me to finish the fine-tuning and operate the rest of the experiments."

"Excellent," Mortimer said. "Then this little incident, though regrettable, doesn't necessarily impact the project."

"Not at this phase."

"We *still* had a major security breach," Butch said. "The question is, what are we gonna *do* about it?"

Kramer held up his hand. "Butch, now just hold it. The first thing we've got to do is just calm down."

Butch did not calm down. In fact, being ordered to calm down just fueled his fury. He stood, leaning over the table, and shouted, "We had a major security breach, Commander, because we've been fucking *negligent!* Negligent to such an extent that there are *comedies* out there that aren't as ridiculous as the way we've handled this!"

Kramer did not raise his voice. "Butch—"

"We've been just sitting around *taking* it and I'm sick of it! Now, *we* allowed the Valdor to dictate the conditions of this contact, and so *we* allowed a Sweg ship to come aboard! *We* compromised our security and enabled an enemy attack!"

"I'm not so sure about that. There was no ship in the Dock Deck, so they couldn't have left in a ship. They simply disappeared. So why would they have needed a ship to arrive?"

"I said I'm not sure *what* happened, Commander!"

"Calm down."

Once again, the "calm down" order just made Butch angrier. "These guys are not Dreb! They can't just disappear and reappear someplace else!"

"Actually, they just might be able to." DuBois spoke in the same tone with which he described gravitational fields or the motions of stars. To him, this was simply a matter of scientific curiosity. "From discussions I've had with the Etuknips, I'm under the impression that part of their physiology enables them to, if I may employ an old cliché, 'fold space'—or, more precisely, fold spacetime in intricate ways. It's possible that they could—"

"Fold space?" Kramer asked.

DuBois nodded. "And make themselves either invisible or to be somewhere other than on Station Post One."

"Yeah, well, there's no Sweg ship on the station," Butch snarled. "I checked all the bays, all the slips, there's nothing in the Dock Deck or berthed to any of the entry tubes. I even checked the Nautabot airlocks. Nothing. All that's there are the *Frontier*, our Ironman shuttles, and our QV Fighters and D-4000 fighters—which, by the way, I wouldn't mind using to go after Ophelia."

"That's out of the question," Kramer snapped. "We can't have that."

"And why not?!"

"Where do I begin? First of all, we don't have the slightest idea where she is. But more importantly, I made an agreement that we would not interfere with Etuknip internal affairs. Now that Ophelia is off the station, clearly the situation qualifies as an Etuknip internal affair. That was the number one condition specified to me by the Valdor, who have arranged and are mediating this encounter."

"Mediated by the *Valdor?!* I thought *we* were running things now! What do the Valdor have to say about it?!"

Kramer was visibly losing patience despite his attempt to bear in mind Butch's emotional state. "The Valdor are still a powerful force in the Community, Butch."

"So are we!"

"I don't want to alienate them because of this. The Valdor set us up with the Etuknips with the clear proviso that we were not to get involved in their politics. We are not dealing with the Sweg or the Leira, we are dealing with the *Etuknips* as a civilization."

"No matter what—"

"We can't get in the middle of any civil war or dispute or whatever the hell the situation is between the two factions."

"No matter what the Valdor 'set up,' the Sweg invaded our station! They planted a spy on board, took over our security, allowed the landing of a hostile ship and the boarding of our station by hostile forces, and abducted a delegate who was here representing their civilization!"

"And I say again, that's their internal concern. Your security rescreening turned up nothing. They didn't damage the station. They left without harming anyone. It's an Etuknip internal affair."

"It became our affair when they violated our security and invaded our station! Whether harm was done to our people or our equipment or not, our station was compromised!"

"And that's *our* internal affair, and I'm counting on you to fix it."

Butch was exasperated. "I *tried* to fix it! You refused! The problem was the condition *you* imposed that we allow the Etuknips to oversee our security! Am I speaking Striktonese here? Am I seriously the only one here who sees the absolutely commonsense problem and absolutely commonsense solution?"

"You're being insubordinate, Butch," Tobey warned.

Butch knew his face must be as red as blood by now. His temples throbbing, he resumed his seat—more to ease a mounting headache than to heed any irrelevant warnings of insubordination. At the moment he didn't care if he was dishonorably discharged.

Kramer, assuming Butch had been put in his place, said, "I want to hear no more about flying off in the *Frontier* and rescuing Ophelia. Even if we had some clue where in the entire multiverse she is, I would still refuse. We have a diplomatic responsibility. There are things about it I don't like, but what any of us like or don't like is not part of the equation. You knew when you joined the service that your duty would come ahead of your personal feelings."

Butch bristled at that, but he also knew that Kramer was right. At the time he had enlisted, he had accepted that—though now he was quite prepared to throw that assumption on the bonfire along with the rest of his military career. Right now Ophelia was all that mattered to him.

But it was clear now that he wasn't going to get her back by appealing to the chain of command. He calmed himself—not with discipline, but with resolve. If he couldn't do it the right way, he would do it the wrong way. "Okay, Commander. Sorry I was so hot-headed. I won't bring it up again."

Kramer smiled slightly. "I understand how you feel. Anyone else have anything?"

"A concern," Mortimer said. "With Ophelia gone, can we expect to gain the same results from the Kevlon-Tau Converter that we had been expecting?"

"Results can't really be predicted with certainty," DuBois said, "but I see no reason we won't achieve the same results with or without her presence. Of course I can make no guarantees, but as long as we understand the operation of the equipment, then it's simply a matter of putting it to use."

"Excellent. Then I hope to discuss the applications of this technology with you later."

As Mortimer spoke, Butch's ears perked. An idea began to form. It was risky, but he was prepared now to take any risk. The thought of losing Ophelia was more unbearable than the thought of losing his career.

And maybe, just maybe he could still have both.

CHAPTER 18

Kramer poured himself a drink, offered one to Tobey, who enthusiastically accepted. Kramer smiled as he poured his executive officer's drink. By any measure, Kramer's job was orders of magnitude more stressful than Tobey's, or anyone else's on the station. Yet Kramer took the stress in stride, rarely let himself become overwhelmed. But Tobey seemed to internalize it; his nerves were often on edge, he often snapped at people, and Kramer often saw him making desperate gestures during crisis situations.

Sometimes Kramer wondered if Tobey had been the right choice for second-in-command. He did his job well, and he was Kramer's indispensable friend and confidant, but Kramer wondered what he would be like as commander. That was, of course, a distinct possibility; even if Kramer was not killed in the line of duty—or done in by disease or injury—someday, inevitably, he would step down, even if many years in the future. Perhaps Tobey would be ready by then.

Then again, Tobey had assumed command quite a few times when Kramer had been off the station for extended periods and had handled himself well. He was more short-tempered than Kramer, more prone to extremes of emotion, but he knew his duty, he knew the rules, and he knew the station. Command was a hard job, and a stressful one, but it was primarily a supervisory job; there were one hundred professionals on the station who knew their jobs. Even without a commander, the station would probably do just fine most of the time.

"I feel bad for Butch," Tobey said, sipping his drink. "Gives him no excuse to mouth off, but I do feel bad for him."

"So do I." Kramer's thoughts again drifted to his unrequited love for Kiani Fulquist and his aborted engagement to Jill Freeport. "Anyone can see he's fallen hard for Ophelia. Who among us hasn't been in his place?"

"Well...I've never fallen for a blue alien—but I did have fling with Diana Krotus which I'm not proud of."

Kramer nodded, remembering the trouble Tobey had gotten into during his ill-advised romance with the notorious villainess. He didn't say it out loud, but Tobey had been really stupid getting involved with a tyrannical despot responsible for one of the most horrific atrocities in Earth's history. Everyone on the *Silver Streak* had been deeply concerned when Krotus had been found drifting in space in cryogenic suspension, preserved after the cataclysmic Nanotech War of the twenty-third century.

No, Butch's situation was entirely different. Ophelia was alien, but seemed a charming creature—and stunningly beautiful. He could understand how Butch could fall in love with one of the angelic aliens. And watching the budding romance had reminded him so strongly of his own relationship with Jill....

"I know how he feels, Tobey. I kind of went through the same thing myself once."

"What, you had a girlfriend who got whisked away into oblivion by hostile strangers from a cosmic string?"

Kramer knew he had never told Tobey about his lifelong crush on Kiani Fulquist, because he had never told anybody. But Jill... "Have I ever told you about Jill Freeport?"

Tobey's nose wrinkled as he thought. "I don't think so."

"It was back on Fresno B-IV. I met Jill at work and we ended up dating—to tell you the truth, I was in love with her. We thought about getting married—we hadn't really gotten serious about marriage plans, but I was pretty serious about her. I was thinking of marrying her, or at least asking her to. And..." He heaved a deep breath. The memory was still surprisingly painful. "At the height of my plans to ask her—she was driving an aircar from Central Colony to the Mountain Colony and...as near anyone could figure out, she must have fallen asleep. She was too damn stubborn to turn on the autodrive. She ran off the track and hit a rock the size of a house. She was killed."

For a long moment Tobey was silent, clearly unsure how to respond to so horrifying a story. "Well...gosh, I'm...sorry to hear about that."

Kramer shrugged. "I don't talk about it."

"Guess not. Well...let me ask you this, what—uh, what lengths would you go to to get her back if you had the chance?"

"Well...I don't know. I don't really think about the past. The past can't be changed."

"Sometimes it can be."

Kramer took Tobey's point; the Etuknips' control over spacetime had unknown limits. He also understood the subtext of Tobey's question—how far would Butch go to get her back? It wouldn't be the first time he stole the *Frontier* and set off on his own.

He couldn't be allowed to do that, no matter how deep his feelings. The relations with the Etuknips were too important, more important than any one man's heart.

———

As Kramer had anticipated, Butch was back in his privacy pod that evening demanding permission to take the *Frontier* out to search for Ophelia. He had a search plan all laid out; he had pinpointed several contenders for the location of the cosmic string, and determined possible flight paths of any ship leaving Station Post One bound for there. He had worked out a course for the *Frontier* to intersect each of those courses at the most probable point that the alien ship could be found, or at least its fuel trails. And he planned on exploiting the Sweg legend of the pirate from the future in order to terrorize them.

Kramer once again said no.

"Why is this summit with the Etuknips so important?" Butch demanded. "We already have the damn Kevlon-Tau Converter—what's it matter now if we bungle things up with the Etuknips?"

"It's more the Valdor than the Etuknips," Kramer explained patiently. "I made an agreement to stay out of their political situation. Dugrow said the Etuknips had some sort of dicey internal conflict, and that their visit to our station was contingent on our staying out of it. Now, if I violate that agreement, whether we consider it important or not, it's clear that the Valdor would take it as an abrogation of our commitments to the Community, and an admission that we no longer desire Community membership."

"Well, maybe we don't. Personally I think this so-called 'alliance' has brought us nothing but trouble."

"And I don't entirely disagree with you, Butch, but that's not your call to make, or even mine. I don't plan on sabotaging a vital interstellar alliance, especially when we might be on the verge of winning this war, all for your personal feelings. Try to understand that, Butch."

"That makes no damn sense, Commander. The Hyrons are enforcing *us* as being in charge of the Community! The Valdor don't have sticky fingers to say about Community governance!"

"Yes, that's true, but the Valdor are willing to go to war with the Hyrons over it." Kramer knew he shouldn't be telling all this to Butch; he should not have to justify his orders. But he had to make Butch understand how delicate the situation was, and the consequences if he decided to go rogue again.

"The Valdor just came out of a Doomsday War," Butch snarled. "How the hell can they be willing to go to war over this? This makes no sense!"

"It makes no sense to us, but we're not Valdor. Their territoriality seems to be so inbuilt into their psyche that the importance of being in charge is self-evident to the Valdor mind. Now, I don't think the Valdor are in any condition to wage a war, but that doesn't change the fact that they'd be willing to do it. And we can't afford to be caught in the middle; it's a miracle we survived the Doomsday War. The only reason we did is we weren't a major target—but we are now."

"This is nuts. So we just abandon Ophelia after all she's done for us?"

"I'm sorry, Butch, I truly am. But you knew when you signed up that you might have to make sacrifices, that you might have to choose your duty over your personal concerns—no matter how important those concerns might be."

"Is it a *personal* concern that our chief contact with the Etuknips has been kidnapped and might be in mortal danger?"

"Now, first of all, we don't know that. All we know is she's no longer on the station. Secondly, no, that's not a personal concern—that's an Etuknip internal concern, the kind we agreed to stay out of."

Kramer stood, circled the desk, and put a hand on Butch's shoulder. "Butch, I know that I'm asking a great deal of you. This is the kind of thing I used to see the evil, heartless commanding officers do in the immies, and I hated them for it. I never wanted to be in a position to order someone to give up a loved one. So please don't make me make it an order. Please understand the situation and consider what's at risk and make an intelligent decision rather than an emotional one."

Butch nodded. "Right. I understand the situation. I hate it, but I understand it. I won't endanger our agreement with those damn crab monsters." Abruptly he turned and left.

Kramer stared after him, hoping he was telling the truth.

CHAPTER 19

Butch *was* telling the truth: he understood the situation. But that did not mean he was willing to live with it. He would honor his word to Kramer: he would not endanger the alliance with those damn crab monsters. But he believed he could get Ophelia back without endangering that alliance. He believed he knew enough about the Etuknips to pull this off.

He went back to the Dock Deck and worked for a few hours—just to make sure his behavior wasn't suspicious. Then, knocking off work at the end of shift, he went up to the Wheel, hoping to catch Dr. DuBois before he finished for the day.

As he had expected, DuBois was working over, as he did practically every day. The Wheel was emptying out as the day shift went off duty, and the nocturnal skeleton crew filed in for another uneventful night.

DuBois was talking to one of the Etuknips; Butch's heart ached at the sight of this creature that so resembled his lost Ophelia.

"When you get a minute," he interrupted, "could I have a word?"

DuBois glanced his way and nodded, then resumed discussion with the Etuknip. Butch waited for them to finish, tried to judge by what they were saying how long they would be—but they spoke in incomprehensible scientific jargon and high-order math far beyond what Butch had learned in flight school. The longer it went on, the angrier Butch became—not because he was being put off, but because apparently Ophelia could be so easily replaced. That sweet, precious, exotic, smart, kind-hearted ministering spirit had been snatched away and it didn't matter; just insert new Etuknip and pick up where you left off.

"All right, that's it for today," DuBois said. "I'll go over the rest of this tonight and we'll talk about it again in the morning."

"Then retire will I," the Etuknip said in a voice painfully similar to Ophelia's.

Once the Etuknip had gone, DuBois said, "What can I do for you, Captain McCrae?"

"What exactly is this device that you and Ophelia have been working on?"

DuBois picked up the device. Unlike the array of equipment that had been strewn about the Wheel before, this device was small, not at all cumbersome, about the size and shape of a transmitter. "Well, it's a Kevlon-Tau Converter."

"And what exactly does that mean?"

"Well, you'd have to do about two years of graduate school in quantum relativity and astrophysics to really understand it—and even then you probably wouldn't. Are you in the mood to hear a lot of detail about tau particles and kevlons?"

Butch sighed. "Tell me what you think I can understand."

"Well...the tau particle is an elementary particle—I assume you know what an elementary particle is."

Butch couldn't help feeling insulted. "Yeah. That's a particle that isn't made of other particles."

"Yes, essentially correct. They have no sub structure, like say a proton, which is made of three quarks. That makes it a composite particle. A quark is made of nothing but quark. An electron is just an electron. There are basically two classes of elementary particles, the fundamental fermions and the fundamental bosons—"

"Is this part really essential?"

"No, no. Okay, moving on. The tau particle is a lepton, which is one of the fermions that I just mentioned. It has a negative electric charge and a one-half spin. The reason it's significant is because there is a particle in both the Thermian universe and along the cosmic string that the Etuknips come from known as a kevlon. This is a recently discovered particle of incredible strength. Where the tau lepton has a life of two point nine times ten to the negative thirteenth power seconds, the kevlon has a lifetime longer than the projected lifespan of the universe. But like the tau, it has a one-half spin—in fact it's...how should I put this?...associated with the tau because of its short lifespan and penetrating nature. And I'm not sure how to even put this non-mathematically..."

"So put it mathematically."

DuBois shook his head. "I'd have to show you a whole group of equations—actually I'd have to school you in a whole new field of math.

Let's put it this way...the kevlon is a kind of a...there's not even a word for it. A manifestation, I guess, like Moffat energy, of the tau's, um...Well, the tau emits very little bremsstrahlung radiation, that's the radiation that gets emitted when a particle is slowed by interaction with another particle. The interesting thing about the kevlon is that its bremsstrahlung radiation increases in a way that's, uh, tangential, I guess, to the tau as it accelerates. In other words, when a tau is accelerated, its lifespan increases, and as it does, we can see a resonance in an equivalent kevlon—Jesus, I'm not explaining this well. But what I'm saying is that taus and kevlons are interconnected supersymetrically."

"Okay, I can understand that."

"What this device does is convert one kevlon into about a thousand taus."

"Why is that important?"

"Well...the energy released by the reaction appears to be exactly the energy released when a particle of energy from the Thermian universe enters our universe and excites vacuum energy. This expenditure of energy is so tremendous that of course, when you have enough of it, it can trigger a supernova in our universe. And so the reverse is true too—by transferring kevlons to taus, we hope to send a reverse reaction, which would have no destructive effect in *our* universe, but which could be intensely destructive in the Thermian universe."

Butch nodded. "Kind of like how kryptonite would be harmless to Superman on Krypton, but is lethal to him on Earth."

DuBois shrugged. "I'm not too familiar with that religion, but yes, I guess so."

"Okay, so the Etuknips helped you to develop this, I presume, from some kind of personal experience?"

"As I told you, the kevlon is found along the cosmic string that they came from."

"All right...so I assume that in order to carry out this reaction, this thing has to be able to find these kevlons?"

"Naturally."

"So..." Butch thought furiously, trying to absorb what DuBois had told him and weave it into a plan. "So...would it be possible for this device to act as a homing beam to find one of the Etuknips?"

"If you're thinking of using this to track down Ophelia, forget it."

Butch sighed, turned away from DuBois, snarling. "Why?"

"Well, first of all, you'd have to know *exactly* the configuration of kevlons surrounding her body, which is a variable figure. Secondly, I'm not giving this to you."

"Oh, come on!"

"We only have the one, and I'm under orders to use it to study the Thermian universe."

"You wouldn't do me a favor?"

"And have Commander Kramer chew my head off?"

A torrent of conflicting emotions washed over Butch. Anger. Guilt. Frustration. He understood DuBois' position, understood that what he was asking for was unreasonable—and yet, dammit, Kramer's stubborn insistence of cowtowing to the Valdor, at Ophelia's expense, was equally unreasonable, if not downright cruel.

But he knew he would make no more headway with DuBois. "Yeah. Well, thanks."

He turned and left, giving up on persuading DuBois but by no means giving up his quest. He would find a way, and he would sacrifice his career if necessary. Ophelia meant more to him than his commission or his oath or the goddamn Valdor's pride.

He went to his privacy pod, simmering, desperate, his mind racing. What could he do? Who could he go to? Could he steal the device? Unlikely; it would be locked away safely— guarded by Etuknip security. He couldn't fight them. He knew he couldn't solicit Kramer's help. He considered for a moment asking Tobey Dingell for help, but no, Dingell was even more hard-nosed than Kramer.

His brow furrowed as he thought of another potential ally: Tepper.

He actually smiled at that. His greatest adversary might actually be his greatest ally. But he shoved that thought aside. His pride wouldn't let him ask for Tepper's help except as an absolute last resort. And besides, even if Tepper was willing to help, there really was nothing he could do.

Butch lay back on his bed, hands behind his head, and looked up at the curved ceiling. In that moment, his mind wandered involuntarily to a consideration of the station's design aesthetic, which led him in a fraction of a second to think of those who had designed the station—and then the answer occurred to him. He shot bolt-upright on the bed. *Of course! Why didn't I think of it earlier?!*

He drove briskly down the curved corridor, his mind a step ahead of him as he quickly put together his proposal. His plan was still only half-formed when he sounded the doorchime.

"Come in," came a tired voice from within.

He entered, approached the desk, and faced down Zach Mortimer.

CHAPTER 20

Mortimer eyed him from beneath his bushy eyebrows, teetering between a scowl and a smirk. Finally the smirk won.

"Well, Captain McCrae, what did I do to displease you this time?"

"Nothing." Butch kicked at the floor, suddenly ashamed of asking Zach Mortimer, of all people, for help. Not only was it an indignity, but a betrayal of his values. And it began to occur to him how much his job meant to him. Imagine never flying again....

But even that was a better fate than never seeing Ophelia again.

"I'm here to see if I can strike a deal with you."

Mortimer locked his hands behind his head, leaned back, and smiled. "All right, let's talk about it."

God, this would be so much easier if he wasn't so damn smug. "Now, you know something about the Kevlon-Tau Converter that Dr. DuBois and Ophelia have been working on?"

Mortimer's face grew serious. "Yes. I actually know a great deal about it. I've been following their progress."

"Well, I'm glad to hear that; I thought you might be. Because what I was wondering is if you're selling them."

"I have not even manufactured them."

"Yeah, but you *could*, couldn't you?"

"Well, I'm...working on it, yes."

Butch couldn't tell if Mortimer was being coy or not. The clever businessman had a tendency to overpromise, but he also had a tendency to accomplish more than he was willing to disclose. Timing was important in marketing. "Well, so manufacture one and I'll buy it."

"Well, I can't rush these things along, you know."

Again, Butch wondered if Mortimer was being clever or honest; yes, it would compromise the quality of the work to push it on the market before a whole battery of quality checks—but then it was also possible Mortimer was playing for a higher price.

Tired of the avaristic games, Butch said, "Then let's cut to the heart of the matter: what do you want?"

All innocence, Mortimer asked, "Excuse me?"

"*What...do...you...want?!* Whatever it is, I'll give it to you."

"I'm not sure you have the power to give me what I want."

"Name it."

Butch bristled at Mortimer's wide, delighted smile.

"All right: I want the startup codes and access keys for all systems of the Dock Deck."

Butch flushed. Yes, that would be a betrayal of his principles, and Kramer would be very angry, but he probably wouldn't lose his commission over it. "So that you can have control over a major portion of Station Post One."

"Yes," Mortimer said cheerfully.

Butch nodded once. "You've got it."

———

Mortimer promised Butch a working model within two days; he demanded it be sooner. He wanted to begin his quest as soon as possible—before Ophelia could slip through his fingers and, just as importantly, before he could change his mind.

With his mind made up, he went back to work the next morning with a sense of peace. He had committed himself to an irrevocable course of action that may draw him a reprimand or may end his career—and which may or may not reunite him with Ophelia. But at least he knew now what he was going to do, and he would accept the consequences whatever they may be.

He was able to go about his duties without giving away that his mind was on anything else; because for today at least, his mind was genuinely on his job. He was firm in his decision and he would wait patiently for Mortimer to finish his work.

It was at the end of shift that his transmitter beeped.

"Mr. McCrae, this is Zach Mortimer. Would you please come to my business pod?"

"Sure, right away, Mortimer."

He finished logging the day's reports, left instructions for the yellow shift chief, and went up to Mortimer's business pod.

Mortimer was holding a small device—similar to the one DuBois had shown him, but glossy black instead of flat gray, and with the Intercore insignia in one corner.

"You said make it sooner," Mortimer said. "My top priority is customer service."

Butch took the device and turned it over in his hand. "Nice. And you didn't, you know, rush it and do slipshod work?"

"I put priority on making it available to you as soon as possible, but we put it through all the rigorous quality tests that make Intercore products the very best."

Butch tried not to think about all the problems Station Post One had experienced after Intercore's "rigorous quality tests." He examined the device, which looked like nothing more than a flat rectangle with no controls, no lights, no displays. "How does it work?"

"To activate, you depress the button on the side."

Butch felt for a button. "Where?"

"On the right side. The front is the blank side without the Intercore insignia—there. Feel the right side."

"Oh. Got it." Butch pressed, and the black face lit with a light blue display.

"The rest is touchscreen," Mortimer said. "There's a lot of sophisticated stuff about subatomic reactions and things...you won't need that stuff for your purposes. You just want to home in on kevlons...right?"

"Right..." Butch paused, glanced at Mortimer. "I don't remember discussing that with you. How did you know that?"

Mortimer smiled. "Whatever you might think, I'm not an idiot. Anyone could guess what you want this for."

"All right, fine."

"Now, this was designed to detect kevlons in a specific—uh, under specific controlled conditions, but it can locate them from a distance too. I can't promise it will specifically find Ophelia, but you should be able to locate an Etuknip ship or their cosmic string. I should warn you it's a long shot, so I hope you at least have a vague idea of where to look. It's a big galaxy."

Butch was nodding. "Yeah, yeah, I've got a search plan, but the trail's getting mighty cold mighty fast."

"Well, this should help, because, uh, one of the things this system works on is a kind of resonance that subatomic particles have throughout the universe. I'll show you how to play with that and hopefully calculate the point of highest resonance, and that will allow you to home in on what you're looking for. If you know what you're looking for."

"A little technology plus a little luck plus a little Butch McCrae intuition, I'll pull it off somehow."

"And of course there's one more thing—I believe we had a deal."

Butch grimaced; he didn't like this part, but he had committed himself to the deal. From his pocket he withdrew a key and handed it to Mortimer. "Security key for the Dock Deck main computer. Access code is '93green521.' That'll put you into the main security system, but it'll be locked unless you enter the chief's access code— that'll be 'Hamlet1599.'"

Mortimer scribbled on a paper pad as Butch spoke. "I'd like to verify these, of course—then I'll instruct you on the use of the Kevlon-Tau Converter."

"Somebody catches you, the jig is up for me! Look, I went way out on a limb getting this stuff for you. How 'bout we trust each other?"

Mortimer laughed. "Trust the Chief of the Dock Deck to betray his duty? I don't think so. I'll verify this, then we'll see." He held up the key. "Can I access the Dock Deck computer from here?"

"Yeah, any terminal on the station. You ought to know that; you designed this damn place."

"I didn't *personally* design it, Captain McCrae—besides, I don't know what modifications you people have made."

Butch felt sick as he watched Mortimer access the security system. The enormity of what he had done began to dawn on him. He had thought at first the worst he could get is a reprimand, but giving the matter further thought, he realized that if—*when*—Kramer found out, not only could Butch lose his commission, he might go to the brig. For a long time.

"Ah, very nice. It works." Mortimer unplugged the key and placed it in his pocket. "I must say I'm rather surprised; I really thought you'd try to double-deal me. In that case, I'll admit that I fibbed to you. The device I just gave you doesn't do a damn thing. I'll give you the real one now."

Butch was too absorbed in his own self-recrimination to feel angry at Mortimer for his deception. He accepted the real device with grace, and for the next hour Mortimer instructed him on its use.

It didn't take long for him to work out the details on his own, and didn't feel he needed further instruction, but he nevertheless allowed Mortimer to finish his lecture; it wouldn't hurt to have more information than he needed.

And besides, once this was done, there would be no excuse for further delay. It would be time for him to go down to the Dock Deck and steal the *Frontier*. Going AWOL. Abandoning his duty. And his career.

CHAPTER 21

Preparing the appropriate costume was easier than Butch had feared. Long ago, he had performed in a play on the *Silver Streak* based on the legend of Captain Kidd, and the SPACEWEB still had a record of his old costume from that play.

Naturally, of course, he didn't go to the Dock Deck wearing the hat, false mustache, and rubber parrot; those things were in the bag slung over his shoulder. Nevertheless he knew he looked conspicuous in his off-white, laced sleeve shirt, red vest, baggy pants, and big black boots.

The elevator doors opened, and the first thing Butch saw was Elmer Tepper. "Grasshoppers with ketchup, what the hell's *he* doing here?" he muttered. Tepper ought to be up in the Rec Pod getting drunk at this time of day.

Well, there was no avoiding him; he had already spotted him and was coming this way. Butch steeled himself.

"Oh, Butch! Butch, wait up! *Butch!* We have a problem with some of the start-ups in the main Dock Deck computer. Some of the programs won't boot. Looks like they've been hacked; I was thinking the Etuknips might have something to do with it. Any idea what might be up?"

Butch didn't answer; he could think of no answer and he was determined to get out of here as quickly as possible.

"Where are you going?" Tepper pressed.

"I'm going away. I might be gone for a while."

"Uh...I haven't heard anything about it. There's no departure clearance for this morning."

"That's why I'm the Chief of the Dock Deck and you're a lowly sergeant."

"Come on, Butch, what's going on? What are you doing?"

"I'm leaving; that's all you need to know."

"What's going on, Butch? I'm not too happy about the way you're talking."

"No kidding; I never liked the way *you* talk. So why don't you go about your thing and leave me the hell alone."

"Butch, come on now! You've got to tell me what's going on with our systems, because I can't—"

"Zach Mortimer has the startup codes and boot-up cycles for all Dock Deck systems now."

"*What?!*"

The was no point hiding it now; Butch had reached the pressure snake. A quick walk through the connecting airlock and he would be in the *Frontier*. Then some power-up procedures, an automatic checkout, and separation from the power umbilicals and pressure snake, and he would be free of Station Post One. Perhaps permanently.

Tepper was grabbing at his sleeve. "When did this happen?"

Butch jerked free. "Leave me alone, *Tepper*."

Tepper stepped in front of Butch, blocking his way into the pressure snake. "Well, you seem to know something about this! Now—"

"Out of my way, *Tepper!*"

"Oh, wait a minute! I think I've got it! You're leaving; you're going after Ophelia, aren't you? You've got to stop letting your personal concerns—"

"What I do, where I go, is my business, not yours. So I'm leaving. You can either help me or try to stop me. The choice is yours."

Tepper held up his hands. "Well, I'm not going to try to stop you, but I'm going to warn you that Commander Kramer gets wind of this and it's all over for you. I'm telling you, he is dead serious about no interference with the Etuknips' internal affairs—"

"This conversation is over, *Tepper!*"

"What am I supposed to do about the Dock Deck systems?"

"Work it out with Mortimer!"

Tepper followed him through the pressure snake, continuing to press. "And where exactly do you plan on starting your search?"

They stepped over the threshold into the *Frontier*. As if this were any ordinary mission, they proceeded side-by-side into the cockpit. "That would be my business, *Tepper*."

"Yeah, well, maybe it would, but it's my business to notify Commander Kramer that you're going AWOL."

Butch was now powering up, booting up the flight computer, running the fuel pressurization checks. "Is that so? Well, why don't you run along and do that?"

Tepper was silent for a moment, then shook his head. "No. I'm not going to do that."

Butch paused in his startup procedures. He looked at Tepper, confused. "Really?"

"Really. Remember last year, the Ognom? When I was so dead-set on setting that thing free?"

Butch nodded; he remembered, all right. The Ognom was a hard thing to forget. A huge, spacegoing organism, a hundred meters across but only a few microns thick, and glowing with an ethereal light, its vast wings sweeping up and down majestically; Butch could understand why Tepper had thought of it as an angel.

They had dragged the Ognom back to Station Post One, killing it in the process. Believing that its "soul" wanted to be returned to the Ognom Breeding Space, Tepper had decided to hijack the *Frontier*, steal the Ognom's body, and carry it on a perilous quest to that mythical space graveyard.

"You could have turned me in," Tepper said, "but instead, you came with me. Well, I guess it's about time for me to repay that favor. I'll cover your getaway."

Butch was not only surprised, but embarrassed. It was not easy for him to express anything but contempt for Tepper, and he knew the feeling was mutual. What Tepper was now doing must be as difficult as helping to spirit away the Ognom had been for Butch. Quietly, Butch said, "Thanks, Tepper. Now, you'd better back off. I'm getting out of here."

"All right, so tell me what your plan is."

"Why?"

"I told you, I'm going to cover for you—but if you run into trouble, I want to know about it. Maybe I can help."

Slowly Butch realized that Tepper was sincere. He nodded, swallowing any sarcastic retorts, and pulled the Kevlon-Tau Converter from his bag. "Well...I've got this homing device that I bought from Mortimer...in exchange for the boot-up sequence for the Dock Deck. This should help me to home in on Ophelia."

" 'Should'?"

"Well...I'm hoping it will anyway. And..." He pulled out the hat and mustache. "And I'm going under cover." He stuck the mustache to his upper lip, then pulled out the parrot. Its adhesive rubber feet fastened to his shoulder. He withdrew an eye patch from inside the hat and pulled it down around his head, letting the patch flap against his right eye. Then he put on the hat, which sported the Jolly Roger.

He flexed his arm, and the parrot squawked.

"What...the...*hell?*" Tepper asked.

"Arrrgh, matey, I'm the Pirate From the Future!"

"What, that Sweg superstition? Jesus, Butch, you think their legend looks like Long John Silver?"

"Well, it's all I've got to go on."

"You look ridiculous!"

"Maybe, but *they* will never have seen this get-up before."

Tepper shrugged at that.

Butch chuckled; he knew what he must look like. But to Etuknip eyes, this would not be a laughable old human cliché, any more an old Eyuknip cliché would look ridiculous to a human.

Such things existed only in a civilization's cultural context. There was nothing intrinsically funny about Butch's pirate costume; it only looked funny to Tepper because he recognized it from human popular culture. To the Sweg he would be terrifying.

Or so he hoped.

"If they think their ancient prophecy has come true, well, then, they might be willing to cooperate with me rather than, uh, deal with my wrath."

Tepper shook his head, smirking. "Okay. Your wrath. If you say so."

"It's not about what I can actually do to them; it's about what I can make them *think* I can do to them."

"You're taking an awful chance, Butch."

"Well, it's better than sitting around doing nothing."

Tepper said nothing, but Butch could see what he was thinking; this would be their last mission together. If Butch did this, his career was over. The *Frontier* would fly no more with Butch McCrae and Elmer Tepper at the controls.

"You don't understand, Tepper; it's worth ruining my career over. It's worth taking all these crazy chances. Anyway, I don't think there's any permanent harm done. Kramer'll get those startup codes back from Mortimer somehow. And besides, what's the worst that can happen? Mortimer's a pain in the ass, but he's not some sort of cutthroat criminal."

"Depends on who you ask!"

"Point is, he won't use those codes to endanger Station Post One. He has the station's best interest at heart, even if it's just to preserve his own worthless hide because he happens to live here. But whatever goes on on the station, I'm finding Ophelia, whatever it takes."

"And ending your career." Tepper sighed. "Well, I hope you've given some thought to how you're gonna make a living after this."

"Unlike you, I have other skills than flying. I'll be fine. Don't worry about me."

Tepper sat down in the seat Butch usually occupied. "Hey, Butchie—uh, think for a minute what you'd say to me if I was doing this for some broad I'd only known for a few weeks. Would you tell me to go ahead, it's worth it?"

"I don't expect you to understand."

"No? I'm a guy, Butch, I've been there."

Butch shook his head. "No, you've never, *ever* been in a situation like this. No human ever has."

"What, 'cause she's an alien? Let me see if I can guess. 'I've never known anyone like her. She makes me feel complete. We can finish each other's sentences. It's not just the sex, it's not just that she's beautiful, it's as if I've been looking for her my entire life and didn't know it.' Sound familiar? Welcome to the human race, Butchie."

"I thought you said love was a sign of insanity."

"Yeah, I still say. I say because I've *been* there."

Yes, it did sound familiar, and Butch knew perfectly well that he was not experiencing anything new or unique to him. The specifics were different, but the feelings Ophelia inspired in him were the same as in any lovesick male over the generations. It could be no other way; all human males were genetically imbued with the same hormones. Ophelia may be the most otherworldy being ever encountered, but a human male could only react like a human male, just as a QV Fighter could only react with the capabilities of a QV Fighter.

"I'm not going to let it go," he mumbled. "I just can't." More loudly, he said, "All right, back off, *Tepper*."

Tepper took a step toward the door, paused and said, "Well, good luck."

"Thanks."

As Tepper stepped through the door, Butch called after him, "If I get caught, if it comes down to it, I'll deny that you were involved in any way."

Tepper shot him the thumbs-up, then left.

Butch listened to the sound of Tepper's footsteps, heard him step from the metal deck of the *Frontier* onto the thick mesh of the pressure snake. He touched the icon that closed the hatch, then proceeded to charge the main engines.

He waited for the blue light to signal that Tepper had crossed into the Dock Deck and sealed the inner hatch, then he released the pressure snake. He confirmed he was fully switched over to internal power and severed the power umbilicals. He was free of Station Post One—and, he thought, of his career.

"Attention, *Frontier*," a voice crackled, "this is CBC. We show you clear of the station. You do not have launch clearance. Repeat, you do not have launch clearance. Identify yourself."

If only there was a code for a middle finger, Butch thought with a grin. He gently pushed the sensitive hand controller forward. The familiar pulse of the main engine followed, and he was now racing away from the station at two hundred thousand kilometers an hour.

He pulled out his Kevlon-Tau Converter and opened the small checklist Mortimer had made for him, and as he accelerated away from the station he quickly followed the directions to lock on to Ophelia. As he did so, he realized what a long shot this was. *I just blew everything I've worked my whole life to achieve, and it was probably for nothing.*

But I have to try. If I don't try, I'll never be able to live with myself. For the rest of my life I'll feel an inadequacy, a sense of loss, a feeling that I put less than my best effort forward for the one thing that meant the most to me in my life.

———

"Hey, Damon, the *Frontier* just departed without clearance."

Kramer looked up from the list of shift assignments, got up and looked over Tobey's shoulder. Not that he doubted Tobey's word; he just wanted to see for himself.

"Dock Deck, this is Commander Kramer."

"Dock Deck. This is Tepper."

"We're showing that the *Frontier* just departed without clearance. Is it a malfunction or a hijacking?"

"I'm not sure. We've been suffering some malfunctions down here, having trouble with the boot-up sequence. I'm guessing there was a false signal that probably triggered the *Frontier*'s automatic power-up sequence, and that in turn probably signaled the umbilicals and pressure snake to detach. I'll work it out and bring the *Frontier* back under remote control."

"All right, well, take care of that and let me know what's going on. PHC out."

———

Butch anxiously watched not only the signal on his Kevlon-Tau Converter—or his Ophelia-finder, as he called it—but also his distance from Station Post One. As soon as he was at safe distance, he would go to light speed, where the station's fighters could not reach him.

The fact that no fighters had emerged told him that Tepper had indeed covered for him. He wondered what was going on back there. Had Kramer discovered what he had done? Was there now an uproar in PHC? Would fighters come zooming after him at any moment? Or was Kramer simply sitting there, rubbing at his cleft chin and wondering what went wrong? Had anyone noticed Butch's absence?

There. He had crossed the red line, the imaginary line surrounding the station beyond which he sould safely go to light speed.

He had no specific destination, so he simply plugged in the directional vector as the Ophelia-Finder indicated, overrode the light speed computer's failsafe that prevented light speed entry without a destination, and engaged the gravity propulsion system.

The stars outside the window turned red, clustered into a field, and disappeared. He was safely sheathed in a distortion envelope, slipping past spacetime, out of Station Post One's reach.

His old friends back there were no longer his concern. That was now his old life. He turned his thoughts ahead to his new life, and the impossible mission he was resolved to accomplish. The odds had been against him many times before and he had never failed to accomplish a mission. This was no different. After all, he now had no purpose to his life except this task. He would find Ophelia or he would die.

From memory he recited the words of Romeo:

Is it e'en so? Then I defy you, stars!
Thou know'st my lodging. Get me ink and paper,
And hire post horses. I will hence tonight.

CHAPTER 22

Kramer quickly forgot about the odd behavior of the *Frontier*; if Tepper said he would bring it back on remote control, he accepted that. He gave no thought to Butch McCrae, who was off shift. His concern was the apparent loss of control over the Dock Deck systems. He spent the next half hour absorbing reports from different Dock Deck personnel and reviewing the data they sent him.

He looked at the wall clock. Still an hour left until nocturnal shift. "Call a senior staff meeting."

"Right." Tobey sounded unhappy, but recognized the wisdom of Kramer's decision.

Fifteen minutes later, Kramer and Tobey sat at the head of the table in the conference pod with DuBois, Tepper, Jerome Flynn, and Dr. Lazarev. At first Kramer paid no attention to Butch's absence; he wanted to get straight to business.

"I want to know why we don't have any control over the Dock Deck."

"It looks like control's been routed over," Tobey said.

Kramer had noticed that too, but didn't accept what he was seeing. He had matched the many obscure and complex lines of code with the operational manual, but given the complexity of the computer system and the way the different codes interacted, he could well be misinterpreting the data.

"Did you get those start-up codes worked out, Tepper?"

"No," Tepper said. "No, we haven't gotten them worked out yet."

Now Kramer realized that *Sergeant* Tepper was not the one he should be talking to. "Well, where's Butch? Isn't he on it?"

"Ummm...not sure where he is."

Flynn said, "Well, you had no luck in bringing the *Frontier* back on remote control, because it never came back."

"Let's put it together," Tobey said. "Butch's girlfriend disappears, Butch asks for permission to go after her and is denied, the *Frontier* flies off, Butch is missing. Is there a brain cell functioning in this room?"

DuBois cleared his throat, then said in a quiet voice, "I feel duty-bound to mention that Butch did come to me asking if he could use the Kevlon-Tau Converter to track down Ophelia."

"Well, did you give it to him?" Kramer asked.

"No, I specifically told him that it was against direct orders."

Tobey sighed. "Is there anyone on this station who just might be able to duplicate a Kevlon-Tau Converter?"

Kramer closed his eyes, ran a hand through his hair in exasperation. "Ebor, did you give the plans to Zach Mortimer?"

"Well," DuBois stammered, "I didn't exactly *give* them to him, but he's sort of been in on the whole project, helping to furnish supplies and—"

"But *does he have* them?"

DuBois hesitated. "I suppose—he probably does."

"That explains everything. Tobey, think about it."

Tobey nodded. "Butch went to Mortimer and struck a deal."

Flynn said, "Explains where the startup codes for the Dock Deck went."

Kramer laughed in spite of—or perhaps because of—his anger. "What else would Mortimer want than the startup codes and access keys to the Dock Deck?"

"Still, I can't believe Butch would really do that," Tobey said. "He's an unpredictable cuss, but he's always been loyal. He knows his duty."

"He's a man in love." Kramer thought of Jill, of his reluctance to speak to her, of the hesitancy of their relationship—of the fact that he had essentially waited too long, and by the time he was ready to start their life together, she was killed.

And his long, unrequited love for Kiani Fulquist; even now there was no reason he couldn't contact her and ask if she'd like to meet up sometime. As angry as he was, he envied Butch his initiative.

"What do we do?" Flynn asked.

Kramer bit his upper lip, thinking. There was no easy answer to that. Station Post One had no faster-than-light vessels except the *Frontier*. The colonists from Fantasia had invented faster-than-light "supershuttles," and had used those to come to the station when they chose to evacuate their colony—but they had taken those supershuttles with them when they moved off to their chosen new homes. Mortimer was now working on duplicating the supershuttles, but none had been built yet. The only way to go after Butch would be to ask for help from someone with faster-than-light ships.

The logical answer would be to call the *Silver Streak*, but the great Space Star was now way on the other side of the Hyron Empire working on hollowing out and colonizing another asteroid. By the time it got here, the trail would be cold.

He could ask the Valdor for help, but he instantly rejected that option. If they found out Butch was interfering in Etuknip affairs, he could say good-bye to the negotiations, and perhaps even get the human race expelled from the Community. Worst-case scenario, it might even trigger a war.

The only other option he could think of was the Hyrons. Zoran was still patrolling the nearby sectors in the Dreadnought *Kinetic*. He could ask Zoran to track Butch down—but to do that, he would have to rely on Zoran's discretion. Zoran was anything but discrete.

But what other choice was there? The only other alternative was to sit back and let Butch get away with his crazy scheme.

"Flynn, see if you can contact the Hyron Dreadnought *Kinetic*. Tell Commander Zoran I want to talk to him."

Flynn raised his eyebrows, but said, "Yes, sir," and got up to leave.

"Zoran?" Tobey asked. "You really think you can trust him?"

Kramer laughed. "Hell, no! But right now I don't see any other alternatives."

———

"Hello. What do you mean to tell me?"

Butch leaned over the blinking light on the Ophelia-finder, his heart pounding. He checked his long-range scanner. Yes, there was an object on the trajectory indicated by the Kevlon-Tau Converter—something moving, moving at light speed. It had to be a ship. And given the vastness of the galaxy, it was unlikely to be any ship but the one he was looking for.

He swallowed as he nudged his course to starboard. A course correction at light speed was always tricky and had to be handled carefully, but the *Frontier* was a good ship, and the light speed computer made automatic corrections in the engine output for such course changes. There was always a margin for error, but a good ship and a good pilot, which Butch was, usually led to success.

He looked at his star chart, matched it with the computer's reading of the photons striking the distortion envelope, and did some quick mental math. He may be a good pilot, but he wasn't used to being out here on his own, so he was more nervous than usual. But as an experienced pilot, he knew how to swallow those emotions and go about his task.

He checked his calculations by the computer, was satisfied he was on the right course to intersect the ship out there, and relaxed. Fifteen minutes. In fifteen minutes he would be making rendezvous with the ship that *might* be carrying Ophelia.

"Just like I thought; I *knew* you couldn't have gone far. Well, look out—here comes the pirate from the future that you're so terrified of."

Now the tricky part. He would have to entice the ship out of light speed in order to rendezvous and dock. The most direct way of doing that would be to communicate with them, inform them he was the pirate from the future and that he was boarding. But would they be terrified into compliance or terrified into running away? Or would they not believe him?

There was only one way to find out. If he failed, he could always home in on them and try firing a plasma laser. Lasers traveled at the speed of light, but if he could get close enough that the distortion envelopes merged (or "strongly interacted," in space parlance), then the lasers would technically still be traveling at the speed of light—just through a shortcut in spacetime. If he could disable the light speed engine, the alien ship would instantly drop out of its distortion envelope into "real" space. It would be dangerous, and a risk to Ophelia's life if she was on board, but he was confident he could do it.

Anyway, he wondered, could Etuknips die?

He switched to Digicom and sought a handshake with the alien communications computer. Communications, like everything, were complicated at light speed, especially when there was no entanglement between communications devices. He would have to hope the signal penetrated the distortion envelopes and wasn't lost in the hyperspatial turbulence.

He nudged the rubber parrot on his shoulder and muttered, "Polly want a cracker?"

The screen flashed different options at him, and he tried them all in recommended order. He wished he had more training in communications; he was a whiz at navigation, space combat, electronics, and general spacecraft engineering, but although he could use a communications computer and diagnose and fix a few problems, he was no expert at communications.

There. Digicom-7, he had a handshake. The computer ran through a dizzying kaleidoscope of numbers and codes, then signaled, READY.

Butch transmitted, "Attention Sweg ship, I am the pirate from the future. You'll drop out of light speed and become a passive target for rendezvous."

There was no emotion in the reply, but the voice had the same tinny undertone as Ophelia's sweet voice—yet, though it was certainly his own bias, he felt this voice was unpleasant and discordant, as compared to Ophelia's musical lilt.

"The pirate from the future?"

"Yeah, that's what I said!"

"Yet flying a Valdor vessel are you."

"Yeah, didn't you hear me? I'm the *pirate* from the future! *Pirate!* That's what we *pirates* do! We steal other people's ships!"

"Will not surrender we our ship you to."

"Oh, really? You seem sure of that. Looking at all the possible futures and alternate timelines? Well, guess what? We're outside the cosmic string and obeying causality. And I say you *will* surrender, otherwise I'll blast you out of the stars! Care to take your chance against my marksmanship? Or maybe you can flee to the future? Oh, wait, you don't do that, do you? You hide in your little comfy corner of spacetime and dread my coming. Well, here I am!"

There was a long pause. Butch couldn't tell if the Sweg believed him or not.

But finally the discordant voice said, "Dropping out of light speed we are. Standing by rendezvous for."

Butch grinned. "That's more like it!" His pulse quickened at the thought of seeing Ophelia again. He thought back to some of the old immies and movies about eighteenth-century pirates; it was every human male's fantasy come true, storming the bad guy's ship and rescuing his beloved.

If he could pull it off....

CHAPTER 23

Kramer sat, simmering, not amused at all, as the voice of Zoran laughed and laughed and laughed over the entangled radio.

"I must say, this is a delight, Commander Kramer! You asking *me* for help in a secret operation! My, my, you must *really* be desperate! Ha ha ha ha ha!!"

"This isn't a joke, Zoran. The political consequences are dire, not only for us, but for you."

"You talk like that's important to me. Personally I would enjoy a nice little war! *If* the Valdor are really stupid enough to provoke one in their current situation."

"For God's sake, Zoran, are you going to help us or not? If not, just say so and I'll think of something else."

"Are you joking? Of course I'll help! Nothing would delight me more than to have you beholden to me. What a fascinating twist in a Vengeance Quest."

"I thought your Vengeance Quest was suspended."

"It is—for now. But as soon as I have permission, it *will* resume."

Zoran had pledged himself to Kramer's destruction because of an incident last year when Kramer had been forced to order an attack on the *Kinetic* to prevent Zoran from interfering with a Community operation. No real damage had been done, but the humiliation had been enough for the unstable Zoran to declare the ancient Hyron rite of the Vengeance Quest. Like everything Zoran did, it was irrational; but by Hyron law it was also legal. The best the Hyrons could do was to order him into *dutimortis*, a temporary suspension of his Vengeance Quest during a time of urgent duty; and right now that urgent duty was brokering the Hyron annexation of the Community, and enforcing Station Post One's new position as capital of the Community.

"I will lock onto the *Frontier*'s fuel trails and follow it to its destination," Zoran said. "How important is it to you that Captain McCrae be retrieved alive?"

"Most important," Kramer snapped. "I don't want any deaths, none. And if there's any threat to Etuknip lives or potential interference in Etuknip affairs, call the whole thing off."

"Let's get something straight, Commander Kramer: you do not give me orders. I am doing this for my own reasons and I will do it my own way. I will retrieve McCrae alive—but the rest of it depends entirely on how the Etuknips respond. *Kinetic* out."

Kramer sat back in his seat. "This was a mistake."

Without looking up from his screen, Tobey said, "Yep."

Nearby, Tepper was still angry. "I belong on this mission. I may not like Butch, but he's my partner and it's my responsibility to bring him in."

Kramer turned toward him. "Speaking of responsibility, it's kind of funny you didn't notice him getting on board the *Frontier* and powering up for launch."

Tepper said nothing.

Tobey ignored Kramer's accusation and said, "If the *Kinetic* diverts here to let you on board, chances are the fuel trails will be undetectable by the time he begins the search."

"May already be too late," Kramer said.

"Hard radioactive residue lingers for a long time," Tepper muttered.

Tobey was growing impatient. "And in the meantime Butch gets farther and farther away!"

"Okay, enough," Kramer said. "Suffice it to say, everybody involved here has made bad decisions. The Valdor shouldn't have forbad us to meddle in Etuknip affairs, the Sweg shouldn't have attacked us and stolen Ophelia, Butch shouldn't have taken the *Frontier*...and *I* should have fought against putting the Etuknips in charge of our security. And *you*..." He pointed a finger at Tepper. "...shouldn't have let Butch go."

Tepper shrugged. "He's my section chief. What was I supposed to do?"

"Clever dodge, but you still covered for him. But we'll deal with that later. Butch is the one who's really going to suffer." Kramer sighed and said in a softer tone, "Which is too bad, because I totally understand."

———

Zoran continued to laugh for a long time as his tactical officer, Maynar, searched for the

Frontier's fuel trails, and the navigators—Grelbad and the new guy, Harshkan—realigned the navigation platform.

First Officer Melkon stood at Zoran's side, looking out over the vast control center of the giant warship. Melkon had grown used to Zoran's manic moods and no longer watched him nervously as he laughed and laughed; he merely waited until the laughing subsided.

"Well, it *is* amusing, don't you think, Melkon?" Zoran finally asked the straight-faced exec.

"No, sir, I don't feel it is amusing to be called off our course by people who are supposed to be our subjects. I don't think it's amusing to be in the middle of a delicate situation that, if handled wrong, could trigger another war."

"You are cautious; I like that. Just the kind of intellectual balance to counter my wild unpredictability, eh?"

"I didn't say that, sir."

"Yes, cautious. You may never be a commander, Melkon, but you'll live a long time."

"My wife will be glad to hear it, sir."

Zoran laughed.

"I think I've got it, sir," Maynar said. "A trail of hot plasma and soft X-rays pointing from Station Post One toward grid Q-11. Quantum data backtrack shows a Q-splash at five six thirty."

"Can you adjust for time lag?"

"Working on it, but I think it's close enough that we can assume that it's still in grid Q-11, moving at sublight."

"Very well. Helm, set course for grid Q-11."

"Yes, sir," said Helmsman Dramia. The navigators quickly supplied her with the course data, and a moment later she said, "I have a three-tornek course at cruise drive factor nine."

"Then let's get there, no wasting time!"

"Yes, sir."

The *Kinetic* jumped to light speed, the control center reverberating with its commander's booming laughter.

———

Butch could now see the Sweg ship. From appearance alone, he never would have guessed this was a ship built by a mysterious civilization that lived on a cosmic string and could control spacetime. It was a primitive tin can. Were it not for the faster-than-light drive, he would have guessed it was a relic from the early days of Earth's space travel, one of those capsules from the twentieth or twenty-first centuries that couldn't make more than maybe twenty thousand kilometers an hour.

It was gray, cylindrical, and covered with external pipes and bits of instrumentation. There was no blunt cone, for this ship was not designed for any atmosphere entry, but in appearance it was evocative of the Apollo ships of the 1960s. And the reason was obvious; the Sweg were new to space travel. The Leira had been at it for some time, and their ship was much more advanced. He wondered why the Sweg hadn't simply stolen a Leira ship rather than designed this piece of junk.

Then it occurred to him that this may very well be an earlier Leira ship that the Sweg had somehow acquired—and as soon as the thought occurred to him, he became certain of it.

Either way it didn't matter; all that mattered was Ophelia.

The Sweg ship was now moving at a hundred thousand kilometers an hour, and with no gravitational bodies within five light years, was on a dead straight course. This would be an easy rendezvous—*if* the Sweg cooperated.

"Okay, Sweg," he muttered, "we can do this the easy way or the hard way."

He matched velocity with the Sweg ship, then nudged the *Frontier* closer. He had done this many times during rendezvous with Station Post One, but it was never a good idea to become complacent during a docking in space. He watched his ranging and his alignment, moving his finger almost imperceptibly against the super-sensitive hand controller. The Sweg ship grew larger—and as it did so he realized it was a lot bigger than he had thought. He was too busy to switch screens and check its size, but he had thought it was no more than perhaps seven meters long; he saw now it must be at least thirty meters long and maybe ten meters across. At any rate it was significantly larger than the *Frontier*.

But that didn't matter. It was weapons that mattered.

He lined up his hatch with the alien hatch and extended the pressure snake. There was a dull thud, then the clacking of the latches locking into place.

He switched over to the automatic pilot, commanding it to hold station, then, gripping his sidearm, moved aft, opened the hatch, and stepped through the airlock. "Here goes," he whispered. He pulled the trigger opening the outer hatch.

Ahead of him, the pressure snake stretched toward an open hatch. No Sweg appeared to greet him, but the open hatch was a passive welcome—but what lay on the other side of that hatch? Cautiously he stepped through, hugging the sidearm to his face, ready to start blazing at the slightest movement, but also aware that the Sweg might try to use Ophelia as a shield. He hadn't intimated that he was here for her, but he couldn't rule out the possibility that they had guessed his intentions.

He stepped through the open hatch and into the Sweg ship.

And there, his conception of spacetime, past and future, and reality itself collapsed.

CHAPTER 24

There was no way for Butch to comprehend what he was seeing, hearing, experiencing; Shakespeare himself would have lacked the words to describe this place. Clearly the Sweg had somehow brought with them in this ship a portion of their native environment.

The first thing Butch was aware of was himself, standing on the other side of the hatch with his arm around Ophelia, coming this way. After a moment of dislocation, this made sense to him and was reassuring: he must be seeing the future, which meant he must succeed.

Then he saw himself lying dead on the floor, Ophelia grieving over him. And himself in combat with one of the Sweg. And as he slowly became accustomed to the place, he saw that each of these things had a thousand, a million mirror images, stretching through a corridor of infinity—but in which direction that corridor stretched he couldn't say. It hurt to look in that direction because that direction didn't exist. It wasn't up, down, left, or right, it was *that* way, a way that he had never been able to see before, a way that human experience was not geared to see. But he could see it now.

And he wasn't merely *looking* at the other Butches—he *was* each of them. He was not *seeing* the future, he was *in* it.

He knew intellectually that this was normal Etuknip existence, as simple and natural as a human's movement in three dimensions and the flow of time from past to future. To the Etuknips, it was terrifying to leave this behind and enter a three-dimensional universe.

But to *him*, this was maddening.

What happened to him here was a cloud of simultaneous occurrences and many mutually exclusive and incompatible events happening in a point of everythingness. There was no duration to the event, because time here was a spatial dimension, and he had the freedom to move forward or backward or even left and right, through many different timelines—which he now saw were not "lines," but simply other routes to follow in the great dimension of time.

Only later, when coming to terms with the aftermath, was he able to decide on a sequence of events in which things had occurred, and even then he had to disregard a lot of things, because there had been many different outcomes. He had to arrange his memory of the encounter to be consistent with only a single outcome, that which he took with him out of the Sweg ship.

And so, since it is impossible to describe in human terms what happened in the Sweg ship, this is how Butch later decided to remember the experience:

His sidearm at the ready, he darted to the side of the open airlock, then leapt through, ready to fire. For several seconds he was disoriented by the uncomprehendable environment, but he refrained from firing. He became aware of several Etuknips at the far end of the…the *place* he was in. He recognized one as Sambo, the technician who had been on nocturnal shift in the Dock Deck.

One of the Etuknips stepped toward him. "Pirate from the future say you are you, yet human appear you to be."

"What of it?"

"Butch McCrae it is," Sambo said. "Works he on Station Post One."

"Why this foolish action taken you have?"

Butch said, "'I loved Ophelia. Forty thousand brothers could not with all their quantity of love make up my sum.'"

"Ophelia? Referring you are to—" The Sweg captain then spoke Ophelia's name in his own language; even in his discordant voice, the sound of her name made Butch's heart sing. "Our prisoner?"

"Yeah, your prisoner. Bring her to me!"

"Begin I understand to," Sambo said. "He here not is on assignment Station Post One for. He here is on personal a mission."

"I see." The captain stood back and barked an order to a subordinate. "She to you being brought is."

"She better be."

Two subordinates escorted Ophelia into the room. She quickly divined what was happening and said, "Butch, your effort wasted is. No good can you me do."

"Let me be the judge of that. I've pulled off a few miracles in my time. Now, if you guys don't want any more trouble, you'll release Ophelia into *my* care."

"Take her not Station Post One to?" the captain asked.

"Where I take her or don't take her is none of your business!"

"Know you time I steal can. Nothing you can do against us there is. But willing am I to release her to you if not you her take back to Station Post One."

"Telling he is the truth," Ophelia told Butch. "Shift he can realities, change he can the timeline, edit he can what happens. Even if shoot him you, he change can that outcome, because even if killed, still alive he is another timeline in."

Butch realized she was right; in the Wheel, the Sweg had removed the battle from the timeline. That was how they had taken Ophelia. "Okay, then tell me why. Why would you release her to me if you can so easily win?"

"Remove her from Station Post One wanted we to. Throw your project into chaos wanted we to. Sabotage the Leira mission into your universe wanted we to, and end our world's contact with you. That done have we. And releasing her to you no difference makes, since that reality in only one time exists."

"Fair enough. I'm not taking her to Station Post One; I can't go back there anyway. I've fried my bacon there. I don't know where we'll go, but it won't be back there."

"Then her take. Go."

Of course, none of this happened that way. Many things happened at the same time, nor was there a linear progression of events. But when Butch found himself piloting the *Frontier* away from the Sweg ship with Ophelia in the co-pilot's seat, he had to recall the events preceding it in only one way, and in a way with which the human mind could cope.

In actuality there had been many outcomes. He had been killed. Ophelia had been killed. He had gunned down the Sweg. Zoran had arrived and taken him captive. Zoran had arrived and they had killed each other. Tepper had arrived in a supershuttle (which Station Post One didn't have in this timeline, but did in another), and Butch had surrendered to him rather than fighting him.

But in a three-dimensional universe, events can only unfold one way, and cause always precedes effect; so Butch's memory of events which had led up to his present moment *had* to be the way he remembered it.

It took him several minutes to reorient himself, to put his thoughts in order, to come to terms with the fact that *apparently* he had succeeded. He had rescued Ophelia.

"Foolish that was," she told him. "Why destroy your career did you?"

At the moment the only reply he could think of was, "Because." It was as good an answer as any right now, because the alert sounded. "Uh-oh, prox on primary ranging."

"What means that does?"

"It means we've got a bogey."

"What a 'bogey' is?"

"Uh, a target. Another ship just came out of light speed—a big one." From the jumbled memories of the surreal experience aboard the Etuknip ship, he already knew who the bogey was, but he checked the SysTrac anyway. "Uh-huh, thought so. Hyron Dreadnought, and I'm guaranteeing it's the *Kinetic*."

He studied the grid map, trying to figure out the Hyron ship's position relative to his own—for that matter, he wasn't sure at the moment of his own position. Fortunately the computer did most of the math, and even handled the star sighting. Normally he liked to double-check that himself, but right now the approaching Hyron ship was his priority.

A light flashed, indicating the communications computer was receiving a signal. He didn't care to talk to the Hyrons, but curiosity got the better of him. He hit the 'transmit' icon. "Who's there?"

"This is Commander Zoran of the Hyron Axis Dreadnought *Kinetic*."

"Stifle my shock," Butch growled.

"Your commander, Damon Kramer, has requested that I track you down and bring you back to Station Post One. He was quite adamant that he wants you back alive, but quite frankly I am not similarly inclined. Therefore I advise you to surrender without resistance."

As Zoran spoke, Butch watched the tracking computer for the *Kinetic*'s position. He had no idea where he wanted to go from here, and even in limitless space it was dangerous to just point the nose and go in a random direction. But right now he had no choice. "'Go, prick thy face, and over-red thy fear, thou lily-liver'd boy.'"

Glancing at Ophelia, Butch said, "Taking a huge chance here." And he engaged the light speed engine.

"You are such a fool," Zoran's voice said. "Your Valdor scoutship is no match for a—" The rest of the Hyron fanatic's sentence was cut off as the *Frontier* slipped into its distortion envelope.

"He won't give up," Butch said. "He can track us, and worse, we're flying blind."

"Outrun him can we?" Ophelia asked.

"Well, maybe. This baby's fast. But I don't know how fast a Hyron Dreadnought is. I guess we'll find out. Right now, though, I've got to get a fix on our position and we need to decide where we're gonna go."

"Should not you this have done."

"Stow that. You're important to me."

"The Sweg this take will as human interference Etuknip affairs in."

"Hey, it's not. It was me acting on my own, contrary to orders. I'll swear to that. If I have to. But first they have to catch us. Now, please, lemme try to work this out...."

The *Frontier* was now at light speed factor six. It was impossible to see any stars; the distortion envelope wrapped the ship in a warped spacetime, essentially an event horizon. No light could enter or escape. But as the light of distant stars struck the outer part of the distortion envelope, the miniscule impacts registered on the computer and were translated into visual images, providing an accurate window on the outside universe. So Butch was able to work out his position and course—but it took time when hurtling through space at hundreds of times the speed of light.

"Okay...grid eighty-two, bearing ninety-eight point seven six two by plus point eight one zero. That puts us on course for...well, nowhere in particular. Let's take a look at the map of the Community...." He studied the map for several minutes, trying to recall any information on the worlds labeled on the screen. Then he remembered he could access the planets' entries in the complete Community database simply by tapping on any of the worlds on the monitor. "Okay...Narmik. I've heard that name, but...Aw, drat. Extinct. Destroyed in the war. Hell, is there anybody that *wasn't* destroyed in the war?"

"Why not simply back to Station Post One go?"

"Because I'm a fugitive, Ophelia. I can't go back there. Ever. I don't know if I'd be thrown in the brig for the rest of my life or just discharged, but either way, they'd split us up, turn you over to the Sweg or God knows what. I didn't throw my life away to get you back just to lose you again. No, I'll find us someplace we can go, even if we have to fly beyond the Community and find ourselves an uninhabited planet."

The alarm flashed. Butch was startled, then silenced the alarm and tapped the blue light to expand it. "Aw, hell, that didn't take long. It's the *Kinetic*. He's after us." The obvious answer was to go faster, but then he would lose any course data he might try to set. Running faster and faster from the *Kinetic* would accomplish nothing; he wouldn't get anywhere, and eventually he would overrun the ship's capabilities and Zoran would catch up. He might have to turn and fight.

The *Frontier* against a Hyron Dreadnought? Maybe...just *maybe* the advanced Valdor technology in this ship could handle the Hyrons' most powerful warship. Even after a year and a half, Butch had not yet tried out all of the *Frontier*'s features. He remembered the nullification beam; he didn't know how it worked, but it should deaden the systems of even so powerful as ship as the *Kinetic*.

But he would have to be careful. If he terminated light speed, the approaching *Kinetic* could vaporize the *Frontier*. He would have to maneuver a few kilometers out of the way, then terminate light speed before the *Kinetic* could compensate for the change in position. At that point, the *Kinetic* would go rushing past—and the turbulence from its distortion envelope would send the *Frontier* out of control. But Butch was a good pilot and he would be prepared for that. There should be plenty of time to bring the ship under control before Zoran could come about.

"Okay, Ophelia, hang tight, we're gonna stand and fight."

"Good idea is that?"

"Ah, hell, no, but I don't know what else to do at this point." He watched the blip of the *Kinetic* as it closed with him. He nudged to port, hoping the sensors on the *Kinetic* wouldn't register the change right away. Hyperspace travel was tricky, and it was a challenge for computers to keep up with all the relativistic intricacies. There were faster-than-light "ripples" associated with any craft using a distortion envelope, and a lot of data could be discerned from those ripples—but even so there was always a delay, and sometimes the time difference was difficult or impossible to compute.

"Okay, here goes." He gently moved his fingers across the touchscreen, collapsing the distortion envelope and bringing the ship out of light speed.

The effect of the *Kinetic*'s passage was instantaneous—or, technically, *faster* than instantaneous, depending on how one figured the math. The *Frontier* wallowed as if it were a boat struck by a high wave at sea. Butch fought the controls, but was unable to arrest the spin. His pilot's instincts took over—don't panic, stop and think, take it one thing at a time, go easy on the controls. The Hyrons probably hadn't yet noticed that their target had disappeared; he had time.

Slowly he arrested the spin, waited for the gyros to stabilize, and allowed the computer to realign. Depending on how long it took the Hyrons to figure out what happened, he might even have time to compute a new course and make light speed in another direction, beyond all reach of the Hyron pursuers.

Even as the thought occurred to him, he knew it was wishful thinking; there was no getting away from his own fuel trails.

The computer blipped, registering a Q-splash, the telltale sign of a faster-than-light ship changing course. Then came a visible flash of light: the light boom. The *Kinetic* had emerged from light speed somewhere nearby.

"They've caught on," Butch snarled. "They're coming after us."

CHAPTER 25

Butch wasted no time. As soon as he had range and bearing on the *Kinetic*, he pushed the throttle all the way forward, and the *Frontier* sped through space at maximum thrust. At first there was a sense of mild acceleration before the ZPL compensator took over, stifling the inertia inside the ship.

He ignored the warning from the *Kinetic*: "Butch McCrae, this is Zoran. Your strategy is fruitless. Surrender. You cannot hold your own against a Hyron Axis Dreadnought."

"We'll see." Butch tried to remember the sequence to activate the nullification beam, but without the checklist he couldn't quite recall the first step. "Hell with it, let's catch 'em off guard first." With that, he opened fire.

There was no effect on the well-shielded Dreadnought. Still, he was pleased when the enormous warship began to veer off course. He wondered what Zoran was thinking as the small and comparatively helpless *Frontier* rushed pell-mell toward the giant Dreadnought. *He might think this is a suicide mission,* he chuckled. If the Zoran engaged the Zargeron Field, the *Frontier* would be destroyed before it could collide, but debris and superheated plasma could still get through, perhaps enough to do significant damage. It wouldn't be a bad plan were Butch willing to die today—which he was not.

But now Zoran had presented his broadside, which gave Butch a slight advantage. The sensor confirmed that the Zargeron Field was not active, so he let loose with a barrage of plasma lasers. He saw impact points and showers of debris—but then, after a few seconds, his weapons began to dissipate, indicating that the Zargeron Field was now on. He wanted to disable the ship's tracking system, but he had no idea where it was, or if it even had external mounts. He could only hope for the best.

The rear end of the giant warship slipped past, and he was staring at the distant stars. "Okay, I hope that did something, because now we're giving him the slip."

He engaged the light speed engine, and a moment later was an AU from the Hyron vessel.

"Okay, if we're lucky, which we probably won't be, I disabled something important and bought us enough time to get clear, and maybe our fuel trails will have dispersed by the time he gets fully operational again."

"Doubt it I," Ophelia said. "Looked it to me like very little damage did you."

Butch sighed. "Yeah. I know."

But after an hour, there was no sign of the pursuing Dreadnought. Butch had chosen a destination: Sacul, an orange dwarf star which, according to Community intelligence, had two planets with oxygen atmospheres. Although one was very hot and the other very cold, both were amenable to human life—just not very comfortable. There would be other challenges; one received a lot of radioactivity, the other had no life forms with amino acids compatible with the human digestive system; one had no surface water, the other had oceans filled with poisonous algae. But he could deal with those problems. He had the *Frontier* and all its advanced technology, he had his own brains and survival training, and he had the guts and determination to make it work. And if it didn't work, he would still have the *Frontier*; they could leave once the heat was off and look for another place to live.

———

Butch McCrae was obviously crazy, Zoran thought. *Even crazier than me.* He smiled. No one noticed his smile. He stood with Melkon, Maynar, and some navigation experts in the astrogation room. A holographic display of the Community, and a number of adjoining star clusters, filled the room.

After that desperate and suicidal run McCrae at made at the *Kinetic*, Zoran decided to take a more methodical approach. The pursuit was a waste of time; McCrae would keep running, maintaining distance, and no one would accomplish anything. Or he would get desperate and try another death run at the *Kinetic*. Zoran had no concern that the *Frontier* could do appreciable damage to a Dreadnought—though that last encounter had caused some superficial damage, depressurization of some sections, and some deaths of minor members of the crew. So it was better to hold off, figure out where McCrae was going, and ambush him there.

"This is his course," said one of the navigation experts.

"You're sure?" Zoran asked.

"Absolutely. We triangulated with the subspace ripple and measured the acceleration of the wave, then crosschecked with the asymptometer. Margin of error is less than a light year at this point in his course, widening by one light year per day."

"That's the only place he can go," Melkon said. "A main sequence star on the edge of the Zodan Cluster, outside Community space."

"Any information on it?"

"It has never been explored, but it is similar to the main sequence star that belonged to the human homeworld. McCrae must be hoping he can find a habitable world there."

"Or already knows of one." Zoran stroked his beard absently. "The Community may have information that we don't. We must finish updating our database."

"Either way, it's the only star along his course that he has a chance of finding a habitable planet—unless our estimate of his course is grossly in error."

"I'm quite confident that I've plotted an accurate course," the navigation expert said.

"Then we'll let him finish his little journey. How long before he arrives?"

"Eighty-four torneks."

Zoran nodded. "Very well. Plot me a course that brings us to that star from a different angle. We'll see if we can intercept him just when he's beginning re-entry procedures."

———

As time went on, Butch experienced a strange contradiction of emotions. Relief came over him as he became convinced he had lost Zoran, and he began to relax. At the same time, as the adrenaline wore off, it began to occur to him that he had irrevocably altered his life—and Ophelia's. He had embarked on a dangerous journey that must end in a hard life of constant labor, lack of modern amenities, no medical care, and no companionship save that of the woman he loved. And he didn't even know her that well; was he *really* sure he wanted to do this?

But if it hadn't been too late before to change his mind, it was certainly too late now. And when he began to doubt, a mere glance at Ophelia reassured him. Yes, he loved her, loved her enough to sacrifice everything to be with her. Wasn't that the plot of all the great love stories?

The *Frontier*'s clock was synchronized with that on Station Post One, which was in turn synchronized with Butch's circadian rhythm, so at 1800 hours, when he was pretty sure that there was no pursuit, he put the ship on autopilot and escorted Ophelia to the lounge. The alarm was set to go off at full volume should Zoran's ship be detected again, so he was reasonably comfortable with leaving the cockpit.

He had unfinished business with Ophelia.

"Last time we saw each other, I had plans for the evening."

"Wanted you to me show the human way making love of."

"Exactly."

"Told you before did I, parts don't match."

"I know. But maybe we can make it work."

"What if cannot we? Did all this nothing for did you."

"No, that's not true. Even if we can't…well, for one thing, there's still the Etuknip way, which is just, like, zowee. And I love you with or without sex. Being with you is the important part. And even if I couldn't be with you, even if Zoran catches us and I spend the rest of my life on Strydia, I couldn't let the Sweg have you."

"But the Sweg me have do. Only a part of reality this is."

"Well, maybe so. But this is the reality I'm seeing and experiencing, so as far as I'm concerned, it's the one that counts."

Ophelia smiled at that. "As long as in your universe I am, the same way of perceiving things do I, so agree with you I do."

"Boy, it just occurred to me…I really know nothing about you."

"What is it like to know would you?"

"Oh, I don't know…nothing in particular, I guess, nothing I won't pick up on as time goes on. It's just that I've never done anything quite this impetuous. *Close*, but never quite *this* impetuous."

"Beginning to have doubts are you?"

"No! Not a one!" But of course there were doubts. Sometimes his mind wandered to all he had given up, the friends he would never see again, the life he would never live again, the oath he had broken. The pursuit of a crazy Hyron commander who would take great pleasure in killing him. Whenever he stopped to think about it, his gut would start roiling, his pulse would increase, he would feel nauseous and dizzy, and he would, at least in part, wish he had never undertaken this crazy venture.

But again, once glance at Ophelia was enough to quell his doubts. He was not alone; they were in this together.

"What about you?" he asked, sudden concern welling in him. "I never asked you how you feel about it. I guess I've ripped you out of your life. Are you okay with this? What I mean is…how do you feel about me?"

"Express we not do emotions in the same way as you humans. Our emotional responses not quite the same are. 'Love' to me not is quite the same as for you it is. And giving up everything not I am quite, not in the way understand it you. Try I will to find a way explain it.

"My life not like yours is—not linear, not unpredictable it is. Know I everything that happen to me will, only do not I know, because a vast cloud of probabilities it is."

"Okay, I understand that. I know my quantum relativity. The concept blows my mind, but I understand it at least intellectually."

"What mean I is, part of my life always have you been—except that 'always have you been' implies that moving past into future have I been, which not true is. But in all this cloud probabilities of, in all the undefined possibilities and experiences, the brightest spot our love and our life together is. Attracted me this timeline to am I, and pleased am I to be here on this ship you with."

Butch looked away, embarrassed to find tears welling in his eyes. "Well…that's, uh, that's what I wanted to know. Tells me pretty much everything I wanted to hear."

"Glad am I."

"So…are you willing to try?"

Ophelia smiled. "Explore each other's bodies want you to do."

Butch blushed. "Yeah."

"Again, I you remind that will not this work, but a brand of pleasure there is such a thing in."

Butch smiled. "Well, we usually start with a kiss."

"Kissing familiar with I am."

He leaned forward and kissed her. Ophelia put her arms around his neck and pulled him closer. He worked his lips and tongue around hers, and she responded in kind. His body also responded, and he pressed against her. He was surprised when she pressed her groin against his; could her anatomy be more like his than either of them thought?

They parted, Butch licking his lips with the strange, scented taste of her. "You're getting pretty good at that."

"Cheated I did slightly, drawing on the visual images I had seen, imitating you, and incorporating other of our kisses from our future."

"We're going to have a future?"

"On the timeline depends."

"Of course, of course. So now…we kind of take things naturally. I'm going to kind of push you backward onto the bunk and move on top of you. It's not a dominance thing or an attack or anything like that, it's just the way we do things—or at least the way I've always gone about it."

"Know I that attack me never you would."

"Good, good." Gently he pushed her back. The bunk was narrow, intended for just one person—and a pretty small person at that!—but he intended on being so intimate with her that they wouldn't need much space. The rubber bunk squeaked under them, and the pressure of their bodies signaled the lights to dim. Fine with Butch.

He leaned in and kissed her softly. She responded, closing her eyes. She tasted good. She smelled faintly sweet. He put one arm gently around the back of her neck and drew her closer into a deeper kiss. She put her arms around him.

Butch couldn't have said how long the kiss lasted, but they finally parted. Her eyes opened and looked deeply into his.

Self-conscious, he asked, "How do you feel about that?"

Chuckle. "Think I it the sweetest thing it ever have I seen. Certainly my attention you have."

Butch put his hand on her cheek and looked into her dark eyes. "I've always loved you. I'm not asking for anything in return; I just hope I can make you happy."

"Already you have." She rubbed her hand along his cheek, and he pressed his own hand against it, stroking her fingers.

Smiling reassuringly, Butch scooped Ophelia up in his arms, held her under him and kissed her deeply. She wrapped her arms around him and kissed back. Then he kissed her chin, layered kisses down her neck and across the exposed space where her scant garment was open. He kissed just the edge of her breasts, and she gasped in pleasure.

She wrapped her limbs around him and caught him in a playful kiss. He snuck his hand behind her back and swiftly undid the binding holding her garment on. It came off easily, and soon Ophelia was naked.

Before he could get a good look at the hidden and mysterious parts of her anatomy, she assisted a bit in undressing him; casually, Butch wondered if she knew what they were doing.

He massaged one breast with his hand and suckled the other one with his mouth. He was only a little surprised that there was no nipple per se, but there was a sensitive circle the purpose of which he could only guess, and he didn't feel like asking about now.

Ophelia gasped and moaned. Butch kissed her body from her breasts down to her stomach, past her navel, down to the thin and hairless pubic area.

His scientific curiosity did nothing to diminish his excitement as he viewed the alien organ she had been hiding. No, the parts did not match, but there were two protruberances that reminded him of enlarged labia. There was no way in that he could see, but he could easily nestle himself between those flaps and enjoy.

He was on the verge of climax already. He crawled back up to face her, asking, "You trust me?"

"Completely, Butch."

He poised himself as though to enter her, wondered momentarily if she would understand.

"Ophelia, like you said, our parts don't match. I'd like to try, though. Okay?"

"Doing this your way are we," she said. "Do as wish you and do not fear embarrassment. Enjoying this immensely I am."

"Are you ready?"

"About to do what you are?"

He kissed her gently and said, "Make love to you."

Her eyes moistened. "What mean that like I would to know."

He held Ophelia tightly, whispered in her ear, "It's all right; I love you," and thrust between those flaps.

She coughed out a "*Ghah!...*" that might have been pleasure or pain, then gasped.

"Are you all right?" Butch asked.

Her eyes were clenched shut. She didn't answer. She bit her bottom lip. Then her eyes slowly opened, and her breathing became more even. "Uhh," she moaned. "My ovulation sacs are those. Strange and unexpected was that at first. But that…that nice is."

They began to move in unison, her face alternating between a sweet smile and restrained urgency. Finally, as she began to cry out in pleasure, they both climaxed.

For a long time afterward, they lay there, wrapped up in each other's arms, totally engrossed in each other. Sometimes they stared at each other, sometimes they hugged tightly. Mostly they relaxed, enjoying the intimate contact.

CHAPTER 26

Kramer, Tobey, and DuBois met in the conference pod. They had Zoran's update on the pursuit of the *Frontier*—though Kramer was deeply skeptical of the details.

It was clear from the report that the *Frontier* had indeed rendezvoused with an alien ship—a physical ship which had dropped out of light speed at Butch's insistence. A pressure snake had been attached, Butch had gone aboard, and Ophelia had been somehow retrieved. What exactly had happened on board the alien ship was unclear.

Now Kramer's job was to make sense of the whole event; the Valdor were hounding him to present to the Community a full report and an accounting of how and why this had taken place. And the Sweg were not making it easy, publicly accusing Station Post One of interfering in internal Etuknip affairs against clearly defined policy.

Tobey was still poring over the details of Ophelia's abduction. It was generally agreed that she had been taken by the Sweg, but how and when that had occurred was a matter of deep debate—and it annoyed Kramer that Butch wasn't here to contribute personally.

"I can't make heads or tails of Butch's report," Tobey said. "Does any of this make sense to you?"

"According to Butch's report," Kramer said, "when the Sweg kidnapped Ophelia, they just disappeared. Yet they somehow got her to their ship. Are they capable of teleportation, like the Dreb?"

"Well, if the Dreb can do it, I don't see why the Etuknips can't," DuBois said, "but I don't think that's what happened. We talked about their ability to 'fold space,' but in spite of that, I don't *think* the Etuknips have that ability, not the way I thought at first. I'm not clear on exactly what they can do, but teleporting from one part of the universe to another doesn't seen to quite be what it is. We know that they originally came to Station Post One in a ship, and according to Zoran's latest update, Butch rendezvoused with a ship and rescued Ophelia."

Tobey said, "Well, if they didn't teleport, how the fuck did they get her from the Wheel to their ship?"

"I'm only guessing here; we ought to ask one of the Etuknips. But from what they've told me and from what I've seen, I think what they did is 'edited' the chronology of events. I think Butch spotted the Sweg in the Wheel, I think he probably stepped in to detain them, maybe even got into a fight with them—and lost. They took Ophelia and dragged her off to the Dock Deck and to their ship. And then I think they simply removed a period of time, so that Butch remembered walking with Ophelia, spotting the

Sweg, and then all of them suddenly being gone. I'd say if the Etuknips are capable of taking a retroactive nap, they're also capable of reaching back in time and editing out a portion of an event; in this case, the battle they probably had with Butch. From his perspective, they simply disappeared; but from *their* perspective, they had a fight, rushed to their ship, and got away."

Kramer was puzzled. "If they edited out that time, how did the events happen? You can't have an effect if you remove the cause."

DuBois sighed and spread his hands in frustration. "I don't know. But picture it this way: imagine we were looking at a security camera recording of the events aboard Station Post One. Say we were reviewing this conversation. After the fact, we could go in and change the recording, take out a portion of it, so that we skip from one event to the next. Someone watching the edited recording would see a skip and not be aware of the events that occurred in between, even though we are aware of them. That's how I think the Etuknips view our spacetime. They exist slightly outside of it, or at a different angle to it. They see our timeline as something like a recording, something *apart* from them, something they can fool around with."

"Blows my mind," Tobey said.

Kramer chuckled. "And yet they still have to deal with mundane, stupid political problems."

"They're just creatures, not too different from us," DuBois said. "They come from a very different world and have a very different way of interacting with the universe, but they're just people doing their best to live life, just like us."

———

"Is this how you honor your contract?" Zach Mortimer stared Jerome Flynn down from behind his expansive desk. Flynn stood facing him, feeling very much the employee being reprimanded by an angry boss.

"I had my orders, Mr. Mortimer."

"If you check your contract, you'll see that if *anyone* should solicit your work in a way that in any way conflicts with your duties to the company, you are to come to me at once and inform me."

"Well...sir...I didn't think that applied to the commander of the station."

"It applies to anyone and everyone, Mr. Flynn."

"Sir, I understand that policy, but I do work for Commander Kramer, and his orders override yours. He can cancel my lease to Intercore any time for any reason."

Jerome Flynn had worked double shifts since Butch's departure to override Zach Mortimer's control over the Dock Deck—a conflict of interest, since he was an employee of Intercore. But Kramer had given him a direct order and he was an officer. Kramer's orders superseded Mortimer's.

Really, it wasn't difficult to override the security keys and startup codes—the hard part was doing so without corrupting or deleting important program files.

"Am I fired, sir?"

Mortimer sighed. "No. But consider yourself warned: if *anyone*, I don't care if it's President Copenburg himself, asks you to work in conflict

with your duties to Intercore, you are to come to
me *right away*."

"Yes, sir."

"That will be all."

"Yes, sir."

Flynn left Mortimer's business pod,
sweating. He had nothing to fear; if Mortimer
fired him, so be it. He still had a good job in the
Command Section. But Mortimer could be
intimidating when he wanted to be.

As he headed for the Battlehab, he wondered
just why Mortimer was letting him off the hook.
There were other engineers; was *he* that vital to
Intercore? Perhaps. Kramer had already used him
to override Mortimer's takeover of the Dock
Deck; Mortimer could also use him against
Kramer. He was a pawn in both men's eternal
chess match against each other. Somehow it was
both insulting and flattering.

At any rate, Mortimer had to have known his
takeover of the Dock Deck would be temporary.
Not only was it inevitable that the security codes
would be overridden, but to divide computer
control was bad for the station, and the station's
well-being was as important to Mortimer as it was
to Kramer. This had been a symbolic victory for
Mortimer, a way of showing Kramer who was
really in charge.

It was stupid, but it was none of Flynn's
business. He would continue to do his job the best
he could for as long as that job existed.

Which was no longer a sure thing, with the
Community now tearing itself apart over this
Etuknip issue.

CHAPTER 27

"Exactly how long did you think you would get away with this?" Kramer leaned over Mortimer's desk, dominating him instead of allowing himself to be dominated by Mortimer's relentless gaze.

"If I thought in the long term, I never would have become a businessman."

"Well, since we have control of the Dock Deck back, perhaps you'll tell me the truth: did Butch give you the startup codes and access keys in exchange for a Kevlon-Tau Converter?"

Mortimer hesitated, then shrugged, ran a hand through his bushy hair, and said, "Oh, why not tell you? Yes, he did."

"You know, the Valdor, the Hyrons, and the Etuknips are all coming here. The Valdor are making a huge interstellar incident out of this, as are the Etuknips. The Sweg are appealing that we took sides in their internal conflict, while the Leira are accusing the Sweg of being on this station without permission. The Valdor are prepared to expel Station Post One from the Community even at the risk of going to war with the Hyrons. And we've lost our only interstellar spacecraft now that Butch, with your help, has stolen the *Frontier*."

"None of that is my fault. It was Mr. McCrae who did it."

"But *you* enabled him! When he asked you for the Kevlon-Tau Converter, you should have come to me and let me know."

Mortimer laughed, secretly amused by the irony that he had just remonstrated Jerome Flynn for the same thing. "And turn down one of the best deals I've ever made?"

"And what have you accomplished? You gained temporary control of the Dock Deck, you made a fool of me for a few weeks, and for what? Now we're alone, without interstellar transportation, on the brink of losing our alliance with all our vital allies against the Thermians, and at the mercy of multiple hostile civilizations."

"Well, you certainly have your hands full."

"Yes, I certainly do. If I do the proper thing, the responsible thing, and take responsibility for this mess as commander of the station, it could mean a full-scale assault on Station Post One, the other two outpost stations, and the *Silver Streak*. On the other hand, if I make Butch McCrae the fall guy…"

Mortimer grinned. "Community relations are patched over. Throw him to the wolves; he's obviously unstable and unreliable, a man who would destroy his own career and our interstellar relations for a date."

Kramer stood up straight, knowing what he had to do. "There's no choice in the matter."

He left Mortimer's business pod and headed for his own privacy pod. He had a lot of thinking to do. He had already made the choice long before visiting Mortimer, but he wanted to make the point that Mortimer's greed had led to the unfortunate choice between interstellar war and ruining a good man's life.

Mortimer did have a point; Butch had brought it on himself. But it gave Kramer no pleasure. Butch had been a steady and reliable crew member, and was a living legend thanks to his and Tepper's unexpected trip to the Andromeda Galaxy last year. And as abrasive and arrogant as Butch was, Kramer had to admit he'd come to like him. It was a great waste and a great loss.

He thought of Jill Freeport, of Kiani Fulquist, wondered what he would do if given the remote chance of being with either of them; he understood Butch's motivations and could forgive him personally if not professionally. He knew Butch deserved to lose his commission for deserting the station and placing the alliance with the Community at risk—but it was a tragedy that he must now lose everything for the crime of falling in love.

———

The Dock Deck was a blizzard of barely controlled chaos. Representatives of the Valdor, the Etuknips, and several Community worlds in this sector crowded the area, and there weren't enough security personnel to keep them herded together. And not all of them were cooperative.

And more ships were arriving.

Kramer arrived in PHC for green shift, finding that Tobey, unusually, had preceded him and was frantically trying to coordinate ship arrivals.

"Jesus God, we've got to send some Nautabots out and paint some lines out there. There are ships everywhere!"

Kramer hadn't thought it possible to cram so many ships into the small volume of space around Station Post One. It was humbling to think that his station had become the center of the galaxy's attention—and embarrassing. "Well, Dugrow and the Sweg Ambassador both want to see me, so can you handle it here without me for a while?"

"Hell no!"

"Well, sorry. You'll have to try for a little while."

"All right."

Kramer went down to the conference pod to face another strange matter: the Sweg Ambassador refused to be in the same room with Dugrow.

"I you with meet *alone*," she said firmly.

"Why? What's the problem?"

"The Valdor were it who arranged meeting your the Leira with. This a slight was to our side and a threat our way of life to. With *you* will we deal, but on a war footing with the Valdor we are!"

"Come on, Ambassador, let's be reasonable—"

"Impossible it is the Valdor to be reasonable with!"

Kramer couldn't argue with that. "Well, Dugrow is already in there, so I'm afraid you'll have to wait until he and I are done. Then I'll meet with you."

"First or second nothing means me to."

"Good. You can just…skip the time between now and our meeting."

The Ambassador simply stared at him.

"Joke," he said lamely. When she still said nothing, he gave up and entered the conference pod.

Dugrow paced back and forth, his eight jointed legs clattering and rattling with each movement. On Kramer's entrance, he turned his crablike body toward him and leveled his recessed, bioluminescent eyes on him. "Kramer," he said in an unfriendly tone.

"Always a pleasure to see you, Dugrow."

"The occasion is far from pleasurable. Is there a single provision of our agreement with the Etuknips that you have *not* violated?"

Kramer shrugged. "We didn't offer them pork."

"I do not understand. That was not one of the provisions—"

"Joke, joke." *And a stupid one*, Kramer thought. It was hard to think straight under the circumstances. "I'm aware that things have not gone as planned—"

"A ridiculous understatement! Have you seen the swarm of Community ships? Are you aware that the Sweg are demanding your expulsion from the Community? Are you aware that your actions have brought the Sweg and the Leira to the brink of war?"

"I'm aware of these things, Dugrow, and it's to be regretted, but the simple fact is…" Kramer took a deep breath. "The incidents that led to this were *not* acts of Station Post One official policy. They were performed by a single rogue element, without my consent or knowledge."

"You are referring, of course, to Butch McCrae."

"Yes." Kramer felt like a traitor. The station, and all that went on aboard it, was *his* responsibility. It was against all his training and command instinct to deflect responsibility to a subordinate. But what choice was there?

"Yet it is *you* who have persisted in retaining Butch McCrae as a high-ranking member of your staff, responsible for vital components of your station, in spite of my repeated warnings of his mental and emotional instability."

"I won't get into a debate with you about the decisions I made regarding the staffing of my station. You wanted me to stay out of Etuknip internal affairs. May I ask you to stay out of *our* internal affairs?"

"I have never heard such hypocritical nonsense come from your floppy, disgusting mouth before. You flagrantly violate the one most important provision of this contact, and then proceed to ask us to honor that provision with you."

"Dugrow—what is the purpose of this conference? You seem only to want to point out the mistakes we may have made. The question is, what do we do now?"

Dugrow uttered a trilling sound that might have been a sigh. "Very well; for once you are correct. The past is behind us and we must now move forward."

"Very well. Since the fault for this entire mishap lies with Butch McCrae, I suggest that if justice is meted out to him and him alone, we can overcome this unfortunate misunderstanding and proceed as we were before."

"*If* that mentally unbalanced Hyron manages to retrieve him! But in any case, that is not up to me to decide. The Etuknips are the ones whose internal relations have been destabilized by McCrae's irresponsible acts."

Kramer nodded. "Then it's time to speak to the Sweg ambassador. Perhaps she will agree to my terms."

"Then take her these terms: if McCrae is captured, he is to be judged by a Community court, not a human court."

Kramer thought of refusing. He had seen too much of Valdor justice when they had tortured Zach Mortimer for war crimes. He could only imagine what they would do if they got their claws on Butch. But again, he felt he had no choice. Perhaps if the matter were taken up by the Centralized Committee, and therefore by representatives of the entire Community rather than just the Valdor, then Dugrow would not be able to carry out the kind of atrocities that Kramer feared. "Very well. I'll discuss it with the Sweg Ambassador."

"Then since the Sweg Ambassador does not wish to be in the same room with me, I will take my leave of you."

Kramer nodded. Dugrow clattered out of the room. Kramer stepped to the door and, seeing the Sweg Ambassador waiting, said, "Please come in."

The Ambassador followed him into the conference pod, saying, "Brief that was. Did you a productive conclusion reach?"

"I hope you'll think so, Ambassador—is there a name I can call you?"

The Ambassador made a series of squeaks and whistles that Kramer found indistinguishable from any name in the Etuknip language.

"Mackenzie one of your humans me called."

"Very well; then with your permission I'll call you Mackenzie. As I explained to Dugrow, I did not authorize the actions that destabilized your relations with the Leira. It was always my intention to honor the mandate that we stay out of your internal affairs. But we have a single officer who went rogue. He had personal reasons. He stole our interstellar ship and fled from our station, attacked your ship without my knowledge or permission, and I immediately asked for assistance from the Hyron Empire in recapturing him. I'm sure Commander Zoran will be successful in bringing him back here."

"So it to me explained has been. A Captain Butch McCrae. Been told I have that a forbidden romance had he the Leira Ambassador with."

"Yes. When your people took her, Captain McCrae was determined to rescue her. He did come to me to ask permission to pursue her, and I refused. He went anyway. So I suggest that Captain McCrae bear the responsibility for this entire affair, and once justice is done, we can resume relations as before. As per Dugrow's request, I have agreed to let McCrae stand trial in a Community court rather than a human one. Will this satisfy you?"

"In your universe, time cannot turned back be. In this reality, the damage by Butch McCrae done cannot undone be. How will this justice the damage correct?"

Kramer shrugged. "I guess that's up to you and the Leira."

"Understand do you that these events precisely match the horrors in legend foretold?

That the pirate from the future the apocalypse have wrought our people upon?"

Kramer fidgeted. "I've been told something about it."

"McCrae's suffering this will not undo."

"But why can't you simply choose a timeline in which this all *didn't* happen? I understand you have the ability to do that."

"Because in your universe are we. Must we observe cause and effect. If in the cosmic string were we, things different would be, and are different from their perspective. I function must by a single timeline from past to future, and as if cannot I choose timelines must proceed."

"In that case, will you accept these terms?"

"Cannot I promise that the end of this will be, and the capture Butch McCrae of far from certain is, but Butch McCrae's punishment do we demand—as well as that of the Leira Ambassador—" Mackenzie spoke a name which Kramer assumed was the Etuknip name of Ophelia.

"What happens to her is between you and the Leira. I have no say in it." Kramer hated himself for saying that. It was a worse betrayal of Butch than throwing him to a Community court. But once again, what choice did he have? The choice was Butch's doomed love story or the very survival of the Community. He wondered if Butch would understand; and he wondered, as a commander, if he could afford to care whether or not Butch would understand.

"Then take it up with the Leira will I." Mackenzie stood, unfolding her arms in that graceful way the Etuknips had; their alien beauty was enticing, and Kramer could understand how

Ophelia had beguiled Butch. "With your permission, leave will I."

"Thank you for the conference."

Mackenzie turned and left.

Kramer sat back, confused and miserable. Some of the things Mackeznie had said made no sense; he knew that the Etuknips could still manipulate spacetime in this universe. That was how they had abducted Ophelia from under Butch's nose. Why were they shackled to a single outcome in this case? Did it have something to do with the Sweg's fear of the future?

He was too tired to think about it; he merely accepted that their way of life was too alien for him to comprehend. He headed back up to PHC, hoping the day ahead would be less chaotic than he feared.

CHAPTER 28

Shakespeare. Beethoven. What will she think of those geniuses? The thought woke Butch early in the morning and filled him with excitement. He knew now his romance with Ophelia was emotionally and physically fulfilling—now to find out if it would be intellectually fulfilling. He already knew she was intelligent—a genius, in fact—but were their intellectual tastes compatible?

"Do you like stories?" he asked, his eyes drawn to her blue feet as she rubbed them together. She sat on the edge of the bunk, alert since he had emerged from his morning systems checks in the cockpit.

"Mmm, yes," she said.

"Well, I'm a big lover of the classics—human classics, that is. And I was wondering—"

He looked at her, hoping to see some reaction. She was watching him, wide-eyed, mouth drawn down at the sides in curiosity.

"—I've got a pretty extensive library stored in the computer on board ship, something to listen to or watch on long trips. I've got a particular fondness for William Shakespeare, who's considered the greatest dramatist in human history. I'd love to introduce you to some of his best stuff."

A finger went to her chin, and she looked off to her left. Then she replied whole-heartedly, "Love I would if share it me with would you!"

"Good," Butch said, new excitement pouring through him. The thought of sitting down in the crafts/hobby area with Ophelia and watching *Romeo and Juliet* was so...domestic. It brought home all over again that he had really done this, that she was with him...that Ophelia knew *he* existed. "I hope you enjoy. I also hope I can give you the freedom you need ... See, space travel can be very dangerous, and I'll need you to follow the rules of space travel. But at the same time, I don't want to be like your father or something—if you even have such a concept—I don't want to tie you down—"

"Like I to explore and discover, but crazy not am I. Will not I anything do that could me killed get. Know you more space about than do I, and want I you teach to me everything."

"I'm sorry. I guess I don't give you much credit. See, I only know what little snatches of your life that I've seen on the station or that you've told me about. I guess we've still got a lot to learn about each other."

And so the *Frontier* devoured the light years, the lounge ringing with the words of the Bard. Butch selected the Alfred Winter version of *Hamlet*—a word-for-word presentation of the complete play, all four hours of it. It was the finest presentation of Shakespeare Butch had ever seen, and he thought it would be interesting to introduce Ophelia to her namesake.

They sat side-by-side in the rear of the lounge on the makeshift sofa he and Tepper had installed to fold out of the wall. Throughout, he kept glancing at Ophelia to gauge her reaction. Sometimes she asked questions, and he felt obliged to pause the holovid as he answered; consequently, it took all day to watch the play.

Well, not *all* day. There was time for lovemaking when it was over.

That night it was the Dennis McPheron *Romeo and Juliet*, and the next morning McPherson's celebrated *Macbeth*. Ophelia expressed regret that she had no Etuknip entertainment or art available to share, but she sang some Etuknip songs, hypnotizing Butch with her melodic voice. With that strange, tinny undertone to her voice, she managed to sing in harmony with herself, which Butch found fascinating and beautiful. *She can't be real*, he kept thinking. *She's a fairy tale come to life—and she's mine!*

As both had become tired of sitting and interacting with virtual reality, or staring at a screen, Butch decided they should try something else. He pulled out his collection of classics, which he had on his portable book reader, and they read some of Shakespeare, Marlowe, and Milton together. He realized he had *Moby-Dick*, which he hadn't read since high school. He looked forward to sharing that one. It was a pleasant and intimate afternoon.

As the afternoon drew toward evening (as measured by the *Frontier*'s clock), Ophelia said, "Cook us dinner will I. Learned I have cookbooks from on Station Post One. You turn down the lights in the lounge and put on some music. Join you will I shortly."

"Okay," Butch said. "I'll be waiting impatiently."

Ophelia disappeared into the kitchenette, leaving Butch to wonder how skilled her cooking would be. Ordinarily he would flatly dismiss the possibility of anyone learning to cook simply by reading books, but Ophelia was an extraordinary woman.

He turned on his collection of the Best of Beethoven, then changed his mind—Brahms was more appropriate to the setting.

A short time later, Ophelia's head popped through the door. "Butch, could I some help use all this carrying."

"On my way." Butch jumped up to follow her.

As he followed her up the short step into the kitchenette, he reached up and tickled her butt. She swatted his hand away playfully. When they reached the access corridor, Ophelia broke into a run, giggling. Butch chased after her. She barreled around the corner into the computer core. Butch followed, caught up, and grabbed her around the chest. They fell to the floor in the artificial gravity, laughing. She wrapped herself around him and he kissed her.

"Our dinners gotten yet we not have," she said.

"No, we don't want them to get cold. Not that there's much chance of that with us around."

Ophelia wriggled out of his arms and hurried around the corner, calling over her shoulder, "'Better three hours too soon than one minute too late!'"

Butch followed her, shouting, " 'Too swift arrives as tardy as too slow'!"

When he entered the lounge, he found two Thai-themed dinners steaming. They smelled delicious. Ophelia had also prepared a salad for him and cabbage soup for herself.

"I thought you didn't eat our food."

"Used I ingredients from nutrient powders brought I cosmic string from."

"Adapting your system to solid food ought to be…interesting."

"Anything can we do that our minds us set to can," Ophelia reminded him for the thousandth time. She looked around at the soft ambience. "Nice lighting."

"Thanks." The room was usually harsh and bright, the light reflecting unpleasantly off the gray walls, but now it was dim as though lit by candlelight.

They ate in silence for a few minutes, before Ophelia spoke. "You know what to do would I like?"

"What?" Butch asked through a mouthful of spicy noodles and chicken.

"On a planet land."

"Well, that's the idea. Assuming there's one around that star that's habitable."

"Actually…thought I maybe could go we down to one that not habitable is."

"You *would* say that," Butch said teasingly.

"Serious am I. Spacesuits could we wear and not wander too far from the ship. Come on, Butch, exciting will be it. Might we alien life find or something else valuable."

"All right, all right, you've convinced me. As soon as we're done eating, I'll put us on a course for the nearest star with planets."

"I you thank." Ophelia took a bite, swallowed, and said, "Will not you this regret. Nice will it be off this ship to get."

"Don't tell me you're getting cabin fever." On Ophelia's quizzical look, Butch explained, "It's a kind of a claustrophobia. Happens all the time in space flight, it's why we take hypodopaserasenzidine. Basically, being confined in a small space for too long with the same people day-in and day-out drives you bonkers."

She shrugged. "After a while, gets it a little cramped in here. And an adventure this supposed to be is, is not it?"

"Well, you're absolutely right about that."

"As said the ghost of Hamlet's father, 'this visitation is but to whet thy almost blunted purpose.'"

Butch chuckled. " 'My pulse, as yours, doth temperately keep time, and makes as healthful music'."

" 'O Butch, thou hast cleft my heart in twain,' " Ophelia said with finality.

They both laughed. It delighted Butch that she was enjoying Shakespeare, and he was delighted to show her his collection and see her responses—though he also realized the time would come when there was no more for him to teach her...and vice versa. The learning experience was one of the great pleasures of their relationship.

After dinner, they tossed their dishes into the recycling slot and pressed the activate button, then retired to the sleeping quarters. Ophelia plopped onto the bed they now shared and Butch joined her. Her head resting on his shoulder, they watched the monitor screen on the far wall, which delivered the same realtime display as the screen in the cockpit.

"Cannot I wait explore a new world to," Ophelia said, almost cuddling with her words as she always did, her musical voice turning the most ordinary smalltalk into a song.

Butch held her close, thinking of the many adventures that were in store for them.

———

"Interesting." Zoran chuckled as he read the navigator's report. "This star has no name in our computer banks, only the designation AZT-4814. There are no habitable planets there. Why in Blackhaven would McCrae be going there?"

"I don't know, sir," Maynar said, "but based on their fuel trails, there is no other destination. There was a light boom registered on the telerometer at six twenty. Hyperlight registry from Valdor interstellar satellite seven seven eight one confirmed it within two torneks. So the *Frontier* is definitely in that system."

Zoran scratched his beard. "What could McCrae be up to? Well, we'll find out when we catch him. How quickly can you get us there?"

"If we make the course change immediately, we'll be there in four torneks."

"Perfect." Zoran smiled. "I can't wait to see the look on McCrae's face when we bring his little adventure to an end!"

CHAPTER 29

"Oh, fuck! –oh! Excuse my language."

"Quite all right, Butch. Learned I that pilot parlance riddled is with such profanities."

Butch double-checked his readings. There was no doubt: the *Kinetic* had caught up with them. The light boom confirmed it: the huge Dreadnought was here, now, somewhere nearby, probably just over the horizon in a higher orbit, ready to pounce.

"What doing you are?" Ophelia asked.

"Calculating…if I were to break orbit now, enter atmosphere, then he could track us, but he couldn't capture us. But I don't know if we'll make atmosphere interface before he comes into range. On the other hand, if I climb to a higher orbit, we might stay out of his range, pace him. But that's just stalling. Sooner or later one of us would have to make a move."

"We could light speed make and out of here get."

"Yeah, and draw a big finger across the sky for him to follow. No…I think our best bet is to lure him to the surface. Then we'll be on equal terms and we can finish this thing."

Butch frowned at his screen, watching the numbers obsessively as he applied the braking nodes. The ship lost speed, dropping like a stone toward the poisonous atmosphere below. Anticipating landing and making a journey on foot, he wondered if the Hyrons would be stupid enough to engage in a sidearm battle in such an environment.

According to his readings, the pressure was survivable, there were no corrosive gases, so respirators would be fine. Even so, it would be hard to keep a respirator on during a battle of any kind. If he was lucky, the Hyrons would back off. After all, was he really *that* important?

No, he knew, *but Ophelia is….*

The air began to flame around the rims of the windows—and he saw a bright star come into view. It could be the planet's small, asteroid-sized moon or it could be the *Kinetic*. Or it could be one of the other planets in this system. *Don't lose your nerve, Butchie*, he thought to himself. *Go with what you know, not with what your gut imagines.*

Soon a blanket of ions, stripped of their electrons by the friction of the *Frontier*'s passage, masked much of the information coming in—and going out. There were plenty of other ways to track a spacecraft, not the least of which was visually: the *Frontier* was now a brilliant stream of fire across the dark blue sky. And he still had digital photon imagery; the *Kinetic*—if that was what that bright star was—was up there, now at the zenith and moving slowly toward the horizon. But there was nothing it could do from up there short of firing its Annihilatron—and what would be the point of that?

The orange inferno slowly dissipated, the roar of the flaming air outside quieted to the whoosh of high-altitude flight.

He looked at the landing radar. "Damn if it ain't the worst landing field I've ever seen."

The land below was a perilous maze of craggy mountains; he could see no surface that didn't incline at least forty-five degrees. He might hover there, but not land—and even that would be risky, as he had already driven the ship's power reserves below recommended levels. The *Frontier* was a faster-than-light ship, but not a long-range capital ship.

What the hell was I thinking? he cursed himself. *My stupid fantasy of a cosmic star voyage with Ophelia in a ship meant for excursions of a few weeks!*

No choice, then. He had to keep flying and hope he came across level ground. There had to be some; the whole planet couldn't be like this! ...*Could it?*...No, that would mean the whole surface was a mass of tiny tectonic plates, all of them pushing against one another. Impossible.

There...on the horizon...it looked like the land smoothed out into choppy mesas and plateaus. There ought to be a good place to land. The *Frontier* wasn't very big and could make vertical landings and lift-offs; he didn't need a whole spaceport, just two hundred or so square meters of flat land.

The alert klaxon sounded. He was too intent on his ranging and descent to pay attention to it. "Ophelia, can you check what that means?"

"Do not I this ship know how to operate!"

"Shit." Butch looked across at the flashing light, hit the button under it to silence it. The screen below indicated two targets approaching. "Damn. They must've launched fighters as soon as they came out of light speed, otherwise they couldn't have tracked us and closed in on us so fast."

He couldn't watch the landing radar and the ranging of the enemy ships at the same time. They were back there; that was all he knew. And being behind him, they had the advantage. He could come around and fight them, but he was outnumbered and in a bulkier, less maneuverable ship.

Or *was* it less maneuverable? He had never really put the *Frontier* though its paces in atmospheric flight. Perhaps now was the time to find out. "Okay, hang on, Ophelia. We're going into battle."

Never mind that he had never *actually* done this with the *Frontier*; he was a fighter pilot and knew was he was doing. Like all pilots, he knew he was the best pilot in the universe.

He swung the ship around in an arc, climbing to thirty thousand meters. The Hyron fighters blinked on the radar screen, each sweep jumping them closer by a hundred kilometers.

"And...there...we...*go!*" He unleashed a plasma laser barrage, banked, and dove straight down. The radar went out as the radosphere lost its bearings, but Butch wasn't paying attention to that right now. "Hold on, Ophelia." He pulled up on the control stick, pulling eight g's. The ship's internal inertial field wildly tried to compensate, but he could feel some of the pressure. Not that it mattered to him; he knew he could handle up to ten g's; Ophelia was another matter.

Then he heard something in the back break. There was a metallic *snap!*, then a fizzling as of air from a balloon. The attitude indicator rolled sharply to the right. "Uh-oh." He jiggled the control stick back and forth; it moved loosely, the ship not responding.

"What happening is?" Ophelia asked.

"Uh…nothing, don't worry about it." He punched the manual control, gripped the stick again, and pulled. He was now operating on hydraulic controls. This deep in the atmosphere, the ship's twin rudders and ailerons were as good as, if not better than, the field tense. The ship stabilized. He could still fly—but space flight was now out of the question. He had ruined the *Frontier* as a spacecraft; it was now an aircraft. He didn't know exactly what had broken, but based on the sound, he assumed it was just a tank that could be replaced.

Radar reacquired the Hyron ships. He hadn't managed to shoot either of them down, and they were now diving toward him. He made for the craggy mountains, hoping to lose his pursuers in the deep ridges and valleys. It was a risk; one mistake and he would crash. But he was Butch McCrae, and Butch McCrae didn't crash.

The peaks loomed ahead, and his eyes flicked spasmodically from the radar to the view out the windows. If he was lucky…yes, there. Between those two peaks was a deep crevasse. He edged the ship closer to it, noting that the Hyron ships were on his tail as if tethered there. *Well, we'll see how long they can stay on me.*

The *Frontier* was fourteen meters across at its widest point; he would have to watch the scope very carefully as he drove through the narrow channel ahead.

The walls of the crevasse now surrounded them, and Butch recalled the feeling of driving a speeding aircar through the mountains of Beta VII. He wondered what training the Hyron pilots had in such terrain.

"Safe this is?" Ophelia cried.

"Trust me!"

The crevasse turned to the right ahead. Butch nudged the stick—not enough! He pulled harder, and the ship turned. The hydraulic controls of the rudders were not as sensitive as the quantum computer control of the field tense. Damn, it had been a long time since he'd simulated this, and he had been so confident in the Valdor failsafes that he hadn't practiced much. But this was much like a ZR-130 fighter; he just had to use his old reflexes instead of his new. No problem.

But the Hyrons stayed on him—and now they opened fire. The bastards were going to start a rockslide! Well, he could play that game. He fired his aft plasma lasers, aiming above the Hyron ships and leading by about a hundred meters.

Nothing happened. If he did start a rock slide, it was a slow one that was well out of sight in seconds.

There was what he was looking for. The crevasse narrowed. He looked at the radar, which warned automatically of the narrowing obstacle ahead. It narrowed to ten meters—too narrow for the *Frontier*. "Damn!" He pulled up and accelerated.

But with the field tense compromised, the acceleration was slow. The ship's nose turned upward, but it continued to speed forward until the rockets kicked in. As the ship swept inexorably toward that impassable channel, he held his breath, willing that rocket to push them away in time.

They cleared with a few centimeters to spare.

And the Hyrons, their own ships still in pristine condition, were waiting for him in the air. They fired, and he felt and heard the rear of the ship take two hits. Alarms screeched, lights flashed red, and the ship tumbled.

"No choice now, we're going down."

He tried to point the ship away from the mountains, but it was no use. He had no maneuverability. The rudders had been shot away.

But he was not losing altitude. The *Frontier* was actually climbing. A shadow fell over the landscape, and he realized what was going on.

The *Kinetic* had entered the planet's atmosphere. Riding on its antigravity force field, the huge Dreadnought was hovering over him, and had caught him in a gravity beam. Zoran had won; the *Frontier* was being sucked into the huge Hyron Dreadnought.

"Well…looks like we've lost."

"What do to us think you they will do?"

Butch shrugged. "I don't know. But we're in this together. Promise?"

They locked fingers, Ophelia smiling. "Promise."

CHAPTER 30

The first thing the Hyrons did was separate them. For all Butch's kicking and spitting and threatening, he could do nothing as she was dragged from him. It took four Hyron soldiers to restrain him as he was ushered down the hall to Zoran's office/quarters.

Zoran had poured a drink for him, which he threw in the Hyron commander's face.

Wiping his white beard with his hand, Zoran glared at Butch and said, "Melkon, bring me a towel."

"What the hell do you want with me?" Butch shouted.

Zoran sat at his desk, held out a hand as his first officer brought him a towel. As he wiped his uniform, he said, "This is really rather delightful; for once, Commander Kramer and I are on the same side. He contacted me and told me about your…desertion. He wants you back, though I'm not sure exactly why. Or perhaps he simply wants Ophelia and the *Frontier* back. Of course, we invoke salvage rights on the *Frontier*—but perhaps the Valdor will be kind enough to give you another ship, considering how warm and understanding they are."

Over Zoran's laughter, Butch demanded, "What about Ophelia?"

"She is not your concern."

"Bullshit! I'm sick of hearing about politics; she and I have decided to be together, come what may. Do what you want with us, but keep us together."

"That is outside my control."

"Oh, since when? You're even more of a maverick than I am. When did you start obeying orders?"

Zoran laughed. "I do skirt the edge of the boundary, don't I? But I never cross over the point that I'm outside Hyron law. And Hyron policy is to honor Community treaties."

Butch scoffed. "Is that why you annexed the Community and put Station Post One in charge against Valdor policy?"

"Those were my instructions from the Hyron Supreme Council. You see? I acted within the law. You, however, defied official Community policy regarding a *critical* diplomatic function whose importance was stressed to you again and again. Then you stole Station Post One property, deserted your post, attacked an Etuknip vessel…and all this for what? A woman?" Zoran laughed again. "You humans can be so romantic. It's so foolish. Perhaps one day they'll write great epic poems about you, but legally…I would be within my rights to kill you right now."

Now it was Butch's turn to laugh. "I doubt that. I don't know exactly what Kramer said to you, but I imagine he explicitly said he wanted me back alive—if for no other reason than he wants to punish me himself!"

"Actually, yes, that is exactly what he said. But he also said that Station Post One's relations with the Etuknips were of paramount importance, and therefore, if you resisted, I must…let me quote him." Zoran pulled a sheet of paper from his drawer. " 'Do whatever you must.'"

"Well, you've done that. I'm here. Now what?"

Zoran chuckled. "Well, now we head back for Station Post One. But en route, I don't see why I shouldn't have some fun. It's not often I get this chance. My Vengeance Quest against Kramer is on dutimortis, but *you* are the one who actually damaged my ship and prompted my Vengeance Quest. With Kramer on my side against you, I can gain some satisfaction without violating any orders."

"So what, you're gonna kill me?"

"We'll see." With a wave of his hand, Zoran turned his attention to his desk screen. "Take him to the brig."

———

Butch had heard of Hyron brigs. When Captain Richard Cameron had been captured by Mordrax, he had been confined to the brig of the Galactic Cruiser *Stendar* for a long and leisurely journey back to Hyron. Cameron's account of those days was horrific. He had been left to rot in a dark and dank room with no toilet, no amenities, no water. He had been tossed slop for dinner that was probably gunk discarded by the recycling computer as unfit for Hyron digestion. He had been taunted and often beaten by the Hyron guards.

To Butch's surprise, the brig on the *Kinetic* was nothing like that nightmarish account. It was much closer to the brig on Station Post One. A bracelet was attached to his wrist—some sort of tracking device, he assumed—and he was given a blue jumpsuit, but otherwise was allowed to keep his portable book reader and a bag of salted almonds he had brought along. The room itself was well-lit, had a toilet with a privacy screen, a sink, and even a computer terminal—though he didn't know how to work it. He was under constant, and humane, supervision. He wondered if this was because of the benevolent rule of Captain Cameron's lover, Eilonwy, and daughter, Keilah.

Still, he wondered how long he would be confined here. Did Kramer know he had been captured, and that the *Kinetic* was on the way? Zoran might just cruise in circles for months without telling Kramer that the chase was over. No telling how long the erratic Hyron commander would prolong this amusement.

But no matter how comfortable this cell was, he was tortured by the absence of Ophelia, and not knowing where she was or how she was being treated. He thought back on their few days together, alone on the *Frontier*, of their lovemaking, of their enjoyment of Shakespeare, of their conversations. He hung onto those memories. Whatever happened next, no one could take those happy days away from him. He would treasure those memories for the rest of his life. He realized now that those few days were the happiest time of his adult life, the only time he had been completely free and happy.

Zoran came by his cell twice a day. He would step inside, order the guards, "Leave us alone," and then goad him. "Come on, McCrae. I am alone. One-on-one, let's do it. Fight me."

Butch restrained himself; he knew he was at a disadvantage, though he wasn't sure what that disadvantage was. But Zoran would not be goading him into a fight unless he expected to win. So he just stared at the Hyron commander, defiant and silent.

Until....

"You know, your friend Ophelia is much more cooperative than you. I visit her each day right before you. She's quite...compliant, don't you think? It's a lot of fun...even though, as I'm sure you recall, her reproductive system is quite different from ours."

With that, Butch lost control. He charged Zoran, rammed him against the wall, jammed his arm against Zoran's neck, and started to demand, "*What did you do to—*" And then he was suddenly wracked with uncontrollable spasms. He convulsed, gasping, as Zoran laughed.

"Didn't I tell you, Butch? Oh, pardon me. The bracelet we attached to you carries an electrical charge that I can activate at any time simply by squeezing my fist." Zoran held up his hand, revealing a device like one of those prank hand buzzers. "I'm impressed by how limber you are. I always wanted to see a human dance. I should advise you that this device is classified as *less lethal* than a standard pulse weapon, not *non*-lethal."

Butch sagged to the floor, gasping, his heart pounding, his head aching. He tried to curse at

Zoran, but nothing came out but heaving breaths. And then he vomited.

"Oh, do clean up after yourself," Zoran said. "That's disgusting. Look what you've done to my floor. Don't you know my security camera is filming you? No one wants to watch that."

Butch heaved again and more bile came out.

"Oh, please, McCrae! Enough is enough! Be a man! You know, this device was tested on thirty volunteers and none of them threw up all over the place. Spirits of Nomad, what have you been eating? That smells like a slyryth's stink sac!"

Butch finally managed to gasp out, "I'll kill you, you sack of shit, I'll kill you."

Zoran held up his hand, revealing the device. "You want to try?" He knelt on the floor next to Butch, flexing his fingers. "You want to try?"

Butch knew he was beaten. He had lost control, just as Zoran had wanted, then performed as Zoran had planned, and now he was humiliated and helpless, and there was nothing he could do about it. "What do you want?"

Zoran leaned forward and whispered in his ear. "Promise to kill Commander Kramer."

Butch looked up at him, disbelieving. "What?"

"Do that and the bracelet comes off."

"Go to hell!"

Zoran stood. "As you wish. I'll see you later."

After Zoran was gone, Butch crawled to his bunk. A few minutes later, two guards came in to clean up the mess. As they worked, a doctor entered and checked him over. "Are you feeling all right?" she asked in a dispassionate tone.

"Not really!"

The doctor scanned him with a humming, cylindrical device with a flashing red light at one end. "Well, you show a pre-existing cardiovascular condition, but I don't want to draw conclusions about your anatomy, no matter how similar it is to ours. I don't think the shock did any additional damage. No neurological damage either. The Stantashock is usually harmless." She leaned close and whispered, "My advice to you is do whatever Zoran wishes. Give him his little victory and you'll go free in a few days. After that there's nothing he can do." She got up, packed the cylinder in a purse around her waist, and left. The two guards made some groaning noises as they cleaned up the vomit, then left.

Butch fell asleep.

He didn't know how much time had passed when he woke, but he recalled the doctor's advice. Should he take it? Could he simply tell Zoran he would kill Kramer, then forget the whole thing once he was back on Station Post One? Or would Zoran have some further incentive to ensure that Butch carry out the plot? And even if not…he had his honor as an officer and a gentleman. Could he lie to protect his own skin?

Then again, he had already violated his honor as an officer, if not as a gentleman, by deserting Station Post One and rescuing Ophelia against direct orders. What did a little lie matter now? He had already put his personal needs above his duty.

But he still had his dignity—despite what Zoran had just goaded him into. No, he would not promise to kill Commander Kramer. He would just restrain himself from attacking Zoran anymore. He could do that. If Zoran wanted to use the bracelet—well, let him. Butch too had been subjected to stun charges as part of his training. Never as prolonged or as severe as what he had just experienced, but he could take it. He could take anything.

CHAPTER 31

He couldn't take it anymore. He didn't care about Zoran's daily taunts, and he had learned to tune out even the worst of his insults, threats, and gloats. What he couldn't stand was not knowing where Ophelia was. This was unbearable...day after day after day of not knowing.

How long had it been? He asked the guard, but the guard said nothing to him. He asked the doctor who came by each day to check on him, and she answered in Hyron time units that meant nothing to him. When he asked about Ophelia, she said, "She's in another department." What the hell did that mean?

He began to wonder about telepathic communication. He had always considered such things to be bunk, but he was also aware of documented cases in which there was no other explanation. He knew that electronic thought transmission (which had even been called telepathy) had been a standard mode of communication from the twenty-first to twenty-third centuries...but could the *brain* do it?

He didn't think so, but Ophelia was a special case. She could see other timelines. She could manipulate the fabric of reality. Was it beyond question that she could touch his mind with hers? It was worth a try.

So he tried. He closed his eyes, concentrated, tried to feel her presence within him. He tried to forget his conviction that this was total bullshit, because he knew this wouldn't work as long as he didn't believe.

Bullshit, his mind whispered to him.

No, believe. For God's sake, it won't hurt anything to believe, just for a few minutes.

He often felt her presence, though he knew, or at least assumed, that it was only his preoccupation with her that created that sensation. Human emotion was not an objective measure of anything. But then again...maybe...just *maybe*.... Some people had suggested that love was indeed a fundamental force of the universe, something that bound life forms together across the divide of space.

Bullshit!

Some of those who suggested this were highly intelligent (but not scientists). Some had written great works of literature that Butch admired.

Bullshit!

It might work. It just might. He tried. He closed his eyes, concentrated, felt his love for Ophelia, felt the comforting warmth of her presence...her *spiritual* presence...

Bullshit!

...and tried, tried to project his thoughts to her. *Ophelia, can you hear me?...Ophelia, can you sense me? This is Butch. Are you there?*

Was there an answer? Even if not in words? Just a subtle mental acknowledgement? An increase in that sense of her presence?

No. There was nothing. This was bullshit. Telepathy didn't exist. Even if it was possible, the human brain was not equipped for it. Yes, thought transmission was possible, but it required an electronic implant. He was wasting his time, indulging in spiritual nonsense that no thinking person believed in.

But what else was he going to do with his time?

Read. Yes, he still had his electronic book reader. Unfortunately, it had no realtime connection, so there was no way to check the date or time, or to browse the SPACEWEB, but at least he could read.

He was in the middle of Willa Cather's *My Ántonia* and had to admit with chagrin that he wasn't enjoying it. It didn't help that under the circumstances he couldn't concentrate on what he was reading. He had enjoyed the chapters dealing with the saga of the Russian immigrants Peter and Pavel, but he had moved past that and was back to a meandering story that, much as he tried, simply didn't grip him.

There were plenty of other books in his database, but his policy was to stick with one book at a time and always finish it. Maybe he ought to break his self-imposed restriction on this one occasion.

One afternoon Zoran arrived, the expression on his face less smug than usual. "Good afternoon, Captain McCrae."

As usual, Butch sat, impassive, staring at the far wall, refusing to show any reaction.

"Commander Kramer wishes to speak with you." Zoran held out a transmitter.

Butch, stunned, looked down at it, afraid to take it, afraid this was a trap.

"Go on," Zoran said. "I notified him you're here and we're coming, and he wants to speak to you. Go on. Don't you believe me?"

No, I don't. Butch didn't say it out loud, but looked at the transmitter as if it contained the secrets of the universe.

Finally the voice of Commander Kramer issued from it. "Commander Zoran? Commander Zoran, are you still there?"

Zoran lifted the transmitter to his lips. "Yes, Commander Kramer. Captain McCrae is here. He seems unsure whether he wishes to speak to you."

"I'll speak to him," Butch said.

"Well, now." Zoran handed him the transmitter. "That's better."

Butch lifted the transmitter to his mouth and said, "Commander?"

"Yes, Butch. You've led us all on a merry chase. But I've been informed that Zoran finally caught you."

Butch looked up at Zoran, who was stifling a laugh. "Commander? Uh...Zoran caught me a long time ago. We've been en route to you—or so I thought."

Now Zoran did laugh. "Actually we've been patrolling the Community. I've enjoyed our daily sessions so much I didn't want them to end—so I delayed in telling Commander Kramer that I had caught you. I hope it's been no inconvenience."

Don't attack him, don't attack him. Butch held onto his calm. "Did you hear that, Commander?"

"Yes, I did, Butch, and I'm sorry I sent that psychopath after you, but after all, you took our only interstellar spacecraft."

You could've asked the Valdor for help, Butch thought, but he knew that option would have been risky for Kramer, and he saw no value in voicing it. "I found Ophelia."

"So I was told. Zoran promised to deliver her along with you."

"And then what?"

"Well, and then we'll see. This has become a major diplomatic incident. The whole Community is involved now. As for you...no decision has been made. You'll be tried."

Tried? That sounded strange. Why not court-martialed? A problem for another time; it might mean nothing. "What about Ophelia?"

"That's up to the Etuknips. Zoran tells me he'll be arriving here by tomorrow, so you'll know soon enough."

Tomorrow. Tomorrow I'll be out of this hellhole—and maybe reunited with Ophelia.

"Well...looking forward to it, Commander."

"And I'm looking forward to having you back." The tone in Kramer's voice was ambiguous. Just how angry was he? Kramer was not a temperamental man—but then no one had ever pulled a stunt such as Butch had done.

Another day and he would find out.

———

Station Post One was as he remembered, but was surrounded by ships of all shapes and sizes. Kramer had not exaggerated; the entire Community was involved.

Zoran had one of his pilots shuttle Butch over. When he stepped onto the familiar Dock Deck, he was met by Tepper—*Lieutenant* Tepper, he noted with surprise. "Well, well. Looks like my little stunt proved a good thing for *somebody*."

Tepper shook his hand. "Wasn't worth it. This has turned into a real mess—and you and I will never work together again. I gotta admit, I'll kind of miss it."

Butch was uncomfortable with that remark and decided not to respond. He was saved from any further sentiment when he spotted Ophelia in the distance, among a group of Etuknips. "Ophelia!" He started to run for her, but Hyron guards grabbed him. "Aw, let me go!"

"Turn him over to us," Tepper said. "Look, Butch, you're under arrest. Behave yourself, huh?"

"I want to talk to her. They've kept me from her for days."

"Fine, okay."

The guards kept pace with him as he approached Ophelia. She watched him approach, her dark eyes wide and luminous with love. "Hello, Butch."

"Hi. You all right?"

"Hurt me did they not."

"Zoran said that—he implied that he…uh… took liberties with you."

"Questioned me he did. No more."

Butch let out a deep breath, relieved. "Well, here we are. My little escapade got us nowhere… but I'll always treasure the time we spent together."

"Me as well. But for the best was not it. Only helped the Sweg did you. To destroy the Community they seek to, now to take down Station Post One by politics."

"Okay, that's enough," Tepper said. "Butch, I've got to lock you up. Sorry."

Butch leaned forward and kissed Ophelia. "'Sweets to the sweet. Farewell.'" He turned and followed Tepper and the others to the elevator, noting that Kramer and Dingell were not present. Was it that they were so angry they couldn't bear the sight of him? –No, more likely they were too enmeshed in interstellar intrigue to leave PHC.

As Tepper marched him toward the brig, he said, "Butch, I just want you to know I'm doing this because I was ordered to. I'm not enjoying this."

"Tepper, you don't have to explain. You did your job. I'd have done the same thing. I'm the one that went out on a limb here."

And so Captain Randal "Butch" McCrae, Dock Deck chief of Station Post One, decorated pilot, and the first man to visit another galaxy, was confined to the brig awaiting trial for desertion.

CHAPTER 32

Zoran still claimed that there had been no delay in contacting Station Post One when Butch was captured, but Butch and Ophelia both claimed their capture had been some time ago, perhaps as much as two weeks. Whatever Butch had done, Kramer didn't think he was a liar—and such a thing was consistent with Zoran's past behavior. And Ophelia's character was above reproach.

Zoran was back on the *Kinetic*, and that was the way Kramer preferred it. The less Hyron interference here the better—though the presence of the looming Hyron Dreadnought did serve as a buffer between Station Post One and the Valdor, which was somewhat comforting. Somewhat.

Kramer, Tobey, and DuBois examined the reports submitted by Zoran, Butch, and Ophelia, trying to piece together what had happened. Butch's account of the experience aboard the Sweg ship was utter nonsense.

"What the fuck is he saying?" Tobey asked. "What *happened*?"

"Well, I wasn't there," DuBois said. "All I know is what limited information I've been able to glean from the Etuknips. But I think it's obvious that the Sweg ship was carrying a pocket of spacetime from the cosmic string, and so Butch experienced a...I don't know what to call it exactly...a 'zone," I guess, of, uh, open spacetime or something..."

"Quantum foam," Kramer said. "All probabilities are equal on the macro scale."

DuBois shrugged. "I suppose. Yes, that could be. That takes a tremendous amount of energy—or in this case, gravity. I don't really see how that would remain intact in the Sweg ship, but apparently it did. It could be that the interior of the Sweg ship existed in a state of false vacuum with respect to our own spacetime, and it's only a matter of time before...well, before bad things happen."

"Bad things?" Tobey asked.

"Boom," Kramer said.

"Cosmic strings vibrate themselves out of existence," DuBois said, "black holes evaporate —and one of the leading theories of the origin of our universe is that eleven-dmensional spacetime existed in false vacuum and then something tipped it past the breaking point, and..."

"Boom," Kramer said again.

"Yes—three dimensions expanded into the universe we know while eight dimensions curled up into the tiny resonances that make subatomic particles."

"And that's what we laymen call the Big Bang," Tobey said.

"It's one of many theories of what the Big Bang was."

"So what, that Sweg ship could blow up and create a new universe?"

"Boom," Kramer said.

———

Butch had paced his small cell so many times he had worn himself out. He had planned on keeping fit with calisthenics, but what was the point now? Chances were he would never get out of here. His military career was over, his flying days were over, and his life with Ophelia was over.

He sat down, grateful that at least he wasn't in the Hyron brig. Better to be confined by his former friends than his present enemies. At least here he knew his rights.

"Hey Butch?"

Butch looked up, surprised at the familiar voice. "Well, well. *Tepper*. Come to gloat?"

Tepper ignored the comment. "How they treating you?"

"Oh, I'm having a fine time. They just put on a nice performance of *King Lear* for me this morning. And I hear that tonight there's going to be a nice little violin concerto, all for me."

"I thought you might be interested in knowing that Ophelia is okay."

Yes, he was interested. "What do you know about her?"

"Well, she's been staying in a guest pod, hasn't really come out. She's only spoken to Commander Kramer and Mr. Dingell and the acting Leira Ambassador."

"The Hyrons kept her from me. I don't know if she's been hurt or—"

"No, she's okay. Anyway, I don't know if they *can* be hurt. But no, she seems fine."

"Any word on what they wanted her for?"

Tepper shrugged. "Nothing official. But according to the Leira that I've talked to, it seems that what the Sweg wanted to do was to discredit the Leira by coming aboard and destroying their relations with the Community. Naturally, being superstitious, backwards folk, they don't want any contact with the Community or other worlds."

"What *would* they have done to Ophelia if they'd kept her?" As soon as Butch said it, he realized the uselessness of asking. Tepper knew nothing.

"Well, they're not gonna say, obviously, and Ophelia and the Leira don't really think anything would have come of it as far as they're concerned. It's just a political end that they were looking for."

Butch sighed. It was frustrating to feel so helpless—especially after the unrestrained freedom of his all-too-brief space voyage with his love. "I don't suppose she's going to be allowed to see me, huh?"

"Well…I'll try to arrange it. I think Kramer kind of understands why you did what you did, and I think he might allow it. But…" Tepper hesistated.

"What is it?"

"Well…I don't know how to tell you this, but, uh—"

"Well, go on, spit it out, *Tepper!*"

"Well…your trial is going to be a very public one, and it's going to be done in a Community court."

Butch knew he shouldn't be surprised, but he was. His situation was getting worse and worse. "We're going to Klym Valdor?"

Tepper nodded. "The Centralized Committee will be presiding. From what they tell me, it's going to be done in the Valdor style."

"Well...shit." Butch stalked across his cell. "I'm done for then."

"'fraid so. They want a scapegoat."

Butch nodded. "Yeah. I *would* say I knew what I was getting into, but I didn't know it was going to come to *this*."

Tepper nodded. "Yeah. Sorry. I guess things have really unfolded in the worst way for just about everybody."

"Well...anyway...thanks for helping me. You went out on a limb for me and you're lucky you're not right in here with me. I won't tell anyone you were involved."

"Thanks. I'll see if I can arrange for Ophelia to see you."

Butch nodded, went over to his bunk and sat. Tepper stood a moment longer, as if fishing for something more to say, then muttered a quick "See ya," and left.

Tepper, of all people. Butch felt uncomfortable feeling gratitude, and even vague intimations of friendship, for Tepper. But they had been through a lot together. They had fought together, flown long missions together, endured the publicity together when they had visited the Andromeda Galaxy, and risked their lives for each other. They were comrades in arms, and as much as Butch disliked Tepper now, he also knew that someday they would be old friends. They shared the bond of extraordinary experiences, a bond that couldn't be broken by their disparate interests or incompatible personalities. It was a disquieting feeling, and yet he couldn't deny that he had come to regard Tepper with something akin to affection.

He wondered if Tepper would come to visit him in prison.

———

Tepper was as good as his word. That evening he brought Ophelia.

"Butch!" she cried, running to the bars.

Butch ran to the bars and took her hands, aware they were enacting a cliché as old as *Les Misérables*.

"I'll leave you two," Tepper said, slinking away.

"All right you are?" Ophelia asked.

"Yeah, I'll be fine. More important question is, how are you?"

"Fine I am. Treating me well they are, but no contact have I had the Sweg with since came we back here."

"What about the Hyrons? Did they hurt you?"

"No." Ophelia smiled. "Every time Zoran toward me came, edited time did I. Confused him that did!"

Butch laughed, trying to imagine the scene— but her ability to manipulate time still staggered his human imagination, so he gave up trying to envision it. "Well, as long as you're all right. Zoran told me some things that…"

"Only trying to provoke you was he. Told me did he some of the things that on went between the two of you. Wished I that a message to you could I have gotten."

"Yeah, me too." Butch chuckled. "I even tried to contact you telepathically."

Ophelia frowned. "Can you that do?"

"No, no. It was just a sign of my desperation that I even tried. It's all bullshit." He hesitated. "Um…it didn't work, did it? You didn't, uh, 'sense' me trying to contact you?"

"No."

He smiled. "No. 'course not. I didn't think so. Like I said, it's bullshit."

Ophelia grew serious. "In deep trouble you are. They no mercy are going to show."

"Eh, I'll be all right." He said it but didn't mean it. He was not at all sure he was going to be all right. In fact, knowing the Valdor, he would not be surprised if he was condemned to death. But he wasn't going to worry Ophelia with such dark thoughts; maybe he would just land a few years in the brig and they would be together to greet the dawn of the forty-second century.

Changing the subject, he said, "Anyway, you haven't been on board Klym Valdor, have you? Now, *that* is a sight."

"Have I there been. In order to open negotiations you with, first we the Valdor to deal with had."

"Oh." Butch was disappointed he wouldn't have the chance to be the first to show her the stunning vista of the Valdor Artificial World. But even if she hadn't been there before, the chances were they would be separated when they went on board. "Anyway, quite a place, isn't it?"

"Nothing have I to compare it. An alien place is it, as alien as Station Post One."

"Seriously? You don't find it more impressive than our little cluster of pods?"

"Everything outside the cosmic string new and exotic is. Hard it is to compare one wonder to another."

"Huh. Someday I'd like to see your cosmic string—though it'll probably make my head explode. That Sweg ship was already about as much as I could stand."

"Would I to you like to show our world. Would I like to you there take."

Butch frowned. "Can you see the outcome of this? Will we have a future together?"

"Sorry I am, Butch. As long as in your universe am I, locked I am in a single timeline, traveling past into future. And the longer stay I here, the less able am I to see outside this timeline."

"Huh. Wonder why that is."

"Long mathematical explanation for that there is. Someday perhaps explain it to you will I. But for now does not it matter." She took his hands. "Would like to you make love in the Etuknip way."

"Oh!" Butch steadied himself. "I'd love to, but I'm not sure this is the right time and place to—*WHOAAA!!!*"

The combined pleasures of a lifetime once again exploded within him, and he was once again not sure which species' method of lovemaking he preferred.

Once his head cleared, he became aware of Tepper's scrutiny. "Aww...what do you want, *Tepper*?"

"Uh...time's up...are you all right?"

"Fine, fine."

"What the hell were you two doing?"

For the first time, it occurred to Butch that he had no idea what actually *happened* during his lovemaking with Ophelia. What had Tepper seen? "Never mind, *Tepper*." He kissed Ophelia's hand. "Hope to see you soon."

"Will I you see soon," Ophelia assured him. "Make certain of it will I."

Tepper put a hand on her back. "Okay, come on."

As Tepper led her away, Butch called, "Hey, thanks, Tepper."

Tepper glanced at him, nodded, and escorted Ophelia down the hall.

Butch returned to his bunk, smiling. Whatever happened next, they had had this time. No one could take that away. He thought back on their time together aboard the *Frontier*...no one could take *that* time away.

If only he could return to that time, live it over and over in perpetuity. *That* would be Heaven.

CHAPTER 33

The next day they left for Klym Valdor.

Since the Hyrons had impounded the *Frontier*, or what was left of it, the Valdor grudgingly provided transportation to the humans. Butch rode in the back of a Valdor clipper not unlike the *Frontier*. It made him homesick; he had become quite attached to that ship, and not just because of the time he had spent there with Ophelia. His many experiences with Tepper also come to mean something to him. In the past year and a half, he and his adversary had shared a lifetime's worth of adventures. He was going to miss it.

Ophelia, unfortunately, was on another ship, presumably with the other Etuknips. Perhaps they were traveling aboard the Leira ship that had brought them to Station Post One; he supposed that was most likely.

It was embarrassing to be seated here, cuffed to a pillar, treated like a common criminal, but he knew he had brought this on himself. He reminded himself he had knowingly violated orders and gone AWOL, and that if he were ever caught, this would be the result. But it didn't make it easier.

On board this ship with him were Dugrow, Kramer, Tobey Dingell, and Tepper, but they all remained up front and no one, not even Tepper, spoke to him during the whole flight to Klym Valdor.

But he had made this flight often enough to know when they were arriving. He could sense the ship's movements, imagine its passage through the outer hull of the huge metal planet, its orientation inverting so as to fly over the landscape that was affixed to the inside of the outer shell. He imagined the structures sweeping by below, and he was only a little off his time estimate when he felt the ship banking to come to a landing in the spaceport.

As the engine whined down, Tepper rose and approached him. "Well, Butch, here we are." He reached down and unlocked the cuffs. "Let's go." He spoke in a hushed voice, as if self-conscious about speaking too much to the prisoner. Butch rose, presented his wrists so that Tepper could reattach the cuffs. "Not too tight?"

"No, it's fine."

"Okay. Let's go."

Tepper led him to the airlock, and they followed Dugrow, Kramer, and Tobey out onto the metallic surface. It was humiliating; the cuffs, and Tepper leading him like a dog, advertised to anyone watching that he was a criminal. The first time he had come to Klym Valdor, he had been an honored guest, an esteemed representative of a newly contacted civilization. Subsequent visits had been less friendly as the cultural differences between humans and Valdor became more problematic—but he had always at least carried the moral authority of being Station Post One's chosen representative.

Now he was just a criminal being led around in handcuffs. All of Dugrow's insults had been validated.

Dugrow, who stood in the lead at the curb of the metallic street, turned and said, "I have summoned a vehicle which will take McCrae to a detention blockhouse where he will be restrained in the Valdor way until the trial commences."

"What do you mean?" Kramer asked. "How will he be restrained?"

"That is none of your concern. You agreed to conduct this in the Valdor way."

Kramer glanced at Butch, then stepped back and remained silent.

I want to see Ophelia, Butch thought, but he knew it would be useless to make a request. Maybe after he was confined. He had no idea what rights, if any, a Valdor prisoner was granted.

The Valdor vehicle, a self-driving car that ran on a magnetic track, came to a stop before them, and they crowded into the small vehicle. Tepper sat next to Butch in the back, Tobey on the other side, and Kramer up front. Dugrow sat in the driver's seat, though did not touch the controls, and soon they were in motion, riding smoothly over the featureless gray road. No one spoke; the atmosphere was tense and uneasy.

Butch watched out the window as the hive-like structures swept by. Although Klym Valdor had come back to life since the war, there was still noticeably less activity now than before that devastating conflict. Millions of Valdor had been killed when a Throrb ship had plowed into the artificial world at light speed. It was really remarkable that Klym Valdor had survived at all. Most of the surviving Valdor were now working around the clock on the daunting challenge of rebuilding their world.

Butch's thoughts wandered; his imagination filled in some frightening images of what Valdor "restraint" might be like. He imagined a dozen worst-case scenarios for his future; he had heard that since that war, the prison planet Strydia—planet "Hell"—had been occupied by the Community, so there was a genuine chance he might be sentenced there. A fate almost literally worse than death.

He and Tepper had also spent some time on the melodramatically named Asteroid Doom, another unpleasant Throrb prison. There he had been hooked up to a device which had brought his worst fears to life.

He could only hope the Valdor were more humane than the Dreb—but then he remembered the condition Zach Mortimer had been in when the Valdor had returned him after the war. They had exposed him to vacuum, probed all his bodily orifices with devices to "study" him and caused considerable damage, and subjected him to daily psychological torture.

And…would he ever see Ophelia again?

He didn't know how much time had passed when the car finally rolled to a stop. Two Valdor guards awaited. The door hissed upward, and one of them said, "Prisoner, out!"

Butch climbed out of the car, followed by Tepper.

"Remove his restraints."

Tepper obeyed, unlocking the cuffs. One of the guards then gripped Butch's shoulder with a powerful claw while the other affixed a glowing tube around his wrists. The Valdor didn't lock it or tie it, but once it was wrapped around his wrists, it tightened, and with a burning sensation that almost made him cry out, adhered to his skin.

Kramer got out of the vehicle. "I want to see his cell before we leave him there."

"That is unacceptable," Dugrow said. "We had an agreement, and I expect you to do a better job honoring this agreement than you have other recent agreements. Take him!"

Another burning sensation from the cord around his wrists incentivized Butch to follow the guards as they clattered toward a domed building.

"Good luck, Butch," Tepper called. "See you soon."

"Hope so," Butch said.

One of the guards snapped, "No talking!"

They passed through an arch and into a dark chamber. A Valdor sat at a desk. On seeing Butch, he rose and stared at him, his luminescent eyes shining red in the darkness. "So you are Butch McCrae." To the guards, he said, "Scan for weapons."

One of the guards looked him up and down, his eyes blinking rapidly. "No weapons, sir."

"Good. Mr. McCrae, I am Vellis. I am the warden here. You are to be held here until your trial commences. If the trial lasts more than a single session, you will be held at the presidium detention area for the duration. For now, though, you belong to me. Take him to his cell. Number three one."

Without another word, the guards led him to an aperture in the far wall. From there they went down a steep ramp into what looked and felt like a cave. They must be in the division between levels; there couldn't be actual caves here. As vast as the artificial world was, it was nevertheless just a huge space station, a construct. Butch wondered if this mimicked the way the Valdor had lived back on their home planet, which had been destroyed by the Thermians centuries ago.

They came to a small cell. It was a cramped cave with what looked like a stone bench at one end and a hole in the floor on the other. It wasn't hard to guess what the hole was for. He hoped that despite the spare conditions, the hole had some sort of internal plumbing.

The guards shoved him in. The cord around his wrist loosened, and he watched in fascination as it fell away and seemed to vaporize before his eyes. He turned, watched the guards leave, and wondered that there were no bars, nor any visible apparatus to generate any kind of force field. He reached out, then quickly jerked back as his hand hit some sort of electrical field. "Well, so much for that," he muttered. There was still so much he didn't know about Valdor technology.

He walked across the cell, bumping his head on the low ceiling, and crawled onto the bunk. It sure felt like stone. "My third prison inside of a week," he grumbled. In contrast to what he had feared, this place wasn't so bad—though he felt it was the worst of those three prisons. He barely had room to move, and that hole that was to serve his excretory needs looked uncomfortable to say the least. And there was no sign of toilet paper.

But there was no reason to think that confinement in this cell was going to be the full extent of his punishment. That wrist cord and the mysterious force field were reminders that the Valdor had technology he didn't understand. Some sort of bizarre alien torture might hit him at any moment.

He tried not to think about it, tried to sleep.

It wasn't easy.

CHAPTER 34

Butch estimated he had been in his cell for about twelve hours when Warden Vellis arrived with the news that his trial was about to begin.

"That was sure fast. Don't I get to speak to my attorney?"

"That is not the way Valdor justice works."

Butch scoffed. "Is there such a thing as Valdor justice?"

"You will soon find out."

Butch cautiously reached out. "Is this thing…"

"The confinement barrier is deactivated. Leave your cell and present your wrists."

Butch obeyed, though he had no desire to experience that hot cord again. "Look, I won't cause any trouble. If you'd just—"

"Silence! Apply the restraint."

A guard appeared from behind him—*Where the hell did he come from?*—and the claws wrapped another burning cord around his wrists. It tightened, affixed to his skin with that same burning sensation, and Vellis said, "We may meet again. If you are found guilty, you may spend a long time here."

Butch only stared at him.

"Take him away."

The guards marched him down the hall, up the steep ramp, and into the dome. A vehicle was waiting outside. The guards shoved him in, and he found himself riding alone in a driverless car as it sped at reckless speed along the magnetic highway.

Unsupervised as he was, he considered jumping out of the car, but what would be the point? Where would he go? Besides, he was willing to bet that wrist cord would do unpleasant things to him if he attempted it. No, might as well stand trial; perhaps if he had a chance to testify, to tell his side of the story, he might persuade the Centralized Committee to at least give him a lighter sentence. And maybe Kramer had lined up some witnesses in his defense; Tepper had mentioned that Kramer was sympathetic to him.

He wondered if that was true.

As the car came to a stop in front of what, he was not surprised to see, looked like an amphitheater, he tried to open the door—and realized any escape attempt would have been futile; the door was securely locked. He sat and waited patiently until the car came to a complete stop, and after a few seconds there was a click and the door hissed upwards.

Two Valdor guards, along with Kramer and Tobey, waited for him. He stepped out, and again the wrist cord fell away and disintegrated.

"Commander," Butch said, "I still don't know my rights—"

"Be silent!" Dugrow snapped. "As of this moment, you are on trial. You will speak when summoned to testify. Otherwise you will respect the dignity of the court."

Butch had a number of snappy replies to that, but kept silent. He knew anything he might say would damage his case—if he had one.

"Sorry, Butch," Kramer said. "Just to fill you in, the Valdor have named Progin Lanzing of the Quilgot to defend you. I know nothing of her."

"And you?" Butch asked.

"No talking!" Dugrow snapped again.

In a subdued tone, Kramer said, "I'll be testifying against you."

Butch nodded, said nothing more. The Valdor guards marched him under an archway and into the building. As they passed through a tunnel toward an archway leading into the amphitheater, Butch was reminded so strongly of immies about the Roman Coliseum that he fully expected to find himself face-to-face with a gladiator when he emerged into the open.

Instead, there was a stage. The Centralized Committee, consisting of leading members of the Community (those who had survived the war) sat in a circle surrounding an empty chair. The guards led Butch onto the stage and gestured him to sit in the empty chair.

"Well. This is intimidating."

No one silenced him this time. As he sat, he discretely gave the middle finger to the guards. They assumed position behind and to either side of him.

Dugrow mounted the stage and stood next to him. A low, reverberating *bong* rolled through the amphitheater, and the murmuring of the crowd grew silent.

Valdor High Commissioner Goblutz rose and said, "This court is convened. This is case number eight five slash one four two, the Community charges Captain Butch McCrae with negligent sabotage of interstellar relations. Speaking in his defense is Progin Lanzing of Quilgot. Speaking in his condemnation is Administrator Dugrow of the Valdor."

"Figures," Butch muttered.

"The charges will now be read."

"May I speak?" Butch said.

"You may not. Proceed, Administrator Dugrow."

Dugrow stepped forward and said, "Captain Butch McCrae is charged with violation of the terms of interstellar agreement between the Community and the Etuknip Hegemony, specifically item number three, the human race shall not in any way or for any reason interfere with Etuknip internal affairs. Captain McCrae not only pursued a sexual relationship with the Etuknip lead scientist and ambassador, but then violated Station Post One official policy by hijacking the Thermian Scout Ranger provided to that station by the Valdor, intercepted a space vessel of the Sweg, and forcibly extracted the Etuknip ambassador with the intent of fleeing to parts unknown. As a consequence of his actions, the Sweg and the Leira, the two rival factions of the Etuknips, have been brought closer to civil war, and relations between the Community and the Etuknip Hegemony have been grievously imperiled.

"Only the assurance that Captain McCrae would be held responsible for his actions and appropriately punished has moved the Etuknips to reconvene relations. In order to save these vital negotiations, which bring us closer to developing the Thermian Destroyer, we must find Captain

McCrae guilty and sentence him to the maximum penalty under the law. I am therefore asking that Captain McCrae be sentenced to eighty years on Strydia Prison.

"That will be all for now."

"Thank you, Administrator Dugrow. Maiden Lanzing?"

An odd creature rose from the circle of members; Butch did not recall seeing an alien like this before. Progin Lanzing walked on four legs, but, like a centaur, had a torso with two arms. Her head was wide, with outstretched, elfin ears and a beak. It was hard to tell from a distance, but it looked to Butch like she had a single, wide, cyclopean eye above that beak; but perhaps there were two (or more!) eyes in a wide, recessed cavity.

"Members of the Centralized Committee. While it is true that Captain McCrae violated the terms of the agreement between the Community and the Etuknip Hegemony, it must be pointed out that he did so not as an officer of Station Post One or a representative of the human race or the Community. At the moment that he abandoned his post and hijacked the humans' Valdor vessel, he effectively was resigning his commission and was acting as an independent entity, and therefore can only be charged with desertion, subject to human, not Community, justice. It must be further pointed out that these actions were done in response to an unauthorized entry of Sweg into Station Post One, which was in itself a violation of the terms of the agreement between the Etuknips and the Community. Therefore, even had Captain McCrae been acting in an official capacity, his actions would have been justified.

"It was the Sweg, not Captain McCrae, who violated policy. In rescuing the Etuknip Ambassador, Captain McCrae was, in fact, ensuring continuation of the vital negotiations between Station Post One and the Leira. Willful invasion of Station Post One is *not* an internal Etuknip matter.

"If Captain McCrae is guilty of anything, it is of the human crime of desertion, and therefore should be punished not by the Community, but by Commander Damon Kramer of Station Post One. Therefore, I ask that this court be dismissed, and that Captain McCrae be handed over to Station Post One for punishment."

"Denied," Goblutz said. "Now. Captain McCrae, you asked to speak. Now is the time that you may enter a statement."

Butch stood, suddenly uncertain what to say. "Uh...members of the, ah, Centralized Committee, um...look, uh...I don't know anything about your, uh, jurisprudence or all that stuff, but I do know that in my civilization, when a fella is arrested, first thing that's done is he's read his rights. Now, I have no idea what my rights are, I have no idea how this court works, I've had no chance to meet with my, uh, attorney in advance to prepare for this whole shindig, there was no pretrial hearing or anything, and so I object to the whole procedure. I don't deny I broke regulations, okay? I did that willingly and I'm willing to face the consequences, but I don't feel that this is a fair trial, and I'm not afraid to say so. So, uh, that's my statement."

He sat, red-faced, feeling stupid and inadequate; that was far from a Shakespearean soliloquy. He wished he'd had more time to prepare a proper statement, and was sure he had made a fool of himself.

"So entered," Goblutz said. "Administrator Dugrow, present your case."

"I would like to begin by questioning the Sweg Ambassador," Dugrow said.

Butch watched a lovely Etuknip female mount the stage. She looked somewhat like Ophelia—though Butch would never have mistaken this being for his true love. There was something different about the eyes, the way she held her head, the way she moved. No, there was only one Ophelia.

Dugrow said, "Do you understand that the plate on which you are standing will read your metabolic patterns and notify us of any lie?"

The Ambassador looked down at the square on which she stood and said, "Did I not that know, but know I it now."

"Few members of the Community can pronounce Etuknip names," Dugrow said. "I have been informed that the humans have been referring to you as Mackenzie. Do you object to my using that name?"

"Do not I object," Mackenzie said.

"Very well. Do you know the Leira Ambassador, whom the humans refer to as Ophelia?"

"Do I."

"You've had negotiations with her before?"

"Have I."

"Have they been friendly relations?"

"Neither friendly nor unfriendly. Professional keep we them."

"But you have avoided war between the Sweg and the Leira?"

"Difficult it is answer that question to. Time and reality different are our world in. But in order simple to keep things, I will in the affirmative answer."

"Has conflict between the Sweg and the Leira been avoided by strict adherence to a set of agreements between your two factions?"

"Again, difficult it is answer that question to. Time and reality different are. Cause and effect not do follow in the same way my world in as in yours. But yes, a set of agreements have we, and in strict adherence to those agreements conflict avoided is—in many timelines."

"Is this the reason that the Etuknip Hegemony demanded that the Community interfere in no way with your internal relations?"

"Is it."

"When Butch McCrae retrieved Ophelia from the Sweg ship, did that endanger relations between the Sweg and the Leira?"

"Yes."

"How?"

"Our worlds different are. Chronological time applies to us does not. In this universe, different things are. Obey cause and effect must we. Disorienting it is, and close brings it us to the horrors our prophecies of. The Leira negotiations your people with therefore must we stop. That the reason is the abduction for of Ophelia. When rescued her did Butch McCrae, demonstrated did he that the Leira aligned were with the humans, and that the agreements between our factions abrogated were."

"And the consequences of this?"

"Depends that does the outcome this hearing of. But if the Sweg and Leira go to war, destruction our world of likely will it be."

"And what would you consider to be necessary to prevent further conflict between the Sweg and the Leira?"

"Agreed have I to placing on Butch McCrae the full responsibility the event of. If adequately punished is he, then will the Sweg consider closed the matter, despite our concerns ongoing regarding the Leira contact the Community with."

Dugrow turned to Goblutz. "That's all for now."

Goblutz turned to Progin Lanzing. "Would you like to question the testifier?"

"I would." Lanzing approached Mackenzie, her four feet clicking on the floor with the sound of a dog's nails. "Ambassador, who agreed to meet with the Valdor and arrange a summit on Station Post One?"

"The Leira," Mackenzie said.

"No, I mean which individual brokered the agreement?"

"Ophelia."

"Who on the Community's end agreed to the terms of that summit?"

"Believe I Administrator Dugrow it was."

"And among the humans, who was responsible for accepting the terms established by Ophelia's agreement with Dugrow?"

"Commander Kramer."

"Not Butch McCrae?"

"I am logging discontent," Dugrow interrupted. "Butch McCrae is Commander Kramer's subordinate and is expected to abide by Commander Kramer's orders."

"That is true," Goblutz said. "Maiden Lanzing, explain the relevance of your question."

"If you will allow me to continue, the relevance will become apparent."

"Very well, continue."

Lanzing turned to Mackenzie. "Did the agreement entered into by Commander Kramer involve relinquishing his authority over his own station?"

"No."

"Then he, and by extension Butch McCrae, were still responsible for handling security issues?"

"Agreed they to place Etuknips in security positions."

"Yes, but nevertheless, in the event of a security breach, was it not still their duty to deal with intruders according to their regulations and training?"

"Yes."

"Would you not describe unauthorized entry to their Wheel and abduction of a lead representative of an important delegation as a security breach?"

"Would I not! An Etuknip internal matter was it."

"Then tell me, what would a reasonable person expect Butch McCrae to have done when a representative of the Etuknip Hegemony, upon whom vitally important negotiations were depending, was attacked and abducted by unknown assailants?"

"When saw he that Etuknips the assailants were, withdrawn should he have, and accepted that an Etuknip internal matter was this."

"Even when the time frame was edited so that Mr. McCrae was not sure what had happened?"

Mackenzie hesitated. "Still, saw did he that Etuknips was he with dealing."

Lanzig turned to the Centralized Committee. "So. The Ambassador is seriously suggesting that a trained officer primarily responsible for the security of his station should ignore all his training and years of experience, and *allow* an incursion into his station and the abduction of an important dignitary involved in vital negotiations." She turned back the Mackenzie. "And tell me, whose idea was it to impose the restriction on human meddling in Etuknip internal matters?"

There was a long hesitation before Mackenzie emitted a whistling and clicking sound.

Lanzing turned toward Goblutz. "Let it be entered into the record that Ambassador Mackenzie just spoke the name of the chairman of the Sweg Ministerial Council." To Mackenzie, Lanzing said, "How did the chairman of your Ministerial Council come to influence the negotiations with the Community?"

"Knew the Leira did that controversial would be contact world with outside our cosmic string, and so opened talks with the Sweg did the President of the Leiran Science Council in order a palatable compromise could he reach."

"Thank you, Ambassador. Commissioner Goblutz, this line of questioning has been to establish that the conditions imposed on the summit aboard Station Post One were deliberately engineered by the Sweg to weaken the station's security and to maneuver Ophelia into a position in which she could be kidnapped without consequence. Under Community law, this amounts to a Treaty of Disaffection, and therefore can be disqualified. I therefore move that this be done."

Goblutz conferred quietly with the Valdor and other creatures surrounding him, then said, "Maiden Lanzing's point is sound and must be considered. We will recess until tomorrow. The prisoner will be escorted to the court cell."

Two guards approached Butch and he stood, admitting to himself that he was impressed with Progin Lanzing. He might be a step closer to life with Ophelia.

CHAPTER 35

"Court is now resumed," Goblutz said. "After considerable conference with other members of this panel, and consultation with Community legal experts, I have decided to reject Maiden Lanzing's request to disqualify the agreement between the Community and the Etuknip Hegemony."

Butch's heart sunk. During the night he had come to believe Progin Lanzing had built a solid case, and that his acquittal was now imminent. He had even begun to hope he would be reunited with Ophelia by the end of the day.

Instead, a long and grueling day in court still lay ahead.

"Maiden Lanzing," Goblutz said, "do you have further questions for Ambassador Mackenzie?"

"Not at this time," Lanzing said.

"Then it is your turn as questioner."

"I would like to question Commander Damon Kramer."

Butch was puzzled. Dugrow had not rested his case; what exactly was the jurisprudence of this crazy court? Not only had he never been read his rights, but he had never been asked to enter a plea. Was there any presumption of innocence? And he'd thought Kramer was a prosecution witness; why was Lanzig calling him as *her* witness? He wished, now that it was too late, that he had perused the Community database back on Station Post One, read up on Valdor courtroom procedure.

"Commander Kramer, did you agree to the conditions imposed on you by the Valdor's agreement with the Etuknip Hegemony?"

"I did."

"Did this include placing Etuknips in charge of your security in pivotal locations and at pivotal times?"

"Yes."

"Was one of these times during the overnight shift of June 2, 4094?"

"I would have to check my logs, but that sounds right."

"And the next morning there was a discrepancy in the log?"

"Yes…our log dump, which is an automatic log generated by the computer, showed an authorized arrival during the night, but that arrival had not been entered in the official log."

"And who was the Etuknip who was in charge of your arrivals and departures that night?"

"Well, I don't know his Etuknip name, but we called him Sambo."

"Did you question him?"

"No."

"Why?"

"Because he disappeared."

"Was he ever seen again?"

"Yes; Butch McCrae reported seeing him aboard the Sweg ship when he rescued Ophelia."

"Thank you, Commander Kramer. That will be all for now."

Goblutz gestured to Dugrow. "Administrator Dugrow, would you like to question?"

"I would." Dugrow clattered toward Kramer. "I only have three questions, Commander Kramer. One: did you agree to no interference in Etuknip internal affairs?"

"I did."

"Thank you. Two: did Butch McCrae violate that agreement?"

"Yes."

"And three: did you agree that Butch McCrae would take full responsibility for that violation?"

"Yes, I did."

Dugrow turned toward Goblutz. "Why are we wasting time here? Sentence Butch McCrae as I have asked. That's all."

"Very well," Goblutz said. "Please return to your seat, Commander Kramer. Administrator Dugrow, it is your turn as questioner."

Oh, so they take turns, Butch thought. *Okay, fair enough, fair enough.*

"I would like to question Zach Mortimer."

Butch groaned inwardly. *Mortimer would have no compunctions about sending me away for life, if not longer.*

Mortimer approached the stand and raised his right hand.

"What are you doing?" Dugrow asked.

"In my civilization, it's customary to be sworn in before testifying."

"This is not the appropriate venue for me to swear at you."

"No, I mean it's traditional for us to take an oath to tell the truth."

"Of what value is that? Stand on the plate and it will tell us if you lie!"

Mortimer lowered his hand. "Well...very well."

"You have followed the research into the Kevlon-Tau Converter, have you not?"

"Of course."

"You have, in fact, developed your own model in conjunction with the work being done by Dr. DuBois and the Etuknips, is that not correct?"

"I have. Would you like to purchase one?"

"Please just answer my questions, Mr. Mortimer. Did Butch McCrae approach you about purchasing one of your privately developed Kevlon-Tau Converters?"

"Yes."

"And for what purpose?"

"To try to seek out Ophelia, who had been abducted by the Sweg."

"And did you provide him with a unit?"

"Yes."

"And what did it cost him?"

Mortimer fidgeted. "I'd...rather not say."

"You *will* say or you will be found guilty of obstruction of this court!"

Mortimer grimaced. "Well. I've been on your bad side before and I don't care to be there again. Very well, it was in exchange for the access codes to the Dock Deck, giving me complete control of a third of Station Post One—if only for a brief time."

"So Butch McCrae not only violated orders, deserted his post, and violated the terms of the Community's agreement with the Etuknips, but he betrayed his commander by selling you sensitive security information. Is that an accurate assessment?"

Mortimer shrugged. "You could put it that way."

"I have no more questions for this creature."

Lanzing stepped forward. "Mr. Mortimer, was Commander Kramer aware that you had developed your own Kevlon-Tau Converter?"

"I really have no idea."

"Did you *tell* him you were developing it?"

"Well, I included all my research in my daily logs. It's my policy to conceal nothing."

The plate at Mortimer's feet illuminated, and there was a low-pitched buzz.

"The Centralized Committee will note that the witness just lied," Lanzig said. "Mr. Mortimer, please tell the truth. You actually *told* Commander Kramer, in as many words, that you were developing your own Kevlon-Tau Converter?"

"Exactly who is on trial here?"

"Commissioner Goblutz, please instruct Mr. Mortimer to answer my question."

"Answer the question, Mr. Mortimer," Goblutz said.

Mortimer sighed. "I did not explicitly tell Commander Kramer I was developing a Kevlon-Tau Converter."

"Did you tell Commander Kramer that Butch McCrae approached you about purchasing this device to pursue Ophelia?"

"No."

"Did you tell Commander Kramer that he had purchased it, and what you gave him in exchange?"

"No."

"Members of the court, I will pause to point out that Butch McCrae is *not* solely responsible for this violation of the agreement between the Community and the Etuknips, and therefore it is unfair to place the entire responsibility on Mr. McCrae. No more questions."

"Return to your seat, Mr. Mortimer," Goblutz said. "It is your turn as questioner, Maiden Lanzing."

Lanzing turned her slit of an eye on Butch. "I would like to question Butch McCrae."

CHAPTER 36

Butch rose, started toward the plate on the floor.

"Remain seated!" Goblutz thundered.

Butch jumped, startled, and returned to his seat. "Sorry."

Softly, Lanzing said, "The seat is taking your bodily readings. It will tell us if you lie."

"Handy."

Lanzing held up a hand, examined it, then dropped it. "Please tell us about your relationship with Ophelia."

Butch was uncomfortable with the question. He disliked discussing his feelings in public—especially his deepest, most intimate feelings, such as those for Ophelia. "Well…we met on Station Post One, started meeting for lunch, got to be friends, and, uh, finally, uh, we, uh, fell in love. Simple as that."

"As simple as that? Is it common for humans to fall in love with non-humans?"

"Hell no."

"Members of the court, I would like to point out that in addition to developing the Kevlon-Tau Converter, the purpose of the Etuknips' visit to

Station Post One was to foster closer relations between the Community and the Etuknips—and what better way to foster such relations than with this beautiful and extraordinary love story? Now, Mr. McCrae, will you tell us about the night Ophelia was abducted?"

Butch hesistated; that was the night he had planned on trying to make love to Ophelia in the human way; not something he cared to share with the court. "Well, Ophelia and I went to the Wheel for a…a date…and as we were, uh, walking, well, suddenly she pointed out these Sweg—and the next thing I knew, she and the Sweg were gone. I guess something happened, 'cause I have a, not a memory, but an *impression* that I'd been fighting them, but they must've edited the timeline, because the next thing I knew, I was all by myself in the Wheel."

"Then the abduction of Ophelia occurred during a time when you were attempting a romantic interlude with her."

"Yeah."

"I would like the Centralized Committee to consider the emotional state of the prisoner. Not only was he involved in a love relationship with Ophelia, but he was actively engaged in the act of a courtship ritual at the time she was abducted. No civilized society advances to the level of space exploration without the consideration that members of its civilization are individuals with individual needs and drives."

"I am logging discontent," Dugrow said. "Maiden Lanzing is drawing unjustified and inaccurate conclusions about the nature of intelligent life, and insulting the Valdor civilization. I point out that our own civilization is strong *because* we subordinate the individual to the collective. The individual's needs and drives are not justification for disobedience of duty, but are instead things which must be excised in favor of responsibility to the collective. And although the human culture does not exhibit this prioritization to the same extent, it does exist. Butch McCrae took an oath which included the willingless to forfeit his own needs for the sake of his duty."

"The Administrator is correct as far as he goes," Lanzing said, "but human emotional factors can and do play a significant role in their behavior, and do influence their duties. Indeed, their justice system has a provision known as 'extenuating circumstances,' in which extreme personal needs can be considered justification for actions which otherwise would be considered unacceptable. Since this is encoded in their justice system, it is a valid extrapolation that their personal needs are a driving force in their individual lives."

"Commander Kramer," Goblutz said, "do you agree with Maiden Lanzing on this point?"

Kramer stood, cleared his throat, and said, "Commissioner, I must say that you've brought up a complex issue that has driven much of human psychological study and literature throughout our history. But Maiden Lanzing is correct that we do recognize mitigating circumstances—and if Mr. McCrae were being tried in a human court, that is something we might have taken into consideration were it not for the delicate interstellar relations involved."

Butch shifted in his seat uncomfortably. He wished Kramer hadn't qualified his statement with that last part. He might just have gotten off the hook; but Kramer seemed to be saying that he would have been punished to the maximum extent of the law even in a human court—because of the agreement with the Etuknips. He hadn't been sure before, but he was positive now: he was being made the fall guy.

Lanzing turned her attention back to him. "After Ophelia was abducted, what steps did you take?"

"Well, I searched the station, and when it was confirmed that she wasn't on board, I went to Commander Kramer to get permission to go after her."

"Oh, so then you started out by obeying the chain of command?"

"Well, yeah."

"Breaking it only when all other options were closed to you?"

"Of course!"

"The Centralized Committee must consider the frustration Mr. McCrae must have experienced as he attempted to go through channels to rescue the one he loved, only to be thwarted by arbitrary and illogical provisions of an agreement which, as I have demonstrated, were designed to undermine Station Post One's security in order to carry out this abduction!"

Butch raised his eyebrows, startled at Lanzing's assertion. The way she put it, he was the only one on Station Post One who was doing his duty.

"Mr. McCrae, what is the usual punishment in your civilization for desertion?"

"Uh...well...court-martial for one, and if found guilty, generally the punishment is dishonorable discharge and confinement for five years. 'course no one's been found guilty of that since the destruction of our planet, as far as I know."

"Then when you made the decision to go against orders and rescue Ophelia, that is the maximum punishment you expected?"

"Yeah...but I didn't plan on returning, so I didn't plan on, uh, facing a punishment."

"When you attacked the Sweg ship, were you aware that you were violating interstellar agreement?"

"Yes, I was."

"Then why did you do it anyway?"

"I was determined to rescue Ophelia. I didn't care at that point what would be done to me. I had committed myself to a course of action and I was going to see it through, whatever the consequences."

Dugrow interrupted. "Did you consider the consequences to the Community?"

Butch fidgeted. "No."

Lanzing jumped in. "And *why* did you consider the rescue of Ophelia to be more important than the consequences to interstellar agreement?"

"Because I love her, and because I think that the terms of the agreement were unreasonable, and because I think a person's life rates higher than rules and bureaucracy."

"In other words, Commissioner, Mr. McCrae used the brain he was given rather than robotically following the terms of an agreement that he could see was engineered for Station Post One's disadvantage. Although he did not at the time know the intricacies I have pointed out here, he in his military experience knew that something was wrong. He acted for his personal reasons, yes, but also because, as an officer, he could see that his people had been maneuvered into a vulnerable position. I have no more questions."

"Dugrow?" Goblutz said.

Dugrow clattered toward Butch. "Mr. McCrae, I would like to repeat my previous question. When you deserted your post, hijacked an interstellar spacecraft, and attacked an Etuknip vessel, did you consider the consequences to Community relations with the Etuknips?"

"As I already said, Dugrow, the answer is *no!*"

Dugrow turned toward the Centralized Committee and spread his claws. "What more need be said? Mr. McCrae has just convicted himself. I have no more questions."

"Thank you, Administrator Dugrow," Goblutz said. "It is your turn as questioner."

"I have no one further to question."

"Very well. Maiden Lanzing, it is now your turn as questioner."

"I have asked all the questions I intend," Lanzing said.

"Very well. The question and answer portion of this trial is at an end. We will now commence the neurological probe."

Butch looked around wildly. "Aahh…what's that?"

Lanzing turned toward him. "Your head will be attached to a neural probe and your brain evaluated for aberrations."

"Wait, I've got no 'aberrations'!"

"Silence!" Goblutz roared. "We will decide that! Neurological probe is a standard part of all

Community trials. Your brain configuration will be compared to the ideal human configuration, and your psychology will be evaluated by one of our psychological experts."

"And what species is this psychological expert?"

"Andrian. Their entire society is structured around the understanding of psychology, and individuals rise to power in their civilization through expertise in psychology. Their knowledge extends to many different species."

Butch had never heard of the Andrians, and he was not comfortable having his mental state examined by an alien of any species—no matter how allegedly knowledgeable in psychology. He was human, and no nonhuman could really understand a human. Hell, humans of different cultures had a hard enough time understanding one another. "I object to this!"

"Irrelevant," Dugrow shouted. "The prisoner will be silent or be sedated!"

Butch realized he had risen from his seat. Surrounded by Valdor, and under the watchful eye of the Centralized Committee and many Community members in the audience, he realized he had better behave. He returned to his seat.

Please, Commander Kramer, speak up for me here, he thought. *I know you're mad at me, and you have every right to be, but come on, this is way out of proportion to what I did.*

Kramer remained seated, saying nothing.

A new creature emerged from the audience, slithering snakelike onto the stage despite the fact that Butch saw four—no, six—appendages on its slender, furry body. It undulated toward the

Centralized Committee, made a series of complex gestures with the four limbs.

"This is Leefer," a voice said.

Butch realized then that the four limbs did not belong to the furry snake, but to a creature the same color who rode nestled into its back. It was that creature who now spoke.

"The Chief Agronomer of East Lorekmadrok and elected representative of our people to the Community."

Watching the exchange, Butch finally pieced together that the furry snake was the psychiatrist, and the rodent-like passenger some sort of interpreter.

"Leefer has made a full study of human psychology in preparation for this assignment," the rodent said, "and is now ready to commence her analysis of the mind of Butch McCrae."

"Proceed," Goblutz said.

The furry snake slithered toward Butch. It was the size, he thought, of a pretty big anaconda, though its knobby head sported large, warm, brown eyes reminiscent of a dog's, and its mouth curved in what to human eyes looked like a smile.

"Come with us," the rodent said.

"Guards," Goblutz said, "escort Leefer and the prisoner to the examining room."

Again, Butch surrendered to the wisdom of cooperating. He had no desire to be examined by this alien, but those gentle eyes were disarming. Maybe this wouldn't be so bad; maybe Leefer knew what she was doing.

As the guards marched him off the stage, he glanced at Kramer, who looked down and wouldn't meet his eyes.

CHAPTER 37

Leefer coiled at the center of the circle of delegates, the rodent—whom Butch had learned was named "Yren"—gesturing and speaking animatedly. Butch had learned that Leefer could not speak at all; Yren was nestled in her back with tendrils extended directly into her brain and could actually share Leefer's thoughts. More than an interpreter, Yren was a vector who was the vocal side of a dual entity.

Butch sat in his witness chair, drained.

The examination itself hadn't been too bad. He had lain back on a couch, and Leefer coiled her snakelike body around his cranium. Yren then proceeded to ask him questions—some quite irrelevant, like what he'd had for breakfast, what his pulse rate was at rest as opposed to during exercise, and whether he had ever taken a prolonged vacation—and some comically cliché, like "tell me about your parents." But as the examination went on, the questions became more probing and more relevant, more related to Ophelia and the basis of his feelings for her.

"By human norms, Butch McCrae has no mental illnesses of any debilitating kind," Yren said. "He is highly intelligent, though not nearly as intelligent as he tries to project. Leefer believes this stems from a sense of inadequacy as related to a best friend who received higher marks than he in his early education, and admiration for a father whose knowledge of human literature was extensive to a pathological degree.

"His obsessive desire to be better and smarter than everyone else has given him a rather derisive attitude toward many of the females of his own species, whom he tends to find boring. His romantic relationships have been few and brief. He seeks the most intelligent and the most exotic mates he can find. He has a history of dating females of different human cultures than his own, and he regrets that the pigmentations and facial characteristics which once divided his species into four different 'races' have disappeared, as he actively seeks a partner of a different complexion and physical makeup than himself.

"He has long held a secret and obviously unrequited romantic interest in a long-dead human named Hypatia, a librarian of Earth's ancient world reputed to be extremely beautiful and one of the most intelligent and accomplished women of her time. Mr. McCrae grieves that she was brutally murdered and often fantasizes about saving her life and bringing her into his own time, and pursuing a relationship with her. Ophelia is very similar to Mr. McCrae's mental picture of this Hypatia.

"He also finds that his own sexual titillation requires an element of the forbidden, and each time he explores some taboo, he quickly becomes bored with it and must experiment further. As a result of these things, he found a rush of excitement with the exotic and wholly non-human

Ophelia. He found himself confronted with an entirely alien culture which he delighted in exploring, and also in dazzling a mate—whose knowledge of human culture was extremely restricted—with his own extensive knowledge of human literature. As a result, he relished the chance to display his own intelligence to one who knew no better.

"Leefer's conclusion is that Butch McCrae has mild cases of narcissism, inferiority, obsession, anhedonia, and paracosm, none of which he was aware of and none of which were extensive enough to interfere in his daily life. But they did result in the construction of a personal world in which he was the hero of a play and Ophelia his romantic interest, and the actions of which he is accused formed the subplot of an adventure story which he was writing in his own mind. There was thus a slight detachment from reality which prevented Mr. McCrae from fully appreciating the consequences of his actions, both to his own life and to his people's relations with the Etuknips.

"Leefer's recommendation to the Centralized Committee is that Mr. McCrae be prevented from further contact with Ophelia or any of the Etuknips and be placed into elemental psychotherapy to recondition his mind to focus on his own people and his job, and to find satisfaction in the company of the human females available to him on Station Post One. It is Leefer's opinion that lengthy prison time will only exacerbate his condition and lead to further problems later. Thank you."

Butch's fists tightened on his armrests at the suggestion that he be prevented from further contact with Ophelia. That was not acceptable; he was prepared to take any punishment—as long as he had a chance of seeing Ophelia, at least on occasion.

He also felt Leefer's diagnosis was bullshit.

"We will now commence the third phase of the trial," Goblutz said, "the deliberations on sentencing. The prisoner's presence is not required for these deliberations. He will be removed to the court cell."

"Sentencing?" Butch asked. "What about the verdict?"

"Silence!" Goblutz shouted.

"If I may," Lanzing said, "the human justice system is predicated on the presumption of innocence. I think Mr. McCrae does not understand that he was already judged guilty before the trial began."

"What McCrae understands or does not understand is no longer relevant. His part in the trial is concluded. We will begin proceedings. Remove him."

Butch stood, glaring at Goblutz. Then he looked at Dugrow, who had turned away and seemed to be consciously ignoring him. "Got your way at last, didn't you, you lumbering oversized beetle," he grumbled.

He looked out at the audience, saw Kramer nibbling on his thumb, Tobey watching him with a grim expression—but where was Ophelia? Surely she was here somewhere!

The guards ushered him off the stage toward the entrance in the rear, and he caught no glimpse of his love. He wondered if he would ever see her again.

———

He lost track of time as he lay on his bunk in the cell. He Valdor ignored him, and as there was no night or day on Klym Valdor, he had no way of marking the passage of the days. He received meals at irregular intervals, so he couldn't even measure time by the number of breakfasts and dinners.

It might have been days, weeks, or months before he finally had a visit from Kramer.

"Ah, Commander." As he spoke, Butch realized his mouth was dry. *I'm not nervous... they just haven't been giving me enough water.* "I hope you're not expecting an apology, because I don't regret what I did."

Kramer shook his head. "Butch, you amaze me."

Butch smiled. "Well, I'm an amazing guy."

"I would think a *little* contrition would be in order."

"I did what I felt I had to do. I know about the chain of command and all that, but you don't rise to my position without being trained to use your own brain. What you did was wrong, Commander. It was wrong. What the Valdor did was wrong. What I did was right. I'm the only one on the whole station who did what was *right*. Maybe it was against the regs, maybe it was a violation of orders, but dammit, Commander, dammit, *dammit!* What I did was *right!*"

"I'm not here to argue right and wrong with you, Butch. The Centralized Committee doesn't do courtroom procedure the same way we do; they don't want to see you again. They've pronounced sentence, and they sent me to tell you."

Butch swallowed, his mouth dry. His forehead felt cold. "Yeah?"

"I won't beat around the bush. They've decided to sentence you to twenty years on Strydia."

Butch felt faint. *Strydia. Planet Hell.*

He had never been there, but he had heard the stories. Strydia was a giant world, its surface gravity two or three g's. The entire planet was a blanket of molten lava, the prison located within a huge orbital tower. The deeper down the tower you went, the higher the gravity. Cages were suspended over the swirling cauldron of molten lava, prisoners condemned to an eternity of heat and torture that often ended in the big dunk in the Lake of Fire far below....

He had known Strydia was a possibility, but hadn't really believed it.

"What...what the hell happened to that psychiatrist's recommendation of just therapy?"

Kramer shook his head. "They took that into consideration and rejected it. They felt the consequences of your actions were so serious that a more severe punishment was warranted." He paused. "For whatever it's worth, I spoke up in opposition to this judgment; I argued that you should be returned to Station Post One and I would see to your punishment."

"Yeah, I can imagine how well *that* went over."

Twenty years! He tried to recall where he was, what he was doing, twenty years ago...the second year of the *Silver Streak*'s flight from Earth...he'd been just a kid at the time....

"Just to give me an idea what I'm in for… how long have I been sitting here waiting for the sentencing?"

"Two days."

Two days!! Impossible! He thought it had been *weeks!* "My God…"

Strydia!! "Have, uh, conditions improved any on Strydia since the Valdor took it over?"

Kramer sighed. "Well…the Throrb are still running it; they're just running it under the auspices of the Community."

"Jesus." He shook his head, clenched his eyes, and said forcefully, "I *still* don't regret what I did."

"Butch…putting aside what you've done to relations between us and—"

"Oh, don't give me that! It's the Valdor government and the Etuknip government that decided to act all ridiculous about this! There's *no reason* why any of this should have happened!"

"Look, the political realities are what they are."

"Yeah, I remind you who it was that made the decision to go along with the crazy idea of having Etuknips looking after our security! If that hadn't happened, that Etuknip ship would never have gotten on board and none of this would've happened!"

"I can't argue with that."

"I don't hear *you* apologizing, so I'm sure not going to!" Butch was aware he was being blatantly insubordinate, but what the hell did it matter now? Could it get any worse than twenty years on Strydia?

"I'm not asking for your apology, Butch. I just want to ask you…was she really worth it?"

Strydia...twenty years on Strydia...Was she worth it? He thought back on their time together aboard the *Frontier*. A few days. Were those few days worth twenty years? Were those few days worth a lifetime? He would never again fly a spacecraft. He would sit in prison while his youth dried up. He would never see Ophelia again. He would very likely die there. Were those few days worth it?

"Look what's happening to us," Kramer continued. "Look what's happening to you, to your life. *Was she worth it?!*"

Butch turned away, looked at the floor, the mottled tiles, the small metal drain. He swallowed again, determined not to let his voice crack, and said, "What do *you* think?"

"But what do you get out of it? Her career is ruined, your career is ruined, you'll never be together. You're going to spend twenty years on Strydia, renowned as the most horrible and unpleasant prison in the galaxy."

Gee, thanks, that helps.

"Why?" Kramer pressed.

Butch met his former commander's eyes. "If you really have to ask that question...I have to wonder if we're even human anymore."

CHAPTER 38

The unpleasant business having been done, it was time to return to Station Post One. No one said anything as they filed into the Valdor ship that would take them home. There had been no discussion of giving them a new TSR to replace the *Frontier*, and Kramer had no idea the current state of Station Post One's relations with the Valdor.

But he had secured permission to take Butch home. He had explained to Dugrow and Goblutz the human need to tidy up personal affairs, and to his immense surprise, they understood and agreed. So although Butch would be confined to the brig, he would be allowed two weeks to communicate with anyone he wished—including Ophelia.

The state of affairs with the Etuknips was as nebulous as that with the Valdor, but Ophelia would remain on Station Post One for at least a few days, until the Etuknips sent word of what they wanted to do next.

In fact, it was less than twenty-four hours after their return to the station that Tobey reported a communication from the Etuknips.

"Damon, word from the Etuknip Hegemony. They're breaking off all contact with the Community as well as Station Post One as a result of this incident."

"Oh, God." Kramer rubbed his temples. He thought he had mollified the Sweg by railroading Butch. This just wasn't right.

"And they are demanding the return of the Sweg as well as Ophelia. Evidently both Mackenzie and Ophelia are to be punished for what happened here."

Kramer frowned. "I figured they might punish Ophelia, but Mackenzie?"

"Yeah, apparently she masterminded the abduction of Ophelia, so she's to be punished along with the chair of the Sweg ministerial council. They violated treaty by manipulating the agreement to arrange the abduction. But even so, the Etuknips want no more to do with us."

All of Kramer's sympathy for Butch evaporated in that moment. *Damn him! Damn him and his overactive libido and his selfishness and his irresponsibility! If he had just followed orders, none of this would have happened!*

But Butch's defender had made an excellent point: the terms of the deal had been influenced by the Sweg, maneuvering him and Station Post One into a position in which Ophelia could be kidnapped at their whim. It was a bad deal, and Butch had tried to warn him so. Yes, Butch was guilty of all charges, but really it was the Sweg who were at the bottom of all of this, and it was *they* who should be punished.

And now it was all for nothing. Butch was being punished and the alliance was *still* falling apart. Too bad the Valdor had the final say; he would like to rush in and grant Butch a full pardon right now.

Instead, he would have to deliver the bad news to the Valdor. "Well, if you'll excuse me, I'll be in my privacy pod. Get Dugrow on the line and transfer it down there. I'd rather do this in private."

"Gotcha," Tobey said.

By the time he arrived in his privacy pod, his realscreen was already alive with Dugrow's image.

Sighing, he sat at his desk facing the screen. "Dugrow. We've received a message from the Etuknip Hegemony."

"Yes, I know. It was simulcast to us. We are aware that they are breaking off contact with the Community."

Kramer nodded, letting out another heartfelt sigh. "Then you know that the whol affair with Butch McCrae is now academic."

"I warned you," Dugrow said in a low, menacing voice. "How many times have I warned you that Butch McCrae is unstable and abrasive and—"

Kramer's hold on his temper gave out. "Unstable and abrasive?! What do *you* know about 'unstable and abrasive'?! You make McCrae look like a spotless saint!"

"Exactly what do you mean by that?!"

"I mean that from the moment our civilizations came into contact, you've withheld information from us, you've treated us like enemies, you've made unreasonable demands, and on top of it all, you *pushed* us into a treaty with the Community that we hadn't had time to properly consider!"

"I want to hear nothing more from you, Commander Kramer! The Valdor hereby break off relations with you! I've warned you about that before and the warning stands! And I intend to immediately recommend to the Centralized Committee that you be expelled from the Community."

"Fine! If you want to invite war with the Hyron Empire—"

"We won the war with the Alternative Alliance, we can win a war with the Hyrons. And *you* and your pathetic station will be one of the first casualties! I relish the prospect of never having to deal with you again!"

"The feeling is mutual!" Kramer jabbed his finger on the disconnect tab. Then he sat back, trembling. Awareness slowly dawned of what had just happened.

My God, my God, my God...

Just as Butch had to be held responsible for sabotaging relations with the Etuknips, now Kramer would be held responsible for destroying the alliance with the Community. How would he explain this to President Copenburg?

My God, my God, my God, I'll be rotting on Strydia alongside Butch....

What in God's name would he do now? Dugrow had directly threatened Station Post One. Technically the Hyrons would be under obligation to defend the station, but he couldn't imagine Zoran making much of an effort to do so.

How did this happen? What could I have done differently? He knew he would be asking himself those questions for as long as he lived— however long that might be.

But given the situation, and with Butch in his possession—possession being nine-tenths of the law—he came to a decision.

———

Kramer's announcement was broadcast throughout the Community on all entangled channels. Every Community member tapped into the interstellar database could hear him in realtime, even over the many light years of distance the Community covered. The electromagnetic peaks exchanged places instantaneously with the electromagnetic troughs along the entangled wave, teleporting the message instantaneously into all receivers.

He was acutely aware of this as he brazenly violated the Valdor's rules.

"This is Commander Damon Kramer aboard Station Post One. Most of you have been attending, or at least following, the trial of Butch McCrae.

"This trial has been conducted in accordance with Community rules. It has been supervised by the Centralized Committee. But as Station Post One, as enforced by the Hyron Empire, is the command station of the Community, I have reserved to myself the final judgment as to Captain McCrae's sentencing."

He deliberately referred to Butch as "Captain" even though he was presumed to have voluntarily relinquished all rank and privileges when he deserted. Kramer was aware of Tobey's expression of bewilderment. He ignored it and continued.

"In light of the evidence and Captain McCrae's confession, I agree with the Centralized

Committee that Captain McCrae is guilty of all charges.

"*But*...in light of Captain McCrae's superlative performance in the defense of Station Post One, as well as his many accomplishments which are a matter of record...as well as some *mitigating circumstances*..."

Tobey smiled at that.

"...I am rejecting the Centralized Committee's suggestion that he be sentenced to Strydia for twenty years." He was pleased with his use of the word "suggestion," and could just imagine the temper tantrum going on now on Klym Valdor.

"Instead, Captain McCrae is stripped of all rank and is dishonorably discharged, and I sentence him to one year in the brig. At the conclusion of this sentence, he will be given the option of transport to one of our colonies or the Space Star *Silver Streak* in order to pursue a civilian occupation. But he will never again serve in an *official* capacity in the Command Defense Force.

"That is my judgment."

He cut off the transmission.

"Holy fucking shit, Damon," Tobey said. He opened his mouth to say something more, fumbled for a moment, and then repeated, "Holy fucking shit."

Kramer nodded. "That about sums up this whole situation, doesn't it?"

Tobey smirked.

———

It didn't take long for a response to arrive from Dugrow. Kramer refused to receive it, but

Tobey recorded it, and after shift they listened to it in his privacy pod as they reviewed the daily reports.

"I of course heard the pronouncement which you so impetuously broadcast throughout the Community. Your judgment is completely unacceptable. You have defied the primacy of the Valdor, you have invalidated the authority of the Centralized Committee, and you have *again* abrogated an interstellar agreement. Your supposition that the Hyrons will enforce your authority is arrogant at best, treasonous at worst.

"I have consulted with the Valdor government and we are in unanimous agreement that we reject the Hyron occupation of the Community and their reckless elevation of Station Post One to the capital of the Community. We are reasserting our own control over our own sector, and over the Community. For myself, I have had quite enough of you and your entire species. It was a mistake to recruit you into the Community. You are a disruptive force, and the disharmony you cause is greater than the benefit we have received from your membership. The Thermians should have wiped your species out when they destroyed your planet.

"Therefore I am notifying you that I will devote all of my energies to removing you from command of Station Post One, and I have made a formal recommendation to the Centralized Committee that you be expelled from the Community. *Ka-thracch* what the Hyrons have to say about it. This is Dugrow, communicating with you for what I hope is the last time. Klym Valdor out."

Kramer and Tobey sat in silence for a full minute after the transmission ended.

Tobey was the first to speak. "I don't think I've ever heard him so pissed."

Kramer rubbed his temples. "I wouldn't worry so much about his temper tantrums except that he does carry a good deal of weight with the Centralized Committee; in fact he seems to be pretty much at the center of everything the Valdor do."

"Well, I never liked the Valdor anyway, and we've all felt we rushed into joining the Community."

"Don't brush this off so easily, Tobey. If this does result in a war—I'm not saying it will, but if it does, we're out here surrounded by enemies, and if I know Zoran, he'll seize on the chance to destroy us. The only way out of this at this point is to abandon Station Post One."

Tobey looked down at the desk and nodded slowly. "Yeah...yeah, I've been trying not to think about that, but I suppose you're right. This is one bug fucking mess. Damn that Butch McCrae."

Kramer thought of a dozen defenses of Butch, but matched against that was the looming fact of Butch's betrayal. So he only said, "Yeah."

CHAPTER 39

Butch literally did not believe his ears when Kramer told him he was sentenced to a mere one year in the brig. He was sure he had either misheard or was dreaming. It was not possible, simply not possible, that he had been suddenly let off the hook so easily.

Of course, dishonorable discharge and a year in the brig was hardly being "let off the hook," but compared to twenty years on Planet Hell, it was a weekend at the Shakespeare Symposium in Denver. And this opened up the possibility of his seeing Ophelia again—or even having a life with her once that year was up.

"Uhhh…please say that again, Commander… are you saying I am not going to serve *any* of that twenty years on Strydia?"

"As long as I'm in command and you're under my jurisdiction, you are not leaving this station and you're not going into Valdor custody—at all."

Butch paced the cell, still disbelieving. "God…I don't know what to say. Thank you, Commander."

"Don't thank me. I don't think there are any winners today. This decision comes with a high price—I don't even know yet how high. We might all be drifting atoms by the end of the day, depending on how things escalate between the Valdor and the Hyrons."

"Well…why then would you do this for me? I mean, not that I enjoyed being thrown under the shuttle, but I understood why you did it. You were putting the good of the station and the whole Community ahead of me. So why do this for me when there are such consequences?"

Kramer hesitated. "I guess…I'm just sick of the Valdor."

Butch agreed, but did not reply.

"One more thing…You and Ophelia have known each other for only a few weeks, but you've made some life-altering decisions for her—as well as some decisions that have altered our entire interstellar political framework. What if the two of you don't work out?"

"Well, when we agreed to join the Community, did we know whether or not it was gonna work out?"

Kramer smiled. "Touché. You're a pain in the ass, Butch, but I'm going to miss having you around."

"I'll miss being around. –But I still say it was worth it."

Kramer turned, said in a soft voice, "You keep telling yourself that," and walked away.

Now, what did he mean by that? Butch watched him go, pondering his fate. His career was over. He was facing a year in the brig. That was the easy part; the hard part was the prospect of a potential war in which he could not take part—and worse, in which he could die as an innocent bystander. What would become of

Station Post One? What did this portend for the war against the Thermians?

If his own light sentence were the only consequence of his actions, then yes, he would have no doubts. But should millions of intelligent life forms, including perhaps the last of the human race, perish for his personal feelings? No. Of course not. And he couldn't lie to himself: he had known that this was a possible outcome. He had made the conscious decision to place his personal concerns over his duty. So it was a little late now to try to pretend a moral high ground.

Actually, what can Ophelia see in me now? I proved myself an unreliable, irrational traitor who's willing to dump a sacred oath as soon as it becomes inconvenient.

But he had done all this *for her*. Surely that had to mean something. And with her ability to see all times and all outcomes, she must have known this was a possible turn of the temporal dice. He wondered how things may have unfolded in other timelines….

He could find out—if Ophelia was permitted to see him again. And if she was not, if she were taken to her strange, one-dimensional home and forbidden to enter his world again, *he* would go to *her* world. If one-dimensional beings could leave the cosmic string and become three-dimensional beings in this universe, then the reverse must be true…right? That had been DuBois' theory, as he recalled; that the Etuknips had evolved on a planet in the normal universe and then somehow entered the world of the cosmic string, becoming one-dimensional representations of their three-dimensional selves. If they could do it, he could do it.

When? How? He would solve those problems later. He was a problem solver, and no problem yet had stood up against his determination.

Where is Ophelia anyway? It was one thing when the Valdor wouldn't tell me anything. I'm among my own people now, people who should understand. I wish someone would just let me know.

The more he thought about it, the angrier he became. But he also knew that others saw his romance with Ophelia not as a blissful and wonderful tale of love, as he did, but as the cause of everyone's problems. As angry as he was that no one would tell him anything, they might become just as angry should he dare to ask. Well, hell with it; he would ask anyway.

He didn't know how many hours passed as he lay on his bunk, drifting in and out of sleep, before he heard the voice of, of all people, Elmer Tepper.

"Hiya, Butch." There was no disdain or taunting in Tepper's voice; it was a simple and subdued greeting.

Butch replied in kind. "Hiya, Tepper."

Tepper shifted uncomfortably. "Well."

"Well." After a few more moments of uncomfortable silence, Butch said, "Well, tell me whatever you have to say."

"Well…I didn't come to say anything, except—"

"How'd the Centralized Committee take my sentence?" Butch interrupted more to halt Tepper's self-conscious rambling than to spare him the awkwardness of the encounter.

"Well…not well. They voted to censure Commander Kramer and they've convened a sort of a special committee or something to advise, I guess, or something, whether or not to expel us from the Community."

Mentally translating Tepper's fumbling words, Butch deduced that the either the Centralized Committee or the Valdor Authority were voting, and he presumed the outcome was already a foregone conclusion. And though Kramer would be loathe to admit it, it was probably for the best. It had been a mistake to join the Community.

Butch, however, would have preferred if the Valdor, rather than the humans, were expelled. *They* were the real problem. But that would never happen to the founding members. So be it.

"What about the risk of going to war with the Hyrons?" Butch asked.

Tepper shrugged. "I guess the Valdor don't care. These are the same idiots that bumbled their way into the Doomsday War; I guess their pride is more important than their survival."

Butch scoffed, shook his head. "Some things are worth fighting for, some things you just have to let go."

"I guess one of the things worth fighting for is love?"

"I'm not discussing that with you, *Tepper*." Butch sighed. "So I guess that means Commander Kramer stuck his neck out for me for nothing."

"Possibly, but you never know. Some good might come of it."

"*What* good might come of it?!"

"Well, *you* tell *me!*"

"Yeah." Butch detected Tepper's unspoken question—the same question Kramer had asked. *Was she worth it?* As far as Butch was concerned the answer was still a resounding yes—but as the consequences mounted up, he was having a harder and harder time justifying why. At this point was he just telling himself she was worth it, because now the damage was done and he had to deal with the consequences? After a year of life in the brig, and then a life without military benefits and with a dishonorable discharge on his record, twenty years from now would he still consider those few days worth it?

He told himself yes, but his certainty had begun to crack. "All this for a few nights with Ophelia."

"Still say it was worth it?"

Tepper's flippant question brought back his certainty, along with an edge of anger that Tepper even dared to question. "Yeah. Yeah, I—"

"There is one thing I wanted to say to you. Don't know quite how to say it." Tepper shifted his weight, scratched his side, and stared at the floor as he hunted for words. "Uh—"

"Look, just say it!"

Tepper nodded. "Look, you and I have never gotten along, we've got different tastes and everything, you, you're into that high-falutin, high-brow stuff, thee thou thee—"

"Yeah, yeah." It drove Butch crazy when Tepper made fun of the language of Shakespeare; in addition to the presentist arrogance of ridiculing someone who spoke differently because he was a product of another time, it showed a woeful lack of appreciation for the beauty of the Bard's writing. It was one of the oldest and bitterest arguments he had with Tepper.

"—Beethoven and all that stuff," Tepper continued, "and of course I'm into the modern stuff—"

"You're into *crap!*"

Unfazed, Tepper went on calmly, still staring at the floor. "We snap at each other and stuff, but—"

"What are you getting at?" Butch asked impatiently. "What are you trying to say, *Tepper?*"

"Well…if I'm just gonna be flat-out, you know, honest—"

"Come on, now, just say it!"

Tepper took a deep breath, then spat out quickly, "I've come to think of you as a friend." He still stared at the floor.

Now it was Butch's turn to stare at the floor. What could he say to that? Make fun? Pretend he hadn't heard? Return the sentiment? He couldn't imagine sharing a sentimental moment with Tepper, but he had to admit… "Yeah. Well. Yeah. I…uh…thinkofyouasafriendtoo, Tepper."

"Yeah…well…" Tepper looked around, suddenly finding everything in the security section of overpowering interest. "You're gonna be around for the next year, even if you're locked up here, so, uh, I'll stop by and talk to you now and then."

"Yeah. All right, well, thanks for dropping by, *Tepper.*"

"Yep. See you later." Tepper rushed off, a current of breeze swirling behind him.

Butch didn't look up until Tepper's footsteps had receded. It was a funny thing; how angry he had been when he had first been assigned to work with Tepper, how he had dreaded their first assignment together...that unforgettable mission to Ymor where they had first encountered the Dreb...and now...the *Frontier* was gone, his career was over, and Tepper, Elmer Tepper, the idiot who had deleted his Beethoven collection, was a friend. God.

He was going to miss it. Their adventures together, their voyages to new worlds, their long flights in which they barely put up with each other, the post-mission lunches where they bickered incessantly...why, after all, had they insisted on eating together if they didn't enjoy each other's company?

Unthinkable, that. But yes...he realized he had enjoyed Tepper's company. *You never know what you have until it's gone.*

But it was worth it, he told himself again. He thought back on that fantasy-like voyage with Ophelia, the scene of domestic bliss, the promise of unbridled adventure in their future—even the ever-present threat of Zoran's pursuit had added a sad desperation to their love story that added to its romantic appeal. Yes, it was worth it.

He knew he would spend the rest of his life reminding himself that it was worth it.

And wondering if it was really true.

CHAPTER 40

It was like the eve of the Doomsday War all over again. Station Post One sat alone and vulnerable, on the precipice of calamity. All aboard could feel it, even though nothing, as of yet, had happened. Someone in PHC mentioned the archaic but apt saying: "The calm before the storm."

There was a difference, though. On the eve of the Doomsday War, everyone had known that war was at hand. Now...no one was sure. Would the Valdor issue a declaration of war? Would there suddenly be an attack? There had been no word from the Hyrons either, and it seemed certain that Zoran would take the opportunity to see his Vengeance Quest against Kramer fulfilled.

Kramer watched the many Community ships which surrounded the station, not knowing whether they were friends or enemies—or if, like him, they were simply awaiting word. Most threatening of all was the *Kinetic*, which loomed like a giant shark ready to strike. He wondered what Zoran was thinking over there on that behemoth.

There had been no further word from the Valdor since Dugrow's temperamental reaction to

Kramer's proclamation regarding Butch McCrae, and he wrestled with whether he had made the right decision. Legally, no; he had overstepped his bounds. But nor had there been word from President Copenburg out there on the *Silver Streak*, even though he had filed a detailed report to the Congressional Council. He knew the report had been received, because the Congressional computer had sent an automatic acknowledgement.

Some of the Community ships were withdrawing, their governments considering the situation to be over. Kramer considered that a reasonable approach. The conflict need only escalate if members *made* it escalate. Forgetting the whole thing seemed a palable alternative.

But this was not to be.

"Here it comes," Tobey said. "Message from the Valdor."

"Let's hear it."

Dugrow's voice rumbled through PHC. "Station Post One, this is Dugrow. This is the decision of the Centralized Committee. The human race has been judged to have committed egregious violations of interstellar agreement and Community policy. These violations are not isolated incidents, but the latest manifestations of systemic problems with your civilization. Taking into account all aspects of the Etuknip affair, combined with past complications involving your people, a plurality of the Centralized Committee has voted that you are to be expelled from the Community."

Kramer let out a deep breath. He had been expecting that decision, and a tiny part of him had even been hoping for it. But now that it was done, it was a shock.

"Therefore, you have twenty-four of your hours to remove your station from Valdor space or you will come under attack."

"What?!" someone shouted.

"How the fuck are we supposed to do that?" Tobey asked.

"It can't be done," Kramer said. "All we can do is abandon the station and hope someone can give our people transportation out of Community space."

"Wait, wait...maybe the Hyrons or someone can give us a tow."

Kramer laughed without humor. "Can you see Zoran agreeing to that? No, the best he'll do is give us a ride, then take great pleasure in blowing our station to bits."

"And taking you prisoner in the meantime," Dr. DuBois said.

"All right, wait," Kramer said, "get me a channel to Klym Valdor."

"It's still open," Tobey said.

"Very well. Klym Valdor, this is Commander Kramer aboard Station Post One, received your transmission. You must surely be aware that it is quite impossible for us to move our station on such short notice. Would you be willing to devote some of your ships to towing our station, or to transporting our complement to one of our colonies?"

Dugrow's voice came back, "Negative. You now have twenty-three hours, fifty-four minutes."

"He's loving this," Tobey said.

"Well, there's lots of ships out there. Put this on Community widescan."

"Righto…okay, set."

"Attention, attention all nearby ships, this is Commander Damon Kramer aboard Station Post One. You must have heard Dugrow's pronouncement. We have been expelled from the Community and have twenty-four hours to remove our station from Valdor space or be attacked. As you may be aware, our only interstellar ship was crippled and impounded by the Hyrons. Would any of you be willing to tow our station out of Valdor space, or to give our people a ride to one of our colonies? Thank you. Station Post One out."

For the next ten minutes, replies trickled in. They were all variations of, "You are no longer Community members, and we do not wish to alienate the Valdor by providing you assistance."

Only Zoran gave a positive reply; in fact he was downright effusive. "I will give your people a ride, Commander Kramer. It is the least I can do. You may begun shuttling them over to the *Kinetic* immediately. I will look forward to having you on board!"

There was no mistaking the threat in that last part. The complement of Station Post One may or may not be Zoran's guests—but Kramer was to be his prisoner. What choice did he have?

"Attention all personnel. This is Commander Kramer. Station Post One is hereby discontinued. Abandon all work and report to the Dock Deck for transport to the Hyron Dreadnought *Kinetic*."

Tobey, visibly reeling, repeated the order.

It took a long time for the evacuation of the station to begin; a lot of experiments were in progress, and the scientists were loathe to abandon them. It took some prodding by DuBois to get his people moving.

Before anyone could leave the station, though, all the guests had to leave, and that was problematic in itself. Security worked to move the various Community members from their privacy pods and usher them to the Dock Deck, while Tepper was in over his head coordinating departures.

Zach Mortimer was, of course, incensed, and soon marched into PHC red-faced. "What are you saying? Station Post One is *discontinued?!* How dare you make such a pronouncement without consulting me! Does President Copenburg know about this?"

"He'll know soon enough," Kramer said, "but if you'd rather stay here and be blown up, be my guest."

"And what is *that* supposed to mean?"

Tobey said, "It means, asshole, that we're going to be coming under Valdor attack in…uh… eighteen hours. We have to be out of here one way or another before then."

"So we're going to just roll over and not even put up a fight?"

"What would you suggest I do?" Kramer demanded. "We can't fight the Valdor and you know it! If you want to blame someone for this, blame yourself for selling McCrae that Kevlon-Tau Converter! You wanted control of the Dock Deck—well, now none of us get *any* of this station!"

Mortimer stood gaping.

"It's your choice," Kramer finally said. "The rest of us are leaving. Stay if you like. Maybe you can single-handedly fight off the Valdor. Or strike a deal with them. Want to give it a try?"

Mortimer's face softened. "I know you did your best. I apologize for my part in this. The situation is regrettable, but in the end it might be for the best." He turned and left.

Kramer and Tobey exchanged looks.

"Well," Tobey said, "he sure changed colors fast."

Kramer glanced at the door through which Mortimer had departed. "That is the weirdest man I've ever met."

———

The Etuknips were now departing. The Sweg were already gone, and what might happen on their bizarre one-dimensional world was the source of endless speculation—and Dr. DuBois had his hands full explaining to curious questioners (who still resisted abandoning the station) the temporal realities of the Etuknip world, especially since he didn't understand them himself.

With the Sweg gone, Ophelia was in the custody of the Leira, and even as the Leira interim ambassador urged immediate departure, Ophelia requested to see Butch one last time. The new ambassador agreed on the proviso that Commander Kramer approve.

"We'll be evacuating the station after the last of you have gone," Kramer told her. "Still, for the next two weeks—wherever we all are by then—Butch has the privilege of meeting with anyone he wishes. So yes, you can see him. But remember, until you depart, we can't evacuate, so please make it brief."

"Believe me, Commander Kramer, only best interests of your station have I heart at. Will I not endanger you any way in."

Kramer was tempted to point out that she was already at the center of everything that had happened to them, but he could not resist her earnest face, her expressive eyes, and her charming smile. He had to admit he could understand why Butch had fallen in love with her. "All right, go see Butch."

Butch was still in his cell; in the frantic evacuation preparations, no one had thought of the lone prisoner who had started this whole mess. But he had heard the announcement, and the noises of running feet and equipment being shuffled around gave the unmistakable sign of big doings aboard Station Post One. He paced, restless, wondering when or if someone would come to take him away.

He was caught between anger and guilt that the station was being abandoned. It was another reckless overreaction by the Valdor—and it was also entirely his fault. But what else could he have done? Just let the Sweg take Ophelia?

(Well, yes, she would have told him. From her perspective, all probabilities were equal.)

But that was bullshit. For *him*, all probabilities were *not* equal, and there was no way he was going to sit around and—

There she was! "Whoa!" He ran to the bars, eagerly seeking the beauty of his love's face. Those large, dark eyes. That flowing blue hair. That perfect, ethereal, idealized body. What was she doing here? Was *she* taking him away? Would she take him to live and love with her forever in her eternal reality on the cosmic string?

"Ophelia, what are you doing here?"

"Come you to see, to you comfort."

"Hey...I made my bed."

Ophelia craned her neck to see into the cell. "No bed there is here, only uncomfortable metal bench."

Despite the circumstances, Butch smiled. Ophelia could always bring a smile to his lips. Looking at her, he remembered now why it was worth it; why that journey aboard the *Frontier* had been so pleasant. Had Zoran destroyed them, he would have died with a smile on his lips. "No...I mean I knew the consequences when I went after you."

"So too I did. But I not did interfere. I *could* have."

"What could you have done?"

After a long pause, Ophelia said, "Never have come here in the first place."

"Well...I guess. I'm glad you did; otherwise I'd never have known you."

"Would you not have known what missing you were—but *I* would. I knew would I you love—wanted to know you, to that experience. Was I selfish."

Butch's mind reeled. She had known before meeting him that she would know him and love him? How long had she known? All her life? "*Selfish* that you wanted to know me? Nah. Like I told *Tepper*, it's worth it."

She shook her head; a mannerism she had picked up from Butch. "Your life ruined is. Community matters worse are, your people expelled are, war at hand is. Where can go you now? What can do you now?"

"Doesn't matter; I've got you."

She nodded; another mannerism she had taken from Butch. "Then have me...one last time."

Dread welled up in Butch's gut. "Last time? What do you mean one last time?"

"Not meet again will we. For what I have done, never I to leave string world. You cannot there live."

Butch blinked back the tears he didn't want her to see. " 'Parting is such sweet sorrow.'"

"So for nothing have come I, have ruined your life, have damaged the Community, have forced you to this station abandon...but...I can still fix."

"What do you mean?"

"By...taking out my visit."

It took a moment for Butch to understand what she meant, and when it sunk in, he found it hard to believe; she was saying she could have shifted the timelines, edited time as the Sweg had done in the Wheel. "What—what—you mean—you mean changing the past so that we never met?"

She nodded. "And reconnecting time before all this happened with...other time."

"Other time?"

"Time..." She frowned. "...over *there*. Where we never met."

"No! No, Ophelia, don't do that. If I never see you again, if I never fly a fighter again, if I never roam free again, don't—don't you see?— it's *worth* it, because...because...you're everything to me. None of the rest of that means anything next to you."

"Would not you that say if never had met we."

Butch took her hands and squeezed. The tears were coming now and he couldn't stop them. At the moment Tennyson was more appropriate than Shakespeare. "''Tis better to have loved and lost than never to have loved at all.'"

"Better to have than have not. Come, Butch, one last time."

She took his hands in hers, and again they shared a lifetime of lovemaking. The ecstasy washed over him, a wave of pure joy, of an eternity in the heaven he didn't believe in. Breathless, he gasped, "I'm *never* gonna get used to that!"

"Will you not," Ophelia said. "Never will you again it experience. Never will have you experienced."

"Whoa! What about you? If you—*if* you do this, will you still be punished?"

"Yes," she said quietly.

"Then don't do it!"

"I punished will be either way. You can I save. But knew you I always will."

"Don't do it," Butch sobbed desperately.

" 'Good night, good night, a thousand times good night.'"

And she did it.

EPILOGUE

For Butch McCrae, nothing had happened. He and Tepper and Mortimer had just used their captured Hyron Galactic Cruiser to fight off the Striktonese superweapon, and the Valdor had just announced that mysterious aliens from a cosmic string, creatures called Etuknips, would be coming aboard the station. For Butch McCrae and Elmer Tepper and Commander Kramer and Tobey Dingell and Ebor DuBois and Jerry Flynn and Marfida Lazarev and Zach Mortimer, Station Post One was as it had always been—and they anxiously awaited the Etuknips.

Butch was angry about the many concessions Kramer had made to the Valdor regarding the Etuknips' visit. As for the Etuknips themselves, he felt nothing, for he had never met one. He was curious to meet creatures who allegedly lived on a cosmic string, but he was more concerned about the perplexing fact that they were to be put in charge of the station's security, which was, in his eloquent assessment, bullshit.

But Kramer's mind was made up.

But then something very strange happened. The Etuknip ship arrived as scheduled—but then was suddenly gone, as if it had never been there.

There was much consternation aboard Station Post One until Dugrow contacted Kramer and informed him that, for reasons unknown, the Etuknips had decided to cancel their summit.

It was unfortunate, but these things happened sometimes when dealing with beings as alien as the Etuknips.

As far as Butch was concerned, it was just as well. Now he wouldn't have to deal with creepy aliens poking around security areas.

Yet as Butch McCrae went about his life with no pain, another being out in the cosmos felt enough pain for them both, as she remembered and sorrowed for what had so briefly been—and yet took solace in the knowledge she had not shared, but kept close to her heart; for in one of the infinite timelines, she knew that she and Butch would meet again.

AUTHOR'S NOTE

In chapter 10, I make the rather extraordinary statement that Planck's Constant was the most important scientific discovery of the twentieth century. Really, I only said that to raise eyebrows; I don't think it was more or less important than numerous other discoveries in relativity and quantum mechanics. But it is a very important discovery.

It occurred to me that if you ask a random person on the street to identify Einstein's most important contribution, he or she would likely say "E=mc^2" or "the Theory of Relativity." But if you ask them what Planck's Constant is, you would likely get a blank stare. So I thought it would be fun to assume that future science would elevate this rather obscure (but important) discovery to a much more exalted status.

I would like to thank my friend Gregory Hall for once again straightening me out on a few concepts, and for pointing out that there are pitfalls in any nonmathematical explanation for a mathematical concept.

Greg pointed out to me that it's a misconception to say that electrons can only exist in discrete energy levels and cannot exist in between; this is true only for an isolated atom. The universe consists of condensed matter too, and in those cases electrons exist in a near continuum of energy states—which are much closer in energy than Planck's Constant suggests.

That being the case, I trust that readers and scientists alike will forgive any oversimplification on my part.

I made up quantum relativity, and I have no precise idea of exactly what it is. If I did, I would publish it and revolutionize physics and make a million dollars. I went out on a daring limb by making the chonon identical to the Planck Time. I should point out that the Planck Time is merely the smallest possible amount of time between two connected events; it is *not* an attempt to quantize time. But considering the way concepts in quantum physics interconnect, it seemed reasonable to me that the chronon, if it exists, would be the same unit of time.

As to the notion of life on a cosmic string— as so often happens, I thought I was breaking new ground there, but then I learned that *Star Trek: The Next Generation* explored this same concept. It's starting to look like there's nothing new in science fiction.

As long ago as 1884, the idea of life in a two-dimensional universe was proposed. Edwin Abbott's famous novella *Flatland* became the basis for understanding the concept of higher dimensions—i.e. a totally flat life form would have no concept of the third dimension, just as we three-dimensional life forms can have no concept of a fourth dimension.

In June of 2019, James Scargill of the University of California published the findings of a study that concluded that life is indeed possible in a two-dimensional universe. Although a two-dimensional universe is quite a different thing from a cosmic string, I did draw upon his study to develop the world of the Etuknips, and to justify the idea that a one-dimensional world might contain sufficient complexity for life to exist.

Scargill based his conclusions on two-dimensional computer neural networks which simulated biological brain networks. Life, or at least intelligence, is essentially information plus energy; if information can exist on a cosmic string, then this science fiction writer argues that life could exist. Scargill is quick to point out that his study proves nothing—but proof is not necessary to the science fiction writer. We deal not in the proven, but in the possible (or the not-quite-impossible).

There are several models regarding the nature of time. Anyone who has seen the *Back to the Future* movies will be familiar with the notion that traveling back in time and changing the past will create an alternate timeline. This is a logical progression of the many-worlds interpretation of quantum mechanics—which has been an important plot point in *Voyage Into the Unknown* before.

It boggles the mind to imagine that there might be alternate versions of ourselves in parallel universes that are slightly different from our own, and the idea seems like pure fantasy—but many scientists take it seriously.

Consider a simple beam of light from a flashlight; it travels both as a wave rippling through spacetime, and as a series of discrete particles, which we call photons. You can try a simple experiment to observe this paradox; try cutting two vertical slits in a piece of cardboard and then shining a flashlight through those slits against a wall. Like an ocean wave crashing between the pilings of a pier, the light wave will wash through the slits and then merge again.

However, the wall will absorb the light in discrete patterns; two slits of light that match the slits in the cardboard.

So what happened to the rest of the light? Where is it?

The same phenomenon applies to electrons, which is crucial, since electrons are components of matter. It defies common sense, but electrons are not actual *things*, but waves of probability, which we call wave function. They only exist as particles when they interact with other particles. The wave function can tell us where the electron *probably* is—for instance, in its ground energy level in a carbon atom in your body. But the wave function also tells us that there is a lesser probability that it might be in an excited state, in a higher shell in that atom. Or in a different atom. Or in a different person's body. Or out on Pluto. Or on the other side of the universe.

Every electron could be *anywhere*.

Photons, electrons, all elementary particles show this perplexing property. So how do we explain this?

If an electron could be *anywhere*, then maybe it is *everywhere*. But since, in a three-dimensional spacetime, it can only be in one place at a time, we can only observe it in the ground state energy level of that carbon atom in your body. It exists in another location *in another universe*. And if you follow this train of thought to its conclusion, since all matter is made of atoms, with the placement of their electrons crucial in the physical makeup of matter, then there must be an infinite number of realities, accounting for every imaginable possibility—and a few unimaginable ones!

So any time you make a decision, for instance whether to turn right or left at an intersection where you're not sure where to go, you in fact make *both* decisions. Thus in one reality you reach your destination, and in the other you find yourself lost. That means that every day, you fracture the universe into many different realities with every decision you make.

Therefore, an errant time traveler who interferes with history would not *change* history, but would simply create a new timeline—just like when Biff created the dystopian alternate world of 1985 by giving his teenage self in 1955 the 2015 edition of the *Grays Sports Almanac.*

It is a rather messy solution to the problem of quantum mechanics, and some have pointed out that it defies the conservation of matter and energy to spontaneously create billions, *trillions* of new universes with every random event every day. In my novel *Dreams of the Stars* I proposed two additional temporal dimensions to give the universe room for all these alternate timelines; I'll leave it to the scientists either to laugh at my speculations or seriously to consider them.

Kip Thorne reached a different conclusion in his research into wormholes. His equations indicate that a particle moving backward in time would fulfill, rather than change, the past. We saw this in the obscure but excellent movie *Somewhere In Time*, in which Christopher Reeve, planning to travel backward in time, checks a hotel registry from 1912 and discovers his own signature, even though he has not yet made the trip.

Consider the paradox: Marty McFly could therefore not go back in time and prevent his parents' meeting, because he would therefore never have been born, and would not exist to go back in time...and so nothing would have prevented his parents' meeting, so he *would* exist to go backward in time, so he *would* prevent his parents' meeting...and so you see that we're backed into a logical conundrum.

These paradoxes are one of the reasons I tend to avoid time travel in *Voyage Into the Unknown*—but it's hard to avoid, given my fascination with black holes and relativity, and in this case, cosmic strings. The assumption I make is that it's possible to send *information* backward in time, but impossible to send *matter* backward in time.

Whatever the truth may be, the science fiction writer is still free to explore the possibilities. There remain many unknowns in this bizarre universe—and the more secrets we discover, the more mysteries present themselves.

WHAT IS IT?
An Explanation of the Cosmic String

Since this book deals with the idea of creatures who live on a cosmic string, I thought it might be a good idea to explore exactly what a cosmic string is. I tried to do so within the body of the novel, but you can't really delve deeply into scientific concepts in a work of fiction lest you slow down the plot. Some science fiction readers know a lot about science, others don't; it's my unenviable job to try to write for the whole spectrum, and to decide just how much scientific exposition to include in the book.

So now that you've read the whole book—or at least I assume you have—we can go a little more thoroughly into the idea of cosmic strings. Assuming you don't already know what they are.

Cosmic strings were first proposed in 1976 by British field theorist Tom Kibble—who also predicted the Higgs boson, which won him a Nobel Prize in 2012 when the Large Hadron Collider detected that elusive particle.

Firstly, a cosmic string is entirely unrelated to the strings of string theory; strings are one-dimensional resonances with ten hypothetical dimensions curled up in them. Their resonances are measured as elementary particles. This explains why our universe consists of three dimensions, when math works in ten dimensions. Strings are not proven to exist, but string theory is one of the most pervasive "theories of everything."

In *A Galaxy in Ruin*, I make the erroneous statement that cosmic strings are related to the strings at the center of elementary particles; that was a mistake in my research, and I revised that in the "flashback" to that scene at the beginning of this book. If the inconsistency bothers you, let's just say that by the forty-first century, future science determined that the two are related.

Anyway, a cosmic string is an entirely different thing.

Let's go back to the Big Bang.

Today there are four fundamental forces of nature—or five, as scientists at ATOMKI (the Institute for Nuclear Research) at the Hungarian Academy of Sciences, led by Dr. Attila Krasznahorkay, have reportedly discovered a fifth force, called X17—but let's just stick to the old familiar four forces, which are electromagnetism, strong nuclear force, weak nuclear force, and gravity.

At the time of the Big Bang, these four forces were united as a single unified force. Then, about 13.8 billion years ago, for reasons that remain unknown, all the space and time and matter and energy of the entire universe, which were then coiled into a point of zero volume, exploded. In a billionth of a billionth of a billionth of a billionth of a second, the unified force split into the four (or five) forces we know today.

The universe itself underwent a sudden, and very rapid, phase transition, as when water freezes into ice. An ice cube is never perfect; there are imperfections. There are multiple nucleation points, or points where the freezing process begins, and so the crystal lattices don't align perfectly. Ice cubes have cracks, walls, bubbles—imperfections that stretch from one end of the cube to the other.

The same is true of the universe—or *should* be. They are literally "wrinkles in time." Cosmic strings are not physical objects, but imperfections in spacetime itself. But although they are not physical, they do have gravity—or perhaps it would be more accurate to say they *are* gravity, since gravity itself is a deformation in spacetime.

In the book, I compare cosmic strings to black holes, only stretched from one end of the universe to another. That's not quite true, since black holes contain the mass of supergiant stars, where cosmic strings have no mass at all. But although cosmic strings have no mass, their gravitational attraction makes them *seem* to have mass—and quite a lot of it. The exact amount depends on the density and level of tension in the cosmic string, and calculations vary depending on how and when the phase transition occurred. But generally they're calculated to have the width of a proton (2×10^{-14} m, give or take a few scientific discoveries), and the mass of the entire planet Earth in one mile.

Spacetime would be distorted around a cosmic string—just as it is around a black hole.

According to Dr. Paul Sutter, astrophycisist at Ohio State University and Chief Scientist at COSI Science Center, you could fly all the way around a cosmic string by making a journey of *less* than 360 degrees.

At this time, cosmic strings have never been detected. It is possible that they once existed, but have now completely disintegrated. As I mentioned in Chapter 2, cosmic strings vibrate, and as they vibrate they shed energy. However, if they do exist, we should be able to detect them by their gravitational waves—ripples in spacetime caused by massive objects moving at high speeds. Gravitational waves were first detected in 2016 by the Laser Interferometer Gravitational-Wave Observatory (LIGO), a pair of huge interferometers in Hanford, Washington, and Livingston, Louisiana.

As a cosmic string vibrates, portions of it will be accelerated to the speed of light—which is possible for a massless object—and result in a burst of gravitational waves which physicist Thibault Damour of the Insititute of Advanced Scientific Studies in Paris compares to the crack of a bullwhip.

But LIGO has failed to find these "whip cracks." This could mean there are no cosmic strings to detect, or it could mean that LIGO is not in the direct path of the crack to detect it.

A better alternative to detecting cosmic strings is from the gravitational waves emitted from their rotation. A loop of cosmic string, like all objects in the universe, would rotate, and as it does so, would emit low-frequency gravitational waves—too low for LIGO to detect. In the early 1980s, Alexander Vilenkin suggested that these loops might seed galaxies, but in 1992, data from the Cosmic Background Explorer (COBE) seemed to rule that out.

But there is another instrument, called North American Nanohertz Observatory for Gravitational Waves (NANOGrav), which times the blinking beams of light from pulsars—which has other implications for *Voyage Into the Unknown* (see Chapter 20 of *Voyage Into the Unknown 9: The Krotus Horror*)—and therefore can detect the timing of gravitational waves. Since the flashing of pulsars is regular, any deviation in their timing would signify the passing of a cosmic string. Since NANOGrav times pulsars from one end of our galaxy to the other, it could detect the passing of a cosmic string with great precision.

As with LIGO, NANOGrav has so far drawn a blank.

In 2035, if all goes well, the European Space Agency's Laser Interferometer Space Antenna (LISA) will be launched. It will be the first space-based gravitational wave observatory. It's possible that LIGO and NANOGrav's failures to detect cosmic strings could be because the frequency of gravitational waves is yet too low for them to detect. LISA might have more luck.

The observatory will actually consist of not one but three spacecraft which will be launched into a triangular formation and separated from one another by a distance of over 5,500,000 miles, a distance precisely monitored to detect the passing of gravitational waves.

Even if LISA fails, however, that will not necessarily signify an absence of cosmic strings. As the venerable Dr. Damour said, "The fact strings come up all the time makes me confident that they exist."

They certainly exist in the *Voyage Into the Unknown* universe, and I'm looking forward to plunging deeper into their mysteries in future adventures!

ADDENDUM

In the Afterword of *Voyage Into the Unknown 11: The Armageddon Strategy*, I discussed a number of methods for achieving a Harry Potter invisibility cloak. Well, as I was putting the finishing touches on this novel, the news broke that a material that can render an object invisible has indeed been manufactured.

In November of 2019, the Canadian company HyperStealth Biotechnology Corporation announced that it had filed four patents for a material it calls "Quantum Stealth."

Guy Cramer, the company's CEO, said, "It bends light like a glass of water does where a spoon or straw looks bent except I figured out how to do it without the water or volume (thickness) of material."

The device uses lenticular lenses, which Cramer explained are "the same material that you see in 3D books and DVD covers and movie posters where by moving side to side, you get a 3D image."

The light coming from the middle of the device is bent from around the sides instead of traveling in a straight line from the object to the eye. The company claims that "It can hide a person, a vehicle, a ship, spacecraft and buildings." Not only visible light is affected, but so is electromagnetic radiation in several spectrums, including thermal, making an object invisible to heat-sensing cameras.

The company expects to sell Quantum Stealth to the Canadian military.

If this sounds like *Star Trek*'s cloaking device, it is. I'm sorry that I have no such device in *Voyage Into the Unknown*; I'll have to consider it.

Watch for

TO CONQUER THE DREB

The next adventure of
VOYAGE INTO THE UNKNOWN:
STATION POST ONE

Coming soon!

VOYAGE INTO THE UNKNOWN

Collect the entire series!

With the Earth destroyed by a supernova, the Space Star *Silver Streak* moves outward into the heavens, a self-sustaining starship housing thousands, settling colonies on other planets…moving outward into the deepest, unknown reaches of space!

Short story collections

VOYAGE INTO THE UNKNOWN: VOLUME ONE
VOYAGE INTO THE UNKNOWN: VOLUME TWO
VOYAGE INTO THE UNKNOWN: VOLUME THREE
VOYAGE INTO THE UNKNOWN: VOLUME FOUR
VOYAGE INTO THE UNKNOWN: VOLUME FIVE
VOYAGE INTO THE UNKNOWN: VOLUME SIX

Novels

VOYAGE INTO THE UNKNOWN
VOYAGE INTO THE UNKNOWN 2: THE VICTORY OF MORDRAX
VOYAGE INTO THE UNKNOWN 3: BACK FROM THE FUTURE
VOYAGE INTO THE UNKNOWN 4: A FOND FAREWELL
VOYAGE INTO THE UNKNOWN 5: THE NEW BEGINNING
VOYAGE INTO THE UNKNOWN 6: THE MIND MACHINE
VOYAGE INTO THE UNKNOWN 7: PASSAGE TO HYRON
VOYAGE INTO THE UNKNOWN 8: THE REIGN OF EDMONDS
VOYAGE INTO THE UNKNOWN 9: THE KROTUS HORROR
VOYAGE INTO THE UNKNOWN 10: THE THERMIAN MENACE
VOYAGE INTO THE UNKNOWN 11: THE ARMAGEDDON STRATEGY

Station Post One

THE PRIEST MONSTER
UNEASY ALLIANCE
COUNTDOWN TO WAR
A GALAXY IN RUIN
LOVED AND LOST